MOONLIGHT

MOONLIGHT

Part 3 of
The Four Lights Quartet

FERGUS

O'CONNELL

THAMES RIVER PRESS

Moonlight

An imprint of Wimbledon Publishing Company Limited (WPC)
Another imprint of WPC is Anthem Press (www.anthempress.com)
First published in the United Kingdom in 2013 by
THAMES RIVER PRESS
75–76 Blackfriars Road
London SE1 8HA

www.thamesriverpress.com

© Fergus O'Connell 2013

The moral rights of the author have been asserted in accordance
with the Copyright, Designs and Patents Act 1988.

All the characters and events described in this novel are imaginary
and any similarity with real people or events is purely coincidental.

A CIP record for this book is available from the British Library.

Cover photograph by Rosie Selman

ISBN 978-0-85728-095-4

This title is also available as an eBook

This book is dedicated to the memory of Lewis Friday, died of wounds 25 May 1917 and buried at Boisleux-au-Mont, France

If in this book harsh words are spoken about some of the greatest among the intellectual leaders of mankind, my motive is not, I hope, the wish to belittle them. It springs rather from my conviction that, if our civilization is to survive, we must break with the habit of deference to great men. Great men may make great mistakes.

—Karl Popper, *The Open Society and Its Enemies* (1945)

Author's Note

In 1914, in Central Europe, there was a political entity known as the Austro-Hungarian Empire. Today's Austria was a part of that empire. For simplicity, throughout this book, I have referred to the Austro-Hungarian Empire as simply 'Austria' and anything related to it as being 'Austrian.'

PART 1

Chapter 1
Saturday 27 June 1914

Henry is taking much longer than usual.

And now Clara is afraid she is going to laugh. Just as she did that other time. The time of *The Pickwick Papers*. And that's what's trying to creep into her head again now. That book. That blessed book. Oh dear God, don't let it. Oh please, don't let it.

From where she is, Clara cannot see very much. She is on her back, her head raised on her two pillows, nightdress pushed up above her waist and her legs wide apart. The room is in darkness as it always is on these occasions but, as a concession to the warm summer night, Henry drew back the curtains before getting into bed. By the ambient light from outside she can see the ceiling and a shadowed version of Henry's moustachioed face.

She can smell him though – a mixture of toothpaste, meat, wine, brandy and the cigar he smoked in the restaurant before they came home. And she can hear him – hear his breathing which has now become something of a gentle pant, like a runner who has settled into a rhythm. She deliberately focuses on all these details because she is trying to keep her mind off *The Pickwick Papers*.

This is what happened last time.

He had taken her to dinner at the Trocadero. It was Saturday night – their usual night for this. As always he ordered a large, sizzling, bloody steak. She often wondered whether there was a connection between the slab of barely cooked meat that he ate and the eagerness he always felt afterwards. And she never liked this other connection between him 'taking her' to dinner and the act which is invariably required to follow. There is something vaguely prostitutional about it. (Is 'prostitutional' a real word, she wonders?)

Anyway, they came home and she could tell that he was aroused. He held an arm around her waist as they walked up Horn Lane to the house. As soon as they got inside, he went to kiss her on the lips. However, at that same moment she turned her head, looking in the hallstand mirror as she took off her hat. The result was that the kiss ended up sliding somewhat sloppily along her cheek. It was a wet kiss, that of a man who had drunk most of two bottles of red wine and finished off with a couple of brandies.

Mrs Parsons, the babysitter, emerged from the kitchen. Had Clara been by herself, Mrs Parsons would probably have been all set for a chat, but she knew better than to do that with Henry there. She put on her hat and coat and hurried out the door.

Henry followed Clara up the stairs as far as the door of the girls' room. Clara looked in as she always did on the sleeping occupants while Henry continued on to their room. Her fear that she would find them not breathing was not as pronounced as usual – the wine had also helped to relax Clara – but she listened silently until she had reassured herself that everything was well.

She went to the bathroom, washed her face, brushed her hair and teeth and then, returning to the bedroom, changed into her nightdress, putting her dress away carefully in the wardrobe. Meanwhile, Henry had changed into his pyjamas and, in slippered feet, headed for the toilet. She heard him there. The wooden seat and its cover made a solid thunk as they were lifted and set against the pipe that ran down from the cistern. Then came a long splashing as the wine and brandy went the way of all fine drink. Henry farted. And then she waited for the hollow sound of the seat and cover to be returned to their resting place on the bowl. No such sound came. Instead she could now hear that Henry had moved to the bathroom, which was closer to the bedroom. The tap ran and he softly hummed some tune or other.

She slipped into bed and, taking a jar of cream from her bedside locker, she moistened herself. When he returned, he clambered in beside her. He lay on his back for a few moments.

'A very pleasant night, don't you think, my dear?' he said.

'Very pleasant,' she replied.

It flashed through her mind that he might actually be too tired and was about to announce that he was going to sleep. But moments later her hopes were dashed. He turned to her and began to kiss her. She closed her eyes trying to surrender herself to the sensation and wondering if it would trigger anything down in her groin. Nothing stirred. After some more kissing he turned over, simultaneously rolling onto her in what she assumed he had intended to be one smooth movement. In reality it didn't quite work out as neatly as that. Crablike, he moved on his elbows, rolling his hips until he seemed to be happy with his position.

These days he was as fat as a font. His round belly pressed down on her. He had been so slim and athletic when she first met him. How had he gone to seed so quickly? And at such a young age? He was younger than her, for God's sake – by three years – only twenty nine. *And* she had borne two children. The belly was the thing that she hated most though. If you touched it with your hand and pressed it, it was solid and cold, like hard rubber – hard and unyielding. (Could you tell a person's personality from their belly?)

She felt him groping for the hem of her nightdress. As he began to drag it up, she did it for him – the whole thing felt a bit more voluntary that way. He raised his bottom to clear the way for her but even then she had to tug it past his belly which remained pressed against hers. She settled the nightdress just above her waist. She assumed that he wouldn't be bothered with her breasts tonight. She could feel his bulge pressing against her groin and then his thing slid through the opening of his pyjamas. Guiding it with his hand he pushed into her. She had not put the cream in far enough and his dry skin snagged on hers. It was uncomfortable rather than painful and she uttered a short intake of breath. The sound seemed to arouse him so that after a few perfunctory thrusts while resting on his elbows, he rose onto the palms of his hands. (Clara wondered if perfunctory was the same as cursory. She must remember to look them both up in the morning.) From time to time he made various noises – little gasps, louder groans – and gradually the intensity of his movements increased. She could sense the strain on his arms – they seemed to be almost vibrating with it. His breathing became heavier.

His body began to scissor to and fro and it was at this moment, when it looked like he was riding, that she thought of *The Pickwick Papers*.

Dickens. She *loved* Dickens. Later, much later, James would point out the pun to her, but she wasn't aware of it that night. She just remembered Messrs Pickwick, Winkle, Tupman and Snodgrass. Mr Winkle's repeated failed attempts to mount the horse under Mr Pickwick's guidance. The horse eventually losing interest and going home. Mr Pickwick then approaching the other horse, the one pulling the chaise and how this takes off with Mr Tupman and Mr Snodgrass. (Henry continued with his own galloping while she was thinking about all of this.)

She remembered that her copy of *The Pickwick Papers* had a picture in it of the chaise on its joyride. Mr Tupman has just tried to escape the runaway chaise by leaping from it. As a result he has landed head first in a bramble hedge – only his legs and his fat bottom in their tight white breeches protrude. Mr Snodgrass is in the air, having also parted company with the chaise. The horse and chaise are going over a humpbacked bridge and the stone wall of the bridge has ripped off one of the wheels, which is in motion like a child's hoop. Ducks and chickens squawk madly as they try to get out of the way.

It was all too much for Clara. She couldn't help herself. She burst out laughing.

Henry's ardour faded instantly. It was as though *he* had been on the chaise and had been thrown off. The thought of this just made her laugh even more. He shouted at her – she couldn't remember what exactly. But he was angry. Very, very angry indeed. And he stayed so for a good two weeks afterwards. Two weeks of icy silences and no conversation – even when they were in bed together – and no dinner out on Saturday night.

Now, once again, as Henry begins his cantering, that picture from *The Pickwick Papers* is on the periphery of Clara's brain. It is like an eager actor waiting in the wings for his cue to rush onstage. And, dear God, if it does, she is done for.

She feels a smile breaking out on her face. She cannot stop it. It as though her face is acting independently of the rest of her.

The smile widens. Henry is looking directly into her face but she is not sure if he sees her; his eyes have a glazed, faraway look about them. And there is sweat on his forehead. She tries to convert the smile into a beatific look of ecstasy, to give the impression that she is getting as much pleasure from the whole business as he is. Meanwhile Henry trundles on.

And for a little while she is calm again. It looks as though she has the whole thing under control. But then suddenly it comes again, like a contraction in childbirth. She knows what's causing it. It's the sight of Henry and the ferocious exercise he is engaged in. When she first met him he was a sprinter – and a good one, winning medals for his club at sports meetings. Now, she estimates that apart from the walk to and from the station, morning and evening, this sex must be the only strenuous exercise he gets. He is not fit and this is far too much exertion for him. And he looks so, so ridiculous in his sweat-soaked pyjamas, up on his hands, slamming into her. And out again. And back in again. A cowboy on a bucking horse. A soldier who's committed some misdemeanour and now has to do some pointless drill over and over again. A mechanical children's toy with a wind-up apparatus on it. (Oh dear God, no.)

The laughter starts to build like a flood pushing against a dam. And now it begins to splutter out. She tries to control it in the same way one attempts to squeeze out wind when in company when what one really wants to do is a good loud explosion. She splutters again, a bubble or two of laughter escaping past her lips, the vanguard of a great wave of laughter that has now built inside her. Oh my God, she's not going to be able to control this. It's running away from her. Quite frantic now, she holds the next skitter of laughter and manages to convert it into a sigh of abandonment.

'Ohhhhh' is the sound she makes; slow and throaty.

Like a bird replying to a call from another in a distant tree, Henry utters an 'Ahhhh.'

Next she emits an extended 'Ohhhhhhhhhhh' and that seems to clear the immediate wave of laughter that was threatening to spill over the gunwales. But Henry isn't to be outdone and a sound that might have been a slow, almost painful 'Oh yes' escapes from him.

A snort of laughter now escapes from Clara and this time, despite the presence of the children next door, she causes the laughter to become a high pitched 'Ah ah ah ah' as though some exquisitely tender pain is being visited upon her. This causes Henry to begin grunting in a deep, throaty voice, each grunt coinciding with an in-stroke. He sounds like he is doing impersonations of a pig.

And now Clara thinks she can't do this for very much longer. Because now her brain is like a city under siege, assailed from all sides by *The Pickwick Papers*, the mechanical wind-up toy, these ridiculous sounds she hears herself making, this odd conversation of sounds that seems to have broken out between herself and her husband, and finally – the last straw, really – the pig noises. (In some ways the sounds are the most bizarre part because he is normally silent during such operations.)

And why is he taking so long? He is still on the palms of his hands and has pushed off the bedclothes, pounding away. It is starting to hurt now. And he is panting so heavily that it occurs to her he might die while inside her. What would happen then? Would his erection remain, held in rigor mortis? The thought of this just adds another impossible weight to the pressure already on her. A snort of laughter escapes from her. Frantically she manages to transform it, so that what begins as a laugh ends as a groan that might be appropriate to a state of mild discomfort or pain. Henry changes into slow, deep, painful strokes. It is as though the thought that he is hurting her has aroused him even further.

And now his panting has developed into loud gasping interspersed with sounds that might be words. He is oblivious to the noise he is making. And Clara thinks of the girls. What if he wakes them? What if one of them comes in and sees their father like this? He'll be angry and they'll be scarred for life. Clara nearly laughs again and bites her lip – actually bites it hard, painfully. But really, he is being far too loud. She needs to end this – to put everyone out of their misery.

And she knows just how to do it.

She discovered the secret quite by accident one night. It was early on in their relationship and she had been genuinely aroused and enjoying what they were doing. Her hands had been exploring his body – such a beautiful body it had been in those days – and, from the front, she had pushed her hand down between his legs and had cradled his balls in her palm. Then, on an impulse, she had pressed two of her fingertips into the place just behind his balls. The perineum, she discovered it was called afterwards when she looked it up in a medical book at the library. He had groaned spectacularly and climaxed almost immediately. And it hadn't been just that once. Any time after this when she did it, it happened.

So now she makes the move. There is no way she can get her hand down past his belly so she reaches around his back. Down across his buttocks, in the hot dampness between his splayed legs. She really has to stretch but she can feel herself nearly there. She locates his hole and then goes just beyond that. It really *is* a stretch. How much did he eat tonight? (Oh stop, Clara, stop, she says to herself.) Then with one more small stretch she presses in with her fingers. He groans loudly. She maintains the pressure and then she feels his buttocks tighten. That's it – she can take her fingers away now. She does and in a few moments, nature takes care of the rest.

He collapses onto her and lies there for several minutes, his breathing slowly easing. He says nothing. There was a time when she would have stroked his hair but now she lies as though in a coffin, her hands by her side. Eventually he rolls off and out of her, leaving her nightdress and face damp from his sweat and her thighs dripping. She is sore inside. Within moments he is asleep. She can freely welcome all her thoughts now – *The Pickwick Papers*, the image of Henry as a mechanical wind-up toy, the little moaning-whimpering conversation they had, the pig sounds, his penis erect in rigor mortis – but none of these things make her want to laugh now. Where has the laughter gone? It has drained out of her, just as she feels his semen slipping out of her now.

She presses her bunched nightdress into her groin and, holding it there with one hand, she pivots out of bed and onto the floor. She goes to the toilet and then into the bathroom. She takes off the nightdress – it is the one she keeps for such occasions – and puts it in the washing basket. She shouldn't need it again now until next Saturday night. Then she douches with a solution of baking soda. Henry has said he doesn't want any more children – that they couldn't afford another – but he has left her to sort out how to do that. She washes with scented soap and dabs on a faint hint of perfume.

Then, returning to the bedroom with its heavily breathing Henry, she takes a fresh white nightdress from the drawer and puts it on. It is the most expensive one she has. The fragrant crispness and delicate material feel exquisite against her skin. Climbing back into bed, she lies on her back. She caresses herself unhurriedly and for a long time. Then she turns her back to Henry, one leg lying flat on the sheet, the other at right angles, knee raised, and goes to the spot.

She touches herself and slowly, ever so slowly, begins to coax it. She has to stop several times when she becomes aware that her own little noises have become too loud. Then she waits for the silence of the house to return and settle before she resumes. Through the window she senses the vastness of the universe – beyond London, beyond England, out into the sky, moving away from the Earth. She somehow feels that same vastness under her finger. Henry, who has been on his other side, turns so that he lies spooned behind her. He puts an arm proprietorially around her, settling his hand on her stomach. She stops what she is doing, slips onto her back and gently presses him away from her. He obligingly rolls onto his back. She turns away from him again and coaxes herself back to the brink. Then she pushes herself over. She is unable to help herself and cries out, a sound like a surprised gasp. Her upraised leg collapses.

In a distant, blurred, groggy voice Henry asks, 'Everything alright, darling?' She makes no reply and he says nothing else. She can tell that he is deeply asleep. Then, just as her laughter disappeared with no clear reason why, unexpected tears sting her eyes and start to make their hot way down her cheeks, wetting the pillow beneath the side of her face.

And this is how she falls sleep.

Chapter 2
Sunday 28 June 1914

A tree grows in Clara and Henry's back garden not far from where they lie sleeping in their separate post-coital states of bliss. It is a tall tree, well over fifty years old and reaching up past their window. What kind of tree is it? It doesn't actually matter but since you ask, it's a beech tree planted there by Clara's father, George. A countryman by upbringing but forced, like so many, to find work in the city, he brought the tree with him as a sapling from the countryside where he grew up. He planted it here in his back garden as a reminder of all that he loved from his childhood.

They say that women always marry their fathers and, in many ways, this was what Clara did. Maybe this is why she worries so much about Henry because from when Clara could first remember, relations between her parents ranged from anywhere between bad and poisonous. Her mother eventually gave up and perhaps this is what Clara really fears – that she will too and become like her mother.

A bird sits singing happily in the tree. It has been doing so for several hours now ever since dawn broke. What kind of bird? Well, if you must know, it's a blue tit and it is appropriate that it should be a bird that we will follow to make the acquaintance of the next major character in our story. You have already met two major characters so far – Clara and Henry. But now we will travel about seven miles as the blue tit flies to our next port of call. Of course this blue tit isn't going to fly that seven miles. Why would it? It's the summer and there's plenty of food in the immediate neighbourhood. So we shall leave the blue tit to its singing and we will travel the seven miles to

Grosvenor Road ourselves where, even though it is just after five o'clock in the morning, people are astir.

(You're probably wondering why I mentioned the blue tit in the first place since we didn't follow it and it played – and will play – no further part in the story. But that should become apparent, my delightfully curious reader, before this present chapter is out and you have met our next character.)

The alarm clock went off half an hour ago in the house on Grosvenor Road but already Sir Edward Grey is washed, dressed and ready to face the day. Why is he up so early, taking the light breakfast of tea and toast that his single servant has prepared for him at this ungodly hour on a Sunday morning? Why is he not asleep like all people who have laboured hard all week and would welcome an extra couple of hours in bed? And let's face it, the general slothfulness of the Edwardian upper classes is somewhat legendary. Why then is he on the move?

We had better follow him as he leaves the house, dressed in a light summer suit the same colour as his name. He carries no bags or luggage – everything he needs is where he is going – everything that is, except for a parcel of sandwiches and a bottle of lemonade in a canvas bag that his housekeeper has prepared for him. Now that he is gone, she will probably go back to bed herself for an hour or two. In the meantime, the car that his office arranged is already waiting for him at the kerbside, its engine running. With a brisk 'good morning' to the driver, Sir Edward gets in and soon they are on the road out of London, heading south west.

Sitting silently in the back, Sir Edward reflects, as he so often does, on the course his life has taken. For a man who has reached the heights he has, he would have to agree it did not start out promisingly. At university he was not noted for his application to his studies. The Master of Balliol College wrote of him, 'Sir Edward Grey, having been repeatedly admonished for idleness and having shown himself entirely ignorant of the work set him in vacation as a condition of residence, was sent down, but allowed to come up to pass his examination in June.'

Proving however, that everybody's good at something, Grey became university tennis champion. And proving that, while democracy may be the best system we have, it still has its flaws, he was elected as Member of Parliament for Berwick-upon-Tweed, becoming the youngest member of the House. Further surprises awaited him. Gladstone made him Under-Secretary of State for Foreign Affairs. Then, in 1895, when the government collapsed, Grey was out of a job. He could not have been described as having been devastated by this turn of events. 'I shall never be in office again,' he wrote. 'And the days of my stay in the House of Commons are probably numbered. We are both very glad and relieved,' he said, referring to his wife. Twelve years later he became Foreign Secretary. It is a post he still holds.

But today matters of foreign policy are not on Grey's mind. They are in fact the furthest thing from his mind. Because today Sir Edward Grey is going fishing.

He dozes but wakes with a jolt as the car slows to turn into the drive. It is as though his body somehow knows that he is in this place, this almost sacred place. There is no road, scarcely a path – and an ancient avenue of lime trees which leads up to the cottage. The dusty ground under the trees is overgrown with long grass and nettles and burdock. The trees are alive with long-tailed tits. Then the cottage comes into sight and beyond that the ground slopes abruptly down to a water-meadow. This is where the River Itchen flows, swift and silent through great masses of flowering reeds and yellow flags, marsh agrimonies and purple loosestrife.

Grey's cottage is a simple building. Dorothy, his late wife – for he is a widower – used to call it 'a tin cottage.' Its roof is painted red, its walls are covered with trellis so that it appears almost buried in clematis, Virginia creeper, climbing roses and honeysuckle. Amongst all this foliage blackbirds, thrushes, chaffinches, robins and wagtails build their nests. It was meant to provide only basic shelter. Their idea when they built it was that most of their life down here would be lived out of doors. But despite its utilitarian beginnings, Dorothy gave it a dainty charm of its own. There is a little sitting room with a large window opening to the ground. The walls are hung with blue linen and there is a soft blue carpet on the floor. The comfortable chairs and sofa are covered with blue and white chintz and on the wall a bookshelf carries two long rows of books.

Though it has been over eight years since Dorothy died, Grey is most conscious of her absence here. They married in 1885, nearly twenty years ago. She died in 1906. The cottage was something they created together – not just the physical building and its setting but what it meant to them. They spent every weekend during the early spring and summer here, refusing invitations which might have stopped them coming down from London.

Sir Edward remembers back twenty years ago, when they first lived in Grosvenor Road. Because the Liberals were in office, government business would keep him in London until late on Friday night. But on Saturday mornings, he and Dorothy would wake with an alarm clock and then, after hurriedly getting themselves ready, they would walk the mile and a half from their home across Lambeth Bridge up to Waterloo Station. Here, they would catch the six o'clock train to Itchen Abbas, a tiny station just before Winchester. They were familiar figures to the station staff and then it was just a short walk from there up the avenue of lime trees to the cottage. 'It was something special and sacred,' Grey would write, 'outside the ordinary stream of life.'

No outsider was allowed to disturb their peace. Dorothy always felt very keenly the strain of social life. She needed complete rest and felt that the only way she could do her duties in the world was by having a refuge where she could be sure of perfect peace. She made no friends in Itchen Abbas or its surroundings. Instead, communing with nature did for her what religion did for others. It lifted her out of herself, it made her move among big thoughts, a lonely soul and yet in touch with the harmonies of nature till she found her place in it and became part of it.

On Sundays when she was alive, there was no fishing. Instead they took turns reading aloud from Wordsworth's *The Prelude*. The best part of their happiness seemed bound up with the cottage. Dorothy said that there was a great feeling of security everywhere about the cottage. There she could most easily be herself. She once said that she felt she wasn't at all 'a good London wife, but that she was a good cottage wife.'

I feel I have to interject here, reader. You'll forgive me, I hope, for this intrusion. I suspect you are feeling a little sad. A little sorry for Sir Edward, a fifty-two-year-old widower, by himself in his isolated country cottage. Admittedly he has chosen this isolation for himself. And, granted, he has a very prestigious job which I'm sure has its pressures from which it is good to escape. But perhaps, despite all this, you are feeling sad for him. He clearly loved his wife very much and she him, and he misses her greatly. Perhaps you are thinking that people shouldn't be alone. And after all, it's been eight years now since Dorothy passed on. It's a more than respectable time. Perhaps now it's time for Sir Edward to move on and find somebody new, to love again, to marry again. It shouldn't be too difficult, what with his exalted position. I'm sure there are dozens of eligible women who would be only too happy to become the wife of the Foreign Secretary. Sir Edward shouldn't be lonely, you are thinking. He seems like a good and gentle man.

And now I fear I am going to make you even sadder because there are two other pieces of information about Sir Edward that I need to give you. And the first one is certainly going to make you a little bit sadder and pity him even more.

Sir Edward's marriage to Dorothy was what the French tactfully refer to as *un marriage blanc* – as opposed, one assumes, to *un marriage rouge, rouge* being the colour of blood. When they returned from their honeymoon, Dorothy told Sir Edward that she had a strong aversion to the physical side of marriage. She didn't like children and had no desire to have any. This aspect of their relationship seems to have been reasonably well known. It was also considered interesting enough that it was the subject of a report sent back to the German government by its Ambassador in London.

After they had been married a number of years, Dorothy suddenly suggested to Grey that they should now begin to lead a normal married life. Contrary to everything you might have expected, he declined, saying that they were both happy with the life they had agreed on. And so that was the way their married life continued up to her death.

Sad, I think you'll agree. And also a little bit curious, don't you think?

Well, you know it's the job of the novelist to toy with the emotions of their readers, so now let me tell you the other piece of information you need to know. It explains Sir Edward's rather curious response to Dorothy's suggestion for full married relations.

The other thing you need to know is that, while married to Dorothy, Grey was conducting what turned out to be a long love affair with Pamela, Lady Glenconnor. (After Dorothy's death and the death of Pamela's husband, she and Grey would marry.) So now I hope your veil of sadness has lifted a little, my reader. Rather than being sad about Grey or pitying him, perhaps there is much to envy on this sunny day long ago. He has an exalted job. He has no money worries, being highly born and independently wealthy. He will spend a day that I think most men would certainly probably enjoy. He will be alone, in nature, and have time to think. Then, assuming he catches some trout in the Itchen, he will take them back to London where a woman will cook them for him and – quite possibly – he will spend the night in the arms of a woman who loves him. I think you'll agree there is much to be envied there.

Anyway, I digress. Let us return to Sir Edward, who has dismounted from his car. The driver will now drive off to Itchen Abbas, there to while away the hours and steal a surreptitious pint or two of local ale, until it is time to return to London tonight.

Sir Edward unlocks the cottage and goes inside. He opens the windows to air the place. His jacket and tie are quickly discarded and he changes into his walking shoes. Then, gathering up his fishing poles, fishing basket, boxes of flies, folding seat and other paraphernalia, he leaves the cottage door open and heads down to the river. The Itchen is a gentle trout stream rising in the Downs and flowing southwards to the sea. A wooden footbridge with a simple handrail spans it. It is called Grey's Bridge. Standing there, a man can fish for trout in the lucid water below and put disagreeable thoughts out of his head.

Today though, Grey chooses a spot on the river bank. He deposits all his gear and then ties a piece of fishing line around the neck of his bottle of lemonade. Lowering it into the water, it comes to rest on the river bed; the other end he attaches to his fishing basket. The lemonade should cool nicely between now and lunch. Then he begins to prepare his first cast.

It would be hard to imagine a place more placidly beautiful, more attuned to the spirit of the nature-loving, widowed man who had been coming here, weekend after weekend, for almost a quarter of a century. (He was there on the night of Sunday, 2 April 1911, for example, when the census was taken. Then he listed his occupation as 'Secretary of State.')

Here, in March 1894, he and Dorothy began their so-called *Cottage Book*, a nature diary of the seasons at the cottage. In his autobiography, Grey wrote of the *Cottage Book*: 'It began from a desire to leave on Monday something which would tell us what to look for on the following Saturday, and the first entries were written solely for this purpose. But it became much more than that. It was a record of our stay there and of our feelings and enjoyment. It was always left open so that either of us might write in it when we felt moved to do so. The entries made by my wife are marked with the "D"; my own similarly are marked with the letter "E".'

Here Grey can fish in the river below the cottage. In these surroundings he can walk, listen, see (until his sight weakened) and name the birds. For this is the other great passion of Grey's life – and this, dear reader, was why we mentioned that little blue tit at the beginning of this chapter. Because Sir Edward Grey is an ornithologist and – it has to be said – rather a good one.

Sir Edward will be quoted as saying that one has to be happy to write a book. He will write two of them on the two passions of his life – fly fishing and bird watching. In Falloden, his ancestral home in rural Northumberland, he started a wildlife sanctuary consisting of two ponds surrounded by a fox-proof fence. Here he bred many species of duck. At feeding times, shovellers would feed at his feet, teal from his hand and mandarin ducks and robins would land on his head.

Grey is also a lifelong railway enthusiast. The main line on the London and North Eastern Railway passes close to Falloden.

So here we have him – train spotter, birdwatcher, fisherman and Foreign Secretary. This is the gentle man who, apart from anything else, will be managing Britain's fortunes in what lies ahead.

But now we must leave Sir Edward by his placid stream. He intends to fish, bask in the sun, eat his modest lunch, go for a walk.

He calls such walks 'going a trail;' thus, a long walk is 'going a long trail.' But today it will not be a long trail – just enough to make sure that everything in this little world he has created is as it should be.

Then, this evening, he plans to return to London and to being Foreign Secretary again. And tomorrow, though of course he cannot know it yet, will begin the most important thirty seven days of his life. He should try to sleep well tonight because he will sleep far less well or perhaps not at all in the weeks to come.

So let us leave him in the slowly intensifying light of this June morning and let us get ready to travel. For this time we must travel far. Our next journey is no blue tit's flight. We must go east and yes, dear reader, it is a long haul – though not the longest we shall make. But it is an important one because we are going to meet our fourth major character. And lest you start to fret that it's all becoming a bit much – the book about to become three chapters old and already four major characters – don't worry, this character will only appear in this next chapter and then he will be gone. Although he will cast a long shadow – a very long shadow – for the rest of the book and well beyond that.

But how, I hear you ask, can he be a major character if he only appears in this one chapter? Surely he would have to appear over and over again for him to count as a major character? Press on, my puzzled reader, and the mystery will be revealed.

Chapter 3
Sunday 28 June 1914

Y ou may have an idea how it starts. Maybe you once read something or they told you about it at school.

It starts with a royal visit. A royal visit and security precautions that would have made a modern White House Secret Service detail shake their heads in disbelief. It starts in the city of Sarajevo in what was then called Bosnia, part of the Austrian Empire.

The Archduke Franz Ferdinand, heir to the Austrian throne is making a visit to Bosnia in his capacity as commander-in-chief of the Austrian Army. He intends to observe Austrian Army manoeuvres in the hills outside Sarajevo. It has been known since March that he will be in Sarajevo on this day. On the morning of this Sunday, the 28th of June, the royal train steams into Sarajevo where the Archduke is also to open the state museum's new premises. He is greeted by the military governor of Bosnia, Oskar Potiorek. Due to a mistake, three local police officers get into the first car of the Archduke's convoy, along with the chief officer of special security. This means that the special security officers who are supposed to protect the Archduke get left behind (wince).

Franz Ferdinand and his wife Sophie drive into the town in a convertible sports car, a Gräf & Stift Tourer, the third in a convoy of four cars. At Franz Ferdinand's request the soft top of the car has been put down so that the people can see him and he can see the sights (wince). Franz Ferdinand and Sophie sit side by side and Potiorek sits opposite them. In front with the driver is Count Harrach, head of the motor corps. The motorcade's first stop on the pre-announced (wince) programme is for a brief inspection of a military barracks. According to the programme, at 10:00 a.m., the motorcade is to leave the barracks for the town hall by way of Appel Quay (wince). As the car goes along the quay the Archduke asks for the car to be driven slowly (wince) so that he can have a good look around, receiving some cheers from the thin crowds.

As they approach the central police station a young man called Nedeljko Čabrinović steps out of the now-thickening crowds and throws a hand grenade directly at the car (oh my God!). The driver of the Archduke's car, seeing a black object flying towards them, accelerates (well done). As a result, the bomb bounces off the folded-back convertible cover into the street. Its ten second delay detonator causes it to explode under the wheel of the next car, putting it out of action. Duchess Sophie tells the driver to 'Drive on quickly.' Franz Ferdinand says, very calmly, 'I always thought something like this might happen.' The bomb leaves a small crater in the road and wounds the occupants of the car under which it exploded. It also injures members of the watching crowd – in all, a total of twenty people. The Archduke's driver immediately increases speed in order to get the Archduke and Duchess to the comparative safety of the town hall. The Archduke tells the driver to stop while he checks on casualties. This, despite the fact that the Duchess's neck had been grazed and that stopping makes the car a sitting duck for any further attacks (wince).

Meanwhile, Čabrinović swallows a cyanide capsule and jumps into the River Miljacka. It is summer, remember – a hot summer in the Balkans. As a result, the river is only five inches deep – something Čabrinović really should have checked out beforehand. In addition, his cyanide capsule is past its best-by date so that it only makes him vomit. Police drag him from the river and he is severely beaten by the crowd before being taken into custody.

The Archduke arrives safely at the town hall. As you can imagine, he is *very* angry. 'I come here on a visit and I get bombs thrown at me. It's outrageous,' he says to the mayor. As best he can, the mayor makes his speech of welcome. Franz Ferdinand's own speech, spattered with his *aide-de-camp*'s blood because it had been in the damaged car, is brought to him. He reads it in his thin, high-pitched voice.

Officials and members of the Archduke's party discuss what to do next. Franz Ferdinand and Sophie give up their planned programme in favour of visiting the wounded from the bombing at the hospital. Count Harrach takes up a protective position on the left-hand running board of Franz Ferdinand's car, a drawn sword in his hand. The Count remarks that he is astonished there is no military guard to protect the heir to the throne, no soldiers lining the streets; this, despite the fact that there are two Austrian Army corps in the vicinity for the manoeuvres (wince).

'Do you think Sarajevo is full of assassins?' Potiorek replies, dismissively.

(Unbeknown to himself, Potiorek has hit the nail on the head. In all there is a team of *seven* assassins in Sarajevo that day. There are only a hundred and twenty policemen and no soldiers.)

Potiorek decides that the royal car should travel straight along the Appel Quay to the Sarajevo Hospital. However, he forgets to inform the driver (wince). On the way to the hospital, the royal car takes a right turn into Franz Josef Strasse. At this, Potiorek shouts to the driver that he is making a mistake.

While all of this is going on, another member of the assassination team, Gavrilo Princip is in a deep depression. Having decided that the whole assassination thing has been a fiasco, he has gone to a nearby food shop, Moritz Schiller's delicatessen, to cheer himself up (in general, probably a good thing to do if you're having a bad day). As he emerges he is astonished to see Franz Ferdinand's car drive past, having taken the wrong turn.

The driver, alerted by Potiorek and realising the mistake, brakes sharply and stops the car (wince). Then he begins to back up (biggest wince of all). In doing so the engine stalls and the gears lock (oh no).

At this point Princip seizes his opportunity and draws a Browning automatic pistol. A nearby policeman spots him and tries to grab his arm but Princip pistol whips him. (How the history of Europe would have been different had that policeman succeeded.) Then, running to within four of five yards of the royal car, Princip fires two shots into it. Blood gushes from the Archduke's mouth onto his blue uniform and onto Count Harrach's right cheek.

As the Archduke pulls out his handkerchief to wipe the blood away from his mouth, the Duchess cries out to him, 'In Heaven's name, what has happened to you?' With that she slides off the seat and lies on the floor of the car, with her face between his knees.

Count Harrach thinks she has fainted with fright. Then he hears the Archduke say, 'Sophie, Sophie, don't die. Live for the children!' The driver speeds towards the Konak, the government building in the Bistrik district. Count Harrach seizes the Archduke by the collar of his uniform, to stop his head from dropping forward and asks him if he is in great pain. He answers, 'It's nothing!' His face begins to contort somewhat but he goes on repeating, six or seven times, ever more faintly as he gradually loses consciousness, 'It's nothing!' Then, after a short pause, there is a violent choking sound caused by the bleeding. It has stopped by the time they reach the Konak.

The royal couple are carried to a room in the Konak. It is a room next door to the one in which the champagne for lunch is chilling. Sophie is found to be dead on arrival – she has been shot in the stomach. Franz Ferdinand dies ten minutes later from a wound to the jugular vein. Princip is arrested and will end his days in Terezin, a place that will become infamous for entirely different reasons thirty years later.

Things will not go well for Potiorek after this either. After Sarajevo he will lead the Austrian Army in two textbook military disasters at the Battles of Cer and Kolubara. After this he will be retired, a decision which will reportedly make him suicidal. Still, he'll be in a lot better shape than the 225,000 men of the Austrian Army under his command – half its entire strength – killed, wounded or captured on his watch.

But never mind that now because what matters is that the assassination of the Archduke Franz Ferdinand and his wife is the event that kicks off the Group of Death.

But what's the Group of Death, you ask, possibly uninterested-in-sport reader? Read on.

Chapter 4
The Group of Death

As well as being the story of Clara and Henry, Grey and (briefly) the unfortunate Archduke and his wife Sophie, and – as we shall see shortly – some other people, this book is the story of the Group of Death. It is the story of five teams, Britain, France, Germany, Austria and Russia – the Big Five – who played in the Group of Death and how all of them lost.

Ordinarily, the Group of Death is a term used to describe a collection of teams whose quality is exceptional and where qualification from the group will be difficult. In this case, all the teams were exceptional and all of them gave one hundred and fifty per cent. However none of them was particularly well-managed and none of them qualified.

Nobody ever wants to play in a Group of Death. The matches will be hard and qualification doubtful. So it was with this one. All of the matches turned out to be much harder than anybody could ever have believed possible. And who could have anticipated that *nobody* would qualify?

But wasn't there a draw, I hear you ask, to decide who would play whom in the Group of Death?

No, there wasn't. The way to think about it is that the assassination of the Archduke *took the place of a draw*. And the result was that the first fixture to be played would be between Austria and Serbia.

Between Austria and who?

Serbia.

Serbia. Who's Serbia? You said – Britain, France, Germany, Austria, Russia. Who's Serbia? And how can they play? They're not even in the Group of Death.

Well, actually – they are.

They are?

They are, poor, confused reader. I'm sorry. I should explain.

There is a sixth team in the Group of Death – Serbia. The reason I haven't mentioned them up until now is that Serbia is a tiny country. In terms of the Group of Death it is the Faroe Islands of its day. Britain, France, Germany, Austria and Russia are all huge countries with great wealth and enormous empires. Serbia is minute. Yet Serbia will play a key part in the Group of Death. It will lose its first game within minutes of starting. Unbelievably, it will win its second one. And that win will have profound implications for the Group as a whole.

The reason Serbia got into the Group of Death at all is this: Austria believes that the Serbians murdered the Archduke. In this, they are more completely spot-on than they could ever have imagined. The people who killed the Archduke *are* Serbians, but not some disaffected young men or fanatics or nutters. No, they received their orders and weapons from some people very high up in the Serbian military and political establishment. This is because these higher-ups wanted a Serbia independent of Austria, which it wasn't at the time.

So now Austria demands a match with Serbia. In fact, not that it will make any difference, the match will be Serbia versus Austria – a home match for the Serbs. It will be played in Belgrade, the Serbian capital, at 6 p.m. on Friday, 24 July. Shortly after that, the main group will begin.

On that sunny summer's afternoon long ago, Austria completely held the moral high ground. The heir to its throne had been murdered. So had his wife. Any country would quite rightly have been justified in considering this an outrage. It was the Pearl Harbour of its time. Austria had the sympathy of the world. And then, just as with George W. Bush after 9/11, Austria would proceed to throw away this moral advantage entirely.

But let's say no more about that for now. After our visit to exotic Sarajevo – even if under rather unfortunate circumstances – where shall we go next? Well, perhaps now that you know about the Group of Death, well-informed reader, and remembering that the

Archduke and his beloved Sophie lie cold in Sarajevo, maybe we should next make the acquaintance of all of the managers in the Group of Death and find out what they think about this turn of events. It's time to return to London.

Chapter 5
Sunday 28 June 1914

The telegram, when it comes, is delivered by his driver.

Whenever Sir Edward comes down to the cottage, the Foreign Office knows it can contact him via the post office at Itchen Abbas. The post office in turn knows that if a message comes in for Sir Edward, his driver will be around the village somewhere – most likely in the pub. The system all goes like clockwork this afternoon and when Sir Edward hears his driver coming down from the cottage he knows there must be something serious afoot.

Sir Edward is on his canvas folding camp seat beside the River Itchen. He has moved several times since we left him but there is no problem finding him. Four shiny, lifeless trout lie on the grass beside him. The sun is hot – his guess would be that it's about seventy-four degrees – and there is a gentle, feathery breeze. He hears a bird singing behind him up near the cottage and recognises it as a blackcap. The sound is not continuous though, but rather broken up – singing, then quiet, then singing again. He wonders if the bird is still caring for its young.

Judging by the position of the sun, Sir Edward reckons it to be about five o'clock or so. He would have been getting ready to go soon anyway, so he doesn't feel too bad as he tears open the envelope and unfolds the paper. It reads:

Consul Jones to Sir Edward Grey.
Serajevo,
June 28, 1914.

According to news received here heir apparent and his consort assassinated this morning by means of an explosive nature.

'Oh dear,' he says, re-folding the paper and putting it into his trouser pocket.

The driver says, 'Back to London, Sir Edward?'

'I'm afraid so,' he replies.

On the way back to London, Sir Edward ponders what has happened, but he doesn't dwell long on the subject. There is always some kind of trouble in the Balkans. And there will probably be more as a result of this. There'll be plenty of posturing. Maybe some armies will march. There may even be some fighting. But just as in the Balkan Crisis of six years ago, it shouldn't be anything that can't ultimately be sorted out at the conference table.

So, if the question we began with is, 'What does Sir Edward Grey think about the Group of Death?', the answer is that he probably doesn't think there will be a Group of Death at all. He believes there will – possibly – be some kind of a match between Austria and Serbia. If there is a match, its nature will be … well, the opposite to a 'friendly,' whatever that is. (Would one call it an 'unfriendly'?) But apart from that there is no issue.

Sir Edward begins to look forward to eating his fish and wonders if he'll get to see Pamela this evening.

Another person who, if anything, is even less concerned about the dead Archduke – but for an entirely different reason – is the man who will be the Russian manager in the Group of Death. While you may know him as Tsar Nicholas II, his full Sunday name is Nicholas II, Emperor and Autocrat of All the Russias.

The Tsar is another man who is neither particularly suited to nor happy with the job he has been handed. When the Tsar was a teenager, and before he came to power, his father organised some lessons for the young Nicky to explain the workings of the Russian state. A sensible enough thing to do, I think you'd agree, for the young man who would one day assume such vast powers. Nicky's teacher would later fondly recall, 'I could only observe that he was completely absorbed in picking his nose.'

Today the Tsar is doing what we would now call, spending quality time with his family. Of course, while for us that might constitute going out to a pizza restaurant or the beach or the movies or for a bike ride, if you're Emperor and Autocrat of All the Russias, quality time is probably going to be pretty different. And in fact, it is.

The British First Battle Cruiser Squadron is moored in Kronstadt harbour just down the coast from St Petersburg, so the Tsar, his wife and four daughters are paying a visit. The weather was rainy earlier as the Imperial yacht *Alexandria* left the landing stage at Peterhof Palace, the Tsar's seaside retreat, with the Imperial party on board. But happily now the sun has come out, irradiating, as the *Times* will later report, 'the roadstead with the ships of the Squadron dressed in honour of the august visitors.'

The Tsar *loves* this kind of thing. First, he just loves being with his girls. There is his wife, the German-born Alexandra, and then his four beautiful daughters – 'OTMA,' as they call themselves – Olga, Tatiana, Maria and Anastasia. They are all so different. Olga, the eldest, who will be nineteen in November, is a young woman. Then at the other end, there is Anastasia, still a child at thirteen. He loves everything about them. But mainly he loves the fact that they are female. As Tsar, Nicholas gets to meet lots and lots of men. Without exception he finds them a dull, uninspiring lot. Perhaps it is because of the nature of the work they do. They are politicians, diplomats, bureaucrats, generals, admirals. Maybe if they were simple working men or writers or engineers or actors, things would be different, but as it is, he is appalled at how much time he has to spend in their company and how wearying, without exception, they are.

Women by comparison – well, they sparkle. They know what's important in life. His five girls, as he thinks of them, all have their own views. They talk endlessly about all manner of things. They discuss what to wear and how they look and whether dinner was nice and how they'll spend today. In other words, they're concerned with the simple things, the simple things that life should be about – not wars and the grindingly dull stuff of economics and the endlessly subtle (and generally nasty) machinations of politics. The men Nicholas meets every day talk about war and revolution, strikes and riots, traitors and starvation, budgets and geopolitics. In contrast, women inhabit a far softer, gentler world.

And the Tsar, too, thinks of himself as a simple man. That's if you can call a man whose wealth, in 1916, was valued at nearly three hundred *billion* dollars in today's money, simple. But in many ways, he *does* live a simple life. He eats simple food and wears clothes until they are worn out.

He is very much what would be called these days a 'new man.' He loves to spend time with his family. He is really not cut out for leadership. He has one of those traits that are particularly disturbing in a leader. Having no real vision of where he is going, he tends to act based on whom he last spoke to.

The Tsar and his party spend a couple of hours touring one of the battle cruisers, including the engine room and the gun turrets. Now this is something to get interested in. The previous evening, Nicolas read about this ship in preparation for his visit. He knows about its maximum speed – 27 knots – its main armaments – eight 13.5 inch guns – the thickness of armour on the turrets and barbettes, and a host of other technical details. He finds the tour fascinating. The astonishing technology of the engine room. The ghastly power he can only sense when he is given a tour of one of the turrets. He asks questions and the officers are delighted to explain, for example, how the bags of cordite explosive are brought from the magazine to the turret and how the system is completely safe. (In this they will turn out to be very far off the mark but it will be almost two more years, off Jutland in the North Sea, before they find this out.) Nicholas runs his fingers along the paint-coated steel and breathes in the aroma of oil and salt air. The newspaper reports will say that he was in splendid spirits and that he never enjoyed himself more. The Tsar's party has lunch and then leaves in the afternoon to rousing cheers from the British sailors.

How they cheer, these sailors – especially those boys for whom it is their first time in foreign waters. What tales they will have to tell when they return home of the places they have been, the sights and exalted personages they have seen. How they will boast to wives or girlfriends or girls they hope will become girlfriends, of how they have seen the Tsar of Russia and his daughters.

And how many of them will go to the bottom of the North Sea when Beatty's battle cruisers meet the ships of the German High Seas Fleet, in one of the many matches of the Group of Death.

I'm sorry. I digress again. The Tsar's party return to the Peterhof, but there all is in a frenzy. Nine-year-old Alexei, the Tsarevich, Nicholas's son has fallen while jumping from a ladder and twisted his ankle. No big deal, you might have thought – except that Alexei has inherited haemophilia from his mother Alexandra, a condition that she can trace back to her maternal grandmother Queen Victoria. Haemophilia means that blood has difficulty coagulating. The result of this can be that even small wounds are potentially fatal. Alexei is bleeding now and crying with pain. His mother Alexandra is white with worry and terrified because the monk Rasputin, the only man she believes can help her son, is not in the palace. Not only is he not in the palace, he has been visiting his family in Siberia where, for reasons unknown, he has been stabbed by a woman. When the news comes in of the assassination of the Archduke Ferdinand, it hardly registers with a distraught Nicholas.

Nine hundred and fifty miles as the blue tit flies, to the south west in Kiel Bay, all silvery light in the Baltic afternoon, the German manager is at the helm of his racing yacht *Meteor*, competing in the Kiel regatta. Frederick William Victor Albert of Prussia, also known as Kaiser Wilhelm II – Emperor of Germany – 'Der Kaiser' (not to be confused with Franz Beckenbauer) is such a keen sailor that he doesn't just have his own boat. *He's had his own navy built* – a navy that's intended to rival the British Royal Navy. (He once confided to his uncle, Edward VII, that his dream was to have a fleet of his own some day. And now he does.)

Der Kaiser has a stern face and the kind of moustache that the rest of us – well, men at least – can only dream about: bristling and turning up spectacularly at the ends. He is immensely fond of uniforms, of (dare one say it about so exalted a personage) dressing up. But this afternoon he is dressed relatively simply. Immaculate white laced shoes, trousers and jacket with just a little bit of gold braid on the epaulettes; white shirt with wing collar and tiny, fashionable bow tie and a white and blue sailor's cap with some 'scrambled eggs,' as it's known in the navy, above the peak of the cap.

Der Kaiser is heading on a northerly course towards the Danish islands when an aide draws his attention to a steam launch astern which appears to be trying to catch up with them. As the steam launch gets closer, Der Kaiser recognises that it is the steam launch *Hulda* with Admiral Muller waving a signal to heave-to. The Admiral shouts into the wind, 'I bring grave news.' By now the Admiral's boat has pulled alongside the Kaiser's yacht and the two boats are travelling together no more than ten yards apart. The Admiral puts a decoded telegram from the German Consul-General in Sarajevo into his cigarette case and is preparing to throw it across to the Kaiser's yacht. But the Kaiser wants to hear whatever this news is directly from the Admiral's lips. The two boats pull closer together and the Admiral manages to execute a transfer to the Kaiser's yacht, the strong, safe hands of two seamen ensuring that there is no mishap.

'Everything has to be started over again,' remarks Der Kaiser to a saluting Admiral Muller. Admiral Muller is mystified. He thinks that Der Kaiser is referring to his recent efforts to win over the late Archduke to his way of thinking and how these have all been rendered useless by the Archduke's death. This must mean that Der Kaiser has already heard about the assassination. How could that be, since it is the Admiral himself who has come bearing this news?

But then he understands. Der Kaiser means that the *race* will have to be started over again. The Admiral tells Der Kaiser what has occurred in Sarajevo. In recent years Franz Ferdinand and Der Kaiser had become close friends. They had been hunting together only the week before. It's perhaps important to explain exactly what Der Kaiser means when he says that they are 'close friends' From Der Kaiser's point of view, it means that he feels or felt that he had the heir to the Austrian throne in his pocket. At all events, Der Kaiser is very upset. Perhaps there is a feeling of 'there but for the grace of God go I.' If a member of a royal family in one country can be assassinated…

Later, Der Kaiser cables the German Chancellor, Theobald von Bethmann Hollweg saying that 'this cowardly, detestable crime has shaken me to the depths of my soul.'

We have to be careful here but I feel I need to point out, valued reader, that it is possible that Der Kaiser is barking mad. He had a difficult birth. He was in the breech position and no one realised it until too late. To make matters worse, an urgent summons to Berlin's most eminent obstetrician got lost. After ten or eleven hours with his mother in excruciating pain, the attending doctors had pretty much given up on her and the baby. Finally, the famous obstetrician got the message and arrived. With liberal doses of chloroform he managed to manipulate the baby out. The child emerged pale, limp, one arm around his neck, badly bruised and not breathing. The attending nurse had to rub him and slap him repeatedly before he cried. Everyone wept with relief.

It cannot be proved, of course, but Der Kaiser, who grew up to be hyperactive and emotionally unstable, may have been brain damaged at birth.

This brings us immediately to a difficulty. Perhaps it is the central difficulty of this book. We expect the people who are (or whom we put) in positions of authority to be sane. We expect a lot more of them than that obviously but, at the very least, we would like them to be sane. By this we mean we would hope they would make sensible decisions. Ideally, we would like wise decisions – profoundly wise decisions – but at the very least we ask for sensible. And what is sensible? Well, obviously everything is relative but a possible definition of sensible might be – well, 'not mad.' It's not an unreasonable expectation, I think you'd agree. Yet repeatedly throughout history we see decisions that could in no way be described as not mad.

Anyway, let us leave Der Kaiser, mad or otherwise, for now as his yacht cuts through the chilly waters of the Baltic, we must travel again, weary reader. This time to Paris. Or, to be more precise, to the Bois de Boulogne on the banks of the Seine. Here at the Longchamps racecourse, with its famous hill that will test any thoroughbred, Parisian society has gathered because it is the peak of the *Grande Semaine*. Many Parisians have come to the track down the river on steamboats and various other vessels, the trip taking around an hour to the Pont de Suresnes. Strolling around the paddock, men admire the horses and judge the women – or is it the other way round? Women admire the horses and judge each other.

The man we have come to see has come not in a boat but rather in a carriage. He is accompanied by his wife. The band plays. Grey top-hats are raised. White-gloved hands are brought to the brims of kepis. For the man in the carriage is none other than Raymond Poincaré, the tenth *Président de la République* and manager of the French team.

With his bald pate, fringe of hair round the sides and back, moustache and goatee beard, Poincaré looks like someone who should be singing Alfredo in Verdi's *La Traviata* on the stage of the *Théâtre National de l'Opéra*. This afternoon he sits in the Presidential box. He looks grey, serious as though he disapproves of the frivolity going on around him.

Like many of the people he represents, Poincaré is, at best, very suspicious of Germany, at worst, anti-German. The reason for this lies in his childhood. In 1870, during the Franco-Prussian War and when little Raymond was only ten, the Germans overran his native Lorraine, forcing his family to flee from their home in Bar-le-Duc. For two and a half months, he, his mother and brother lived in a series of hotels in Dieppe and then in Belgium while his father stayed at the family home. Bar-le-Duc was occupied by the Germans for the next three years and, following the war, Germany annexed the provinces of Alsace and Lorraine.

But it would be wrong to think that Monsieur Poincaré has a visceral, irrational hatred of the Germans. His patriotism and desire, like all Frenchmen, to regain 'the lost provinces' is coupled with moderation, rationality, a need for order. Some think him cold. One commentator described him as having 'a stone for a heart.' Poincaré trained as a lawyer and so is accustomed to sifting evidence and drawing conclusions. Thus, shortly after becoming Premier and Foreign Minister in 1912, he studied the files related to foreign policy with Germany. His assessment was that 'whenever we have adopted a conciliatory approach to Germany, she has abused it; on the other hand, on each occasion when we have shown firmness, she has yielded.' From this, he drew the conclusion that Germany understood 'only the language of force.'

At four, the most valuable race of the year is due to be run – the Grand Prix de Paris, with prize money worth, in English money, sixteen thousand pounds. Just before four o' clock, when the jockeys are about to go under starter's orders, an officer of the President's entourage hands Monsieur Poincaré a telegram from the Havas Agency. The President reads it and, without any change of expression, passes it to the Austrian Ambassador, sitting nearby in the Presidential box. The Ambassador reads the message. Then, excusing himself to the President, he leaves the box and hurries from the course.

Shortly afterwards the yellow and green colours of Baron Maurice's horse Sardanapale pass the post, winning by a neck. The horse comes in at eighteen-to-five.

The President has put no money on the victor. It's probably not a Presidential thing to do. Still, it's a pity. For if he had, it might have put him in better form for what lies ahead. President Poincaré is a cousin of the famous mathematician Henri Poincaré. Henri is reputed to solve a problem completely in his head before committing it to paper. As events will turn out, perhaps it would have been better if Henri had been president. Then he might have been able to use this skill to solve the problem with which his cousin will shortly be confronted.

So in this chapter you've met the two managers who have inherited their positions – Der Kaiser and the Tsar – and the one who's been elected, Monsieur Poincaré. But now it is time to return to London to see how our other characters – some so-called 'ordinary people' – are spending this afternoon that lounges beneath a cloudless sky across all of Europe.

Chapter 6
Sunday 28 June 1914

Back in Acton Clara rises just after eight that Sunday morning, leaving Henry still sleeping. He likes to lie in on a Sunday and he always sleeps more heavily after sex.

In the bathroom Clara looks in the mirror as she pulls a brush through her blonde hair before tying it up. She thinks her face is too long. But her teeth are good and she has nice lips. Her blue eyes are bright. She has to admit she slept well herself.

While the girls are still asleep, Clara gets some chores done. She has a cleaning lady – Mrs Parsons, who also does duty as the babysitter – who comes in every weekday. But the house is so big that there always seems to be an endless list of things to be done. In some ways it is not the house Clara would have wanted – she would have preferred, and they could have managed with, a smaller one. But she inherited it after her father died. She and Henry discussed whether to sell it but, in the end, they both agreed that it was better to move into it.

They did so for different reasons. Henry thought it could 'only increase in value' – and presumably he knew about such things given that he worked as a manager in an insurance company. Clara chose it because it was where she had been born and brought up, a house she had loved since childhood. There are days though – like today – when the house just feels like a burden. After all, outside sunshine is calling and she finds herself cleaning and washing and dusting and polishing.

While she is the only one up, Clara tries to check on some of the things she wondered about last night. Prostitutional isn't a real word, the dictionary tells her. In terms of gauging a person's personality from their belly, there's nothing she can really look up in the *Encyclopædia Britannica* (11th edition) or the atlas or the dictionary. She just thinks it's something she'll keep in mind whenever she is out and sees or meets people. Cursory *is* almost the same as perfunctory. Even after flipping to and fro between the two entries several times, she still isn't sure if she could explain the difference to somebody else or knows exactly when to use one and when to use the other. And finally, as she closes the dictionary with a soft, papery 'plop,' she realises with a smile that she is never really going to be able to find out about what happens to erections if one is in progress at the time of death. She imagines it would fade but she doubts if there is anyone in the world who actually knows the truth. She gets up from where she is perched on the edge of the armchair's seat and returns the heavy book to its shelf.

After about an hour, the girls wake up and Clara can hear them chattering in their room. They quickly became so loud that she has to go upstairs and hiss at them to come down so as not to wake their father. Ursula is six, born within a year of Clara's marriage; Virginia is fifteen months. Clara gives them some toast and milk and then takes them upstairs where she dresses Virginia. Ursula dresses herself. Later Henry surfaces and Clara makes a big breakfast of eggs, bacon, sausages and fried bread for them all. She will give them something small, just to keep them going, during the afternoon. Then, at supper time, they will have cold slices of the ham she cooked yesterday along with some cold potatoes and tomatoes and lettuce from Clara's small vegetable plot at the end of their large back garden. Henry likes it this way in the summer, whereas in the winter they eat their main Sunday meal at lunch time. After breakfast, with the washing up all done and the rest of the day's meals organised, Clara goes out into the garden.

The girls are already out there, sitting on a rug beneath her father's tree. Ursula has her head sunk in a book. She has blonde hair like her mother's, cascading in natural curls as far as her shoulder blades. Virginia's is still growing and is dead straight reaching to just below her ears. Both girls have rosebud mouths and Clara has a sense – which she thinks is more than just mother's pride – that both girls will be stunners when they are older. It is one of the reasons why she chose Henry. At the time he was slim, healthy, handsome, and she reckoned that he would father beautiful children. In that, at least, she was correct. Virginia especially is one of those people who has been blessed with everything – she has good looks, seems to be highly intelligent and appears to be just a nice, caring person. Virginia calls to Clara as soon as she sees her, saying 'Mama' and waving the rag doll she is holding by one leg.

They spend the afternoon in the garden, the girls playing, Henry reading the paper and dozing, Clara – when she isn't with the girls or looking after feeding everybody – reading *Dubliners* by James Joyce. They go to bed early – Henry has work tomorrow, Ursula has school and Clara is exhausted.

Despite this, she can't sleep. She is a light sleeper anyway. Given that Henry sleeps so heavily – even if he hasn't had sex – there has to be somebody there in case the children wake up. And so when she sleeps, it is fitful. It is as though she drifts just below the surface, ready to float up if the need arises. Such sleep is not refreshing. She sometimes has to take a nap during the day in order to keep going. Then she will ask Mrs Parsons to mind the girls while Clara disappears up to her bedroom for an hour. Mrs Parsons is the most loyal and loving woman in the world. Her children are grown up now. Her daughter is married and living in Lewisham; her son is in the army and stationed in India. She adores the girls and they seem to fill the gap in Mrs Parson's life left by the departure of her own children. But even so, Clara is conscious of what-if-something-happens. The result is that all the nap does is to take the edge off her tiredness.

Tonight as she lies in bed her mind, as usual, is crowded. First come the girls who are both a joy and a sorrow. What if anything were ever to happen to them? She knows she just wouldn't be able to survive something like that; wouldn't *want* to survive. Then there's the house and the things that have to be done tomorrow. What cleaning will she do? Where will she start? A list begins forming in her mind. Clara often thinks in lists. She wishes she didn't but she so often does. And they are numbered lists so that as she works her way through them, she sees in her mind's eye the number of items on the list dropping and she feels like she is making progress.

She also – again in her mind's eye – crosses things off the list as they are done. She sometimes wonders if her life has become nothing more than a succession of days with each day having a list pinned to it and every item on the list crossed off.

Sometimes – as now – the list divides into two lists – the things she will do and the things that can be left to Mrs Parsons. There are some things Clara likes to do herself. Cleaning the toilets – why should anybody else have to clean their shit, as her father might have said. Clara likes to do the cooking though she is happy for Mrs Parsons to prepare everything. And then certainly, before supper, she likes to have Mrs Parsons gone so that they can be together, just the four of them. Sometimes this can be a struggle since, especially if she has had a happy day with the children, Mrs Parsons is reluctant to return home to her solitary life and will keep finding things to do to keep herself from going. This in turn annoys Henry if he returns to find her still there. Of course, he'll be all smiles to Mrs Parsons but Clara will hear all about it later.

What will she cook for dinner tomorrow? Are there leftovers that should be used up? What does she need to buy? Are those pears still fresh? Maybe she shouldn't buy so many next time.

Once she has finished fretting over current things – things that happened today, things that may happen or have to happen tomorrow – Clara moves progressively on to the future. The rest of this week, this month, next month. Even though it is just early summer she thinks about the autumn, when Ursula will return to school. She'll need a new uniform. She's grown so much in a year, Clara can hardly believe it – and no amount of clever seamstressing will make Ursula's present uniform go any further. Clara will have to think how best to broach it with Henry so that he doesn't end up complaining too much about the money. It's not that he begrudges it – she doesn't think he does, anyway – but she never seems to be able to save enough from the weekly housekeeping money for these eventualities. The result is that she always ends up having to ask him for more. And she never knows for sure how he's going to react. Sometimes he hands it over cheerfully – he'll make some remark about it being 'great to have it.' But then other times he'll complain or give her the silent treatment afterwards.

Each year he increases her housekeeping allowance a little with a 'Well prices aren't going *down*, are they?' And he must be right because the additional money doesn't seem to buy any more. She still has to be careful about the cuts of meat she buys and she still makes most of the girls' clothes herself. She had thought that, with his promotion earlier this year, he might increase what she got, and she mooted that with him the night he took her out to celebrate. But he simply said that it wasn't that much, that he'd been given a lot of extra responsibility but not a lot of extra money to compensate him for that. Of course, how much he received or, indeed, how much he earns is and always has been a mystery to her.

So she'll just have to muddle on, she supposes, and put up with whatever she has to put up with when these extra expenses occur. And at least they don't have a mortgage – Henry said that they should clear that with the money she inherited from her father, which they did. And she has a good husband and two beautiful, healthy children. There are so many, many people less fortunate than her.

But then she begins to dwell on how things can change in the blink of an eye. What if Henry were to die? He has explained to her before how she would be taken care of financially, but it still worries her. And perhaps even more worrying than him dying is the thought of him *living*. She always laughs silently when she thinks of this. What she means is what would happen if he tired of her and left her. She would have this house, the girls, no savings and no income. Or would she have the house? Legally, she's not sure what the situation is. When she married Henry did all of her property become his? She keeps meaning to consult a solicitor and find the answer to this question. But where would she find the money to pay a solicitor without Henry finding out? Actually, she knows she could probably find the money and still keep it from Henry if she had to. Maybe the real reason she doesn't do it is that she doesn't really want to know the answer.

Her father made his money by coming to London and opening a stationary shop. As well as selling to the general public he pursued contracts with businesses – banks, insurance companies, offices. At first just paper, ink, ledgers, that kind of thing. But soon he began to offer a service whereby he would take care of all their printing requirements, supplying the special forms they required to run their enterprise. His business blossomed. When she left school, Clara worked there until she got married. It is the only type of work she knows. But now her father is dead, the shop is sold and the time when Clara had an income of her own seems like another age. In fact, it doesn't seem like her life at all, but rather somebody else's – or something she read about in a novel.

And supposing something was to happen to one of the girls? She has finally returned to where she started thinking about all of this several hours ago. Supposing they got sick or had an accident? She would never be able to get over something like that. And the house, while it is big and comfortable like an old pair of shoes, it always seems to need something doing to it. And while Henry was glad to come and live here, and she knows he likes the prestige associated with living in a house like this, he still complains when he has to spend money on its maintenance. And Henry is no good at that kind of thing himself and never helps in the garden. 'I'm no good with my hands,' he says, with an implication that to be good with one's hands is a somewhat demeaning thing. So they have to hire in people – and this costs money. So lately Clara has started trying to do some of these things herself. And to her surprise, she has had some success. Clara, as it turns out, *is* good with her hands.

Whether Henry lives or dies before her, whether he leaves or stays, she worries about growing old. She has two different visions between which she alternates. In one he is not there, the girls are grown up, have left and are living their own lives – married with children, in all likelihood. She really has no life beyond the girls. She sees herself rattling around the house, a shrivelled old woman. What will she do then? Sink into a bottle of gin?

And even more disturbing in some ways is the scenario where she and Henry grow old together. What will that be like then, given that, in some ways, Henry is old now? When it happened, she's not quite sure. He was young when she met him and during their courtship and some early part of her marriage. It's something that mystifies her – she can never quite pinpoint the time when it occurred. Was there a moment or did it happen over a period of time? She can't tell or remember.

And so Clara fills her hours in bed until finally sleep overtakes her tired body and her exhausted mind. On that strange and distant and hazy border between waking and sleep, happier thoughts start to emerge shyly; times when she really was truly, truly happy. People from her life that she knew loved her – her grandparents, for example – her mother's parents. They are dead now but maybe – wherever they are – they love her still. She hopes so. She's not religious in the conventional sense but she often thinks about the people who went before her and views communing with them as a form of prayer. She remembers happy times she spent at home or summers long ago. And in the short periods where she does sleep deeply, she dreams long, convoluted, richly coloured dreams. She often remembers these and speaks about them with her girls over breakfast – as long as their father isn't there.

Chapter 7
Sunday 28 June 1914

Nobody is sleeping at number 2 Ballhausplatz in Vienna. (I promise, weary reader, this will be our last port of call for what has been, I think you'll agree, an exceptionally long Sunday. We shall meet the Austrian manager and, once we've done that, there will be only one major character left for you to meet and we can leave that until tomorrow. So then everyone will be able to go to bed. So let's be done with it, shall we?)

Leopold Anton Johann Sigismund Josef Korsinus Ferdinand Graf Berchtold von und zu Ungarschitz, Frättling, und Püllütz – how about we just call him Berchtold? – is the Austrian Foreign Minister and manager. A wealthy landowner in Hungary and Moravia, Berchtold, through marriage, is one of the richest men in Austria. Amongst many other things, he owns a castle in Moravia – his country seat – surrounded by magnificent forests. That is where he is this afternoon, opening a charity bazaar, when the news of the assassination reaches him. He catches the next train back to Vienna.

Berchtold joined the diplomatic corps in 1893, and although not credited with any great ability – fifty shades of Grey, if you'll pardon the pun – he nevertheless impressed with his courtly manners and aristocratic background. Promotion was consequently rapid. After spells in London and Paris, Berchtold was appointed ambassador to Russia in 1907, serving at St Petersburg until his return to Vienna in 1912 whereupon he took up his appointment as Emperor Franz-Josef's Foreign Minister.

If you want to picture what Berchtold looks like try to imagine a balding and very stern headmaster of an early twentieth-century posh school. In fact, the headmaster is not just stern; he's angry.

There is a permanent anger bubbling just under the surface and ready to break out at the drop of a hat. Perhaps he is sexually frustrated – the headmaster, I mean – and this is where his anger stems from. Berchtold has a little moustache and a permanently slightly irritated look about him. It is that look a headmaster has when a habitually offending pupil is relating a story that the headmaster doesn't believe in the slightest and, rather than listening to the excuse and try to treat it on its merits, the headmaster is already trying to decide what the punishment will be.

At the outset of the Balkan Wars two years ago, Count Berchtold flirted with the idea of war against Serbia, but vacillated and pulled back from intervention at the last moment. The result is that he has a reputation for being weak and indecisive.

When Berchtold arrives in Vienna there are already black flags draped from some of the buildings, looking oddly sinister in the dusty evening sunlight. People stand around in groups reading special editions of the newspapers. When his car stops for an old lady to cross the street, Berchtold hears a voice say through his partly open window, 'We can't put up with any more of this.' The car continues on to 2 Ballhausplatz where his staff is already waiting for him.

Amongst them are Count Hoyos, his *chef de cabinet*, Count von Forgach, Second Section Chief, and Alexander Musulin, Head of Chancery. (Don't worry – you don't need to remember any of these people. I'm just trying to give you a sense of the gathering. Hoyos is the leader of a group of younger diplomats at the Ballhausplatz, known as the 'Young Rebels,' who have always favoured a more aggressive foreign policy as the only recipe to stop the decline or disintegration of Austria.) In the weeks to come, Berchtold will hold daily meetings with these men and their advice will shape his tactics.

Also there is Franz Graf Conrad von Hötzendorf – or Conrad, for short – the Head of the Austrian Army. With his beaked nose, chin jutting out like a ledge on which a seagull could have nested and magnificent moustache, Conrad is the very model of a modern major general. He is a social Darwinist, which is just a fancy way of saying that he believes in survival of the fittest. Which is just a clichéd way of saying that he believes that the struggle for existence is 'the basic principle behind all the events on this earth' and is 'the only real and rational basis for policy making.' Conrad believes it is self-evident that at some stage Austria will have to fight to preserve its status as a great power. Accordingly, he first proposed a match against Serbia in 1906. He did so again in 1908–09, in 1912–13, in October 1913 and May 1914. Between 1 January 1913 and 1 January 1914 – in case anybody should have been in any doubt about his position – he proposed a game against Serbia *twenty-five* times. Since mid-1913, Austria had asked Germany three times for help to play against Serbia. Each time, Der Kaiser had refused.

Conrad is widely regarded as a military genius and so he is the author of numerous books on military matters. He is a great believer in the attack – that armies which fight defensively invariably turn out to be the losers. He doesn't have much time for the new technologies like the machine gun. However, in his book on the Boer War, he does concede that such technologies could make frontal attacks more costly. His solution? Abandon the thought of such frontal attacks altogether? Well, er, no, not really. His solution is that armies are going to have to be bigger – they're going to need more men so that they can force the issue and overcome massed machine guns. If a genius is someone who can foresee the future then Conrad probably *is* a genius. His analysis will turn out to be chillingly accurate when it comes to the Group of Death.

So as you've probably guessed, the mood of the meeting could not be described as conciliatory. Pretty much all the men in the room at number 2 Ballhausplatz are keen on an aggressive war against Serbia. Berchtold is worried about preparing public opinion for any such war but, perhaps judging by the mood on the street this evening, that isn't going to be much of a problem. Anyway, this evening the meeting breaks up and the men go to bed having reached no decision on what action to take.

Chapter 8
Monday 29 June 1914

Henry has been wondering a lot lately whether, seven years ago, Clara had trapped him. He is wondering this now as the train rattles along the Central Line towards his station at Bank. It is such a nice day that he was tempted to take the omnibus and sit upstairs in the sunshine, but in the end habit won out. Henry likes his routine. If he arrives at one of the milestones on his daily journey earlier than usual, it gives him a little lift; if later, he becomes concerned. Not that he is ever late for work. He believes his punctuality, a record as firm as the Bank of England itself, was one of the factors when they considered him for promotion earlier this year and when he subsequently was given the title 'manager.'

He joined the firm as a clerk. His first step up the ladder was when, still as a clerk, he was given responsibility for all of the company's stationary requirements. They already had a contract with Clara's father so Henry's job was just to make sure it ran smoothly. He liked the old man, despite his somewhat gauche country ways. He was honest, easy to deal with, every bit as predictable and reliable as Henry could have wanted and things ran like clockwork.

Except that, one day, quite unexpectedly, they ran out of claims forms. It was during the winter – a particularly cold one – and there had been a lot of water damage from burst pipes and so a surge in claims. Henry probably would admit that he had become a bit complacent after six months in charge of stationary. The old man seemed to do most of the work. It was a cushy number. Except that Henry did have to do *some* work and one of his tasks was to ensure that there were always plenty of forms on hand. He had been careless, lax. Somewhere in his head a little voice had been saying, 'The old man's taking care of it' with the result that he hadn't noticed how quickly the stockpile of claims forms had gone down. It was only when another great batch disappeared and he discovered there was only a handful left that Henry realised he had a problem. A *big* one.

It was a sticky situation. Even now, whenever he thought back to that dreadful day, he felt a momentary chill. It could all have gone so horribly wrong. Work in the claims department could have ground to a halt and it would have quickly become apparent where the fault lay. He's convinced they would have let him go – it had happened to people for less – and without a reference.

Trying not to look like he was panicking, Henry stepped out and hurried round to the stationary store. It was a bleak rainy day with a high wind and he was in a cold sweat. When he discovered that Clara's father wasn't even at the shop, Henry reckoned the game was up.

'Can I help at all?' the girl behind the counter asked.

It was almost as though he hadn't seen her up until then. Trying to keep the tremor out of his voice, Henry explained that he knew that a delivery of claims forms wasn't due until late next week, but he wondered if, by any chance, there were any already printed, since a sudden, unexpected need had arisen. The girl said she would check.

While she disappeared into the back, Henry prayed that she would find some forms. Even ones that maybe had been printed and hadn't quite come up to the old man's exacting standard. Even these. Please God, the old man hadn't thrown them in the bin. Henry looked out unseeing as the rain ran down the plate glass window of the shop. People hurried past. Umbrellas were blown inside out. It was the end – he knew it, could feel it. Even the weather knew it. He pictured himself returning to the firm empty handed and praying that the tiny remaining pile of claims forms would hold out, all the while knowing that they wouldn't. Like a fuse burning its way towards a keg of gunpowder, the last one would finally be taken. Then somebody would ask – brightly, cheerily, in a completely routine sort of way – 'Any more claims forms, Henry?' and then he would have to own up. After that he would be called into Mr Faber, the managing partner's, office. And after that?

After that would come his hat, coat and the door, stepping out into rain-lashed, end-of-the-world London.

'How many do you need?'

He spun round. The girl carried several thick, heavy blocks of forms wrapped in brown paper.

'They're all printed,' she said. 'You just need to tell me how many you need. And we'll have to find some way of keeping them dry while you get them back to the office. Or I can have them delivered,' she added with a smile.

In that moment, Henry felt he had never seen a more beautiful woman. He could have kissed her. The relief he felt would literally stay with him for days. It would remain the first and only time he made such an error. After work he hurried to the nearest pub and downed three whiskies, and it was only when he was going home to the room he rented that he remembered the pretty girl in the stationary shop. She was short with blonde hair and really quite the loveliest face. He recalled her perfect skin and soft blue eyes.

Henry was quite surprised by the effect the incident had on him. His self-confidence soared. Even though he clearly had played no real part in the solution to the problem, he found he walked around the office with something of a swagger now. It was a swagger, which if anything, further increased when Mr Faber said to him one day, 'Seem to be keeping on top of all that stationary business, Kenton.' It was the closest Faber was ever likely to get to a compliment.

The following week, when the old man was supervising a delivery, Henry thanked him for having had the foresight to have extra batches of claims forms on hand.

'Think nothing of it,' he replied. 'That's what we're here for.'

'That nice girl in your shop was very helpful,' continued Henry.

'Ah, you met Clara,' said Mr Jordan. 'She's a good girl is Clara. She's m'daughter, don't you know.'

Henry did it all as it should be done. The old man already knew him, which was an advantage. The next time he met the old man, Henry asked if Clara had a young man in her life. When Clara's father confirmed that she didn't, Henry asked if he might take Clara to tea, perhaps on Saturday at lunchtime, after he'd finished work for the week.

'I don't see why not,' said the old man amiably. 'But you'll have to ask the lass herself – it'll be her decision.'

And that was how it began.

She said yes and they went for tea at an ABC. If he had expected her to be shy or diffident in any way, he was to be surprised. She was confident and, if anything, it was he who came away from their tea feeling somewhat intimidated and inadequate. As well as being pretty, she was well read and seemed to have the same head for business as her father. But all of this only reinforced his desire to pursue her. He could still remember how much he had admired her self-possession and poise. Now, though, as the train clanked along, he wondered if what he had seen as self-confidence wasn't actually the reaction of an animal that has seen its prey and now needed to bring it down.

At the time, he thought that their courtship was the happiest he had ever been in his life. Now he couldn't help feeling that it had all been orchestrated by her, telling him the things he wanted to hear, deferring to him, doing things he wanted to do. Everything had just fallen into place – even the death of Clara's father six months into their courtship. Not that Henry hadn't been sad to see him go. On the contrary, he had been very fond of the old man.

Obviously Clara had no part in the old man's death, but that event too had helped to propel Henry to the altar. Clara's mother had died several years before her husband. Clara had an older brother and, even if she did have lots of aunts and uncles, Henry felt that it was up to him now to take care of her. Clara's brother inherited the stationary business; she inherited the house in Acton and some money. So now they had a place to live. They were married within the year.

At first it had been blissful, particularly when Clara got over the worst of the grief after her father's death. Any fears Henry might have had about the physical side of married life were also quickly dispelled. In the pub he and the other men from the office might laugh uproariously about wives, saying things like, 'Somebody has to hold the beastly thing' but Henry often wondered how many of them were actually joking. Clara had no such reservations – she was uninhibited in a way which, again, he found somewhat daunting. There were times when it was almost as though she was the man. This affected Henry so much so that, for about six months after they were married, he had difficulty getting it up. Again, what he saw then as Clara's understanding and patience in helping him through it had really been her continuing to get what she wanted from their relationship.

But the main thing, the thing that overrode everything else – Henry is now in the lift taking him up to the station exit – was that somewhere along the way, she stopped loving him. That's if she ever had.

He can't pinpoint where this happened. Was it when she gave up working in the shop, which she did almost immediately after they were married? Or when she was pregnant with Ursula? Although, almost all through that pregnancy, she still wanted to have sex. In fact, he had been the one who had been uncomfortable with the whole idea.

'Won't it be able to see us?' he asked, to which she had laughed that laugh of hers that, at the time, he loved so much, but that now grated on him whenever he heard it. At the time he had found it lusty, hearty, full of *joie de vivre*. These days it just sounded rather common.

It is a short walk to the office. It is getting near the time when he must put these thoughts to one side and concentrate on his work. Being a manager has brought with it heavy responsibilities and he will not make the mistake he made before with the stationary – of taking his eye off the ball. These days he gives it his full attention and is often thinking about it long after he has returned home.

They are due to go to Devon on holiday in mid-August. They are going to stay by the sea. It is the first time since their honeymoon that they have been able to afford such a luxury. This morning at breakfast, Clara announced that she was coming into town to pick up some necessities for their trip. She suggested that she and Henry meet for lunch – even if it was only a quick one. However, he demurred, explaining that he would be too busy, by which he really meant he didn't want to be distracted from the task at hand.

But there is a second reason why Henry demurred, and this is also the reason why he is not particularly looking forward to their holiday in August. Because Henry has a secret.

Chapter 9
Monday 29 June 1914

Clara too often wonders how and where things changed. It seems like one day she and Henry were lovers – young, passionate, fun-loving – and the next they had the relationship they have now. But it can't have happened as suddenly as that. Can it?

She has one theory, which is that the marriage itself caused the change. After they left the church it was as though they both suddenly took up roles, as though they were actors in a play. Henry suddenly became the serious, self-important, I'm-the-provider type of person, reading the paper, going off to work, insisting that his shoes were shined and his collars were sparkling white. Before, his landlady had done those things. Without even a murmur, Clara had stepped in and taken over.

And that's the other thing. She first thought that Henry was to blame for this change in their relationship. She realised now that she has facilitated it completely. Just as he took up his role, so she took up hers. She took it as her duty to keep a clean and tidy house, to make sure his clothes were just so and that meals were served up. Since she had no other job, she threw herself heart and soul into this one. But as a result, the other Clara, the independent, opinionated, extroverted Clara who had worked in the stationary shop, became a distant memory.

Her thoughts continued in circles, as all her theories seem to. Didn't all women want this – the nesting, homemaking, child rearing? Yes, she had, but she also enjoyed her other life. And most of all, she just didn't want to be viewed as a sort of combined maid and nanny and sex vessel. (This is a phrase she has begun to use to herself – 'sex vessel.' A vessel as in a container, not a ship. A container for what Henry shoots into her every Saturday night after he has taken her to dinner.)

She had pictured their life after they married would be a continuation of what they had done before. Talking, laughing, sharing what had happened each day. He would go off to work, her job would be the house and eventually the children, but the fun would continue when they were together again in the evening. It would be an equal partnership – he brought in the money, she cared for the house and the family. Surely that was the way it was meant to be. But now, instead, it has evolved into something where, somehow, his job is more important than hers. In fact, not just more important. It is like it is the only job that has any meaning. Hers seems to have been reduced to just skivvying around the house.

The worst part is that she knows it cannot be changed. How could they possibly row back from such a position? Would Henry even want to? Because it seems to her that part of the change is that he now sees her in a different light from when they were courting. She is not his equal any more. He sees her in this skivvy role. She is the maid and nanny with whom he has sex. One night a week, for those few hours when they go to the Trocadero or some such place, he is maybe the man who romanced her again, but even that is fading. The last night they were there, he was very subdued and, after she made numerous attempts to engage him in conversation, she gave up.

So she knows this isn't a conversation she can ever have with Henry. But could she *do* something? They say that actions speak louder than words. Can she start to live the life she pictured? And in doing so, in changing her behaviour, might she cause him to change his?

If she is to do this, if she is to live this other life, the first thing she has to do is change how she feels about herself. Because she has been going along with this idea that his is the only job that matters. Everything she does, from being the first up in the morning to being the last in bed at night, is all centred around making Henry's day go as smoothly as possible. His clean clothes are there when he gets up, his shoes are polished, the children aren't too boisterous at breakfast, one of his favourite dinners is cooked and waiting when he comes home. Henry doesn't really like fish, whereas Clara adores it. As a result, she rarely cooks it.

And then there is the whole business of 'Don't upset your father.' Clara spends literally all the time that Henry is at home trying to make sure she or the children don't do anything to irritate him or annoy him. She sort of knows where this comes from. When Clara was growing up, her parents constantly argued. For some reason that she doesn't at all understand, Clara assumed that these arguments were either about her or that she was to blame for them. As a result she spent much of her childhood trying to ensure that whatever she did wouldn't trigger one of these arguments. She would spend long hours in her room watching the birds that she coaxed onto her windowsill with crumbs of bread. When her mother took to her bed, as she often did, her father would explain that it was her mother's 'nerves,' and as Clara took over the running of the house, she would try to ensure that whatever she did wouldn't upset her father.

Clara is still the same child. She realises this. 'Find the child and you've found the adult' is a favourite saying of hers. Even though she is now a grown woman, in some ways – and this is especially true in her marriage to Henry – she is still the little nine-year-old girl trying to please and not cause any disagreement.

Clara thinks life should be a bed of roses. She is the only person she knows who has ever thought this. When she was at school she had a friend, Genevieve, to whom she once said this. They were talking of what they wanted life to be like when they grew up. Genevieve so ridiculed this idea that Clara never mentioned it to anybody again. Not even to Henry. Not even when they were courting.

Chapter 10
Monday 29 June 1914

'Bother! O blow! Hang spring-cleaning!'

They are probably Clara's favourite words from what may well be her favourite book, *The Wind in the Willows*. They suddenly occur to her now, standing on the dew-drenched lawn of the house in Acton in her bare feet. It is early morning.

A few minutes ago she woke before Henry's alarm clock went off. The room was in darkness. While she would prefer to sleep with the curtains pulled back and be woken by the sun, Henry prefers to have them drawn. She slipped into her dressing gown and slippers and stole silently out of the room. In the bathroom mirror she brushed her hair and then came downstairs. The house was silent; the girls were still asleep.

She loves this time of morning, before everyone else is awake. The hush and then the stirring, the pause before the chord, the breath before the kiss. She goes into the kitchen, opens the back door and then down the three steps to the lawn. Here she takes off her slippers and stands in bare feet on the wet grass. She likes to stand on the earth, likes to imagine the sphere of the world turning slowly with her attached to it. Clara's middle name is Mahala. Her mother told her that it is an American Indian word for woman. Clara likes to imagine that somewhere, right now, an American Indian woman is standing on the Earth just as Clara is doing.

She closes her eyes and lets the sun, which slants into the back garden when it rises, warm her face. She listens to the birds twittering madly. They aren't as loud or as many as they were in spring but it is still quite a performance. Clara *adores* birds. How she loves the spring when the fluff ball baby birds – the 'little babas,' as she calls them – start to appear and get their first flying lessons. They are all well out of the nest now.

And that is when it occurs to her – the Bother, O blow and Hang spring-cleaning. She *won't* stay around the house all day cleaning, dusting, sweeping and minding the girls. She will take a few hours to herself and go into town. She can buy some things for their holiday. And perhaps meet Henry for lunch. Hang spring-cleaning indeed. With this resolve, she slides her feet back into her slippers. Their wetness doesn't bother her. The dew is holy water, beautiful wine.

Henry is already up – she can hear him in the bathroom. She goes upstairs again and calls Ursula. The general hubbub has woken Virginia, who lies happily in her cot until Clara comes to get her. She is such a placid child, unlike her sister at that age. Clara brings Virginia downstairs, pops her into her baby chair and starts to prepare breakfast, talking to her all the while. The table has been laid the night before. She makes Ursula's lunch for school. Meanwhile Ursula and Henry appear and sit at the table. Clara makes tea and ferries toast from the grill to the bread basket. Henry isn't really one to talk much in the morning but, in fairness to him, she feels he makes an effort. He asks – as he does every day – each of the three of them in turn what they intend to do that day. Ursula gets to be asked first.

'We're going to be reading stories in school,' she says.

'And you, Virginia?'

'Papa,' says Virginia happily, between mouthfuls of porridge that Clara is feeding her.

Clara has noticed an interesting thing – though she has never said anything about it to Henry. When Henry is there, Virginia seems to just know a few words – 'Mama,' 'Papa,' 'chair.' But when Henry is at work or in the sitting room, and Clara and Virginia are together, Clara will talk constantly to the child, who then seems to know many more words. She knows 'leg' and 'face' and other parts of the body. She understands when Clara says, 'I'm just going to open the window' or 'Where did I put that spoon?' and will repeat some of the words. It is very curious. Though in another sense, it isn't. Clara thinks – has thought from the first time she clapped eyes on her – that Virginia is an old soul. She has been here before.

'And you, my dear?' asks Henry.

'I thought I might go into town. Pick up some things we're going to need for our holiday.'

'May I come, Mummy?' asks Ursula.

'I come?' asks Virginia, in the same questioning tone.

'Not today,' Clara replies. 'You stay with Mrs Parsons. We three will go some other day. Anyway, you've got school, Ursula.'

Ursula returns to her toast. Clara butters a small piece and gives it to Virginia. There is a knock at the door.

'That'll be Mrs Parsons now,' says Clara.

'I'll get it,' declares Ursula.

'That'll be nice,' Henry says, spreading butter on a crust of toast.

He often does this, referring back to a piece of conversation that occurred a while back. Clara knows that he ignores a lot of what goes on in the house, not to mention what she says. He often doesn't listen because he is reading his newspaper or thinking about work or something else. This is true particularly lately. But it is almost as though there is some other part of his brain that is recording the conversation and then this recording gets checked for anything of significance. Clara has this image of a group of little men in Henry's head listening to the recording, a bit like the dog on the 'His Master's Voice' advertisements. If they hear anything worthy of his attention, they pass it along to him and he comments on it, just as he did now. Clara once told him about the little men in his head but he wasn't at all amused. She keeps it to herself now.

'I wondered if you'd like to meet for lunch?' she asks.

'Oh, I don't think so,' he says, now somewhat more engaged, though his eyes are still on the newspaper. 'I don't think I'll be able to today. Not on Monday. Everything tends to be far too busy on a Monday. Perhaps some other day.'

For a moment Clara is surprised – and hurt. But the feeling passes quickly.

'Of course,' she says, sitting down herself.

She pours some tea and butters a piece of toast. It doesn't matter. Time in town by herself will be just as nice.

After breakfast, Clara goes through everything with Mrs Parsons, particularly the collecting of Ursula from school.

Then, with Virginia in her pram, Clara delivers Ursula to school. After that, leaving Virginia with Mrs Parsons, Clara goes upstairs, bathes and dresses. She puts on a frothy white blouse and a dark blue skirt. She won't need a jacket today – not in Central London, not in this weather. A white hat with a cornflower blue ribbon, some lipstick and she's ready to go.

She takes the omnibus into town. She wanders in and out of shops on Regent Street. She picks up some bargain winter clothes which are being sold off. They won't fit Virginia now but should by the end of the year. She buys each of the girls a little gift – a small packet of sweets for Ursula, a little bar of chocolate for Virginia. Clara goes into an ABC and orders coffee and two cakes. What a beautiful drink coffee is. She rarely drinks it at home. Henry prefers tea and it seems silly and expensive and wasteful just to make it for one. The cakes each consist of two round shortbread biscuits with strawberry jam in between, icing and hundreds and thousands on top. She has loved them ever since she was a child.

She doesn't mind being by herself like this. It seems to her sometimes that she has spent her whole life alone. Her mother began to retreat into herself while Clara was still a child. Clara never knew the reason for this but she wonders if it had something to do with the deep-seated unhappiness that existed between her parents.

The more her mother withdrew, the more her father retreated into his work. By the time she was nine Clara was often – for weeks at a time – running the house, cooking for her father and brother and trying to jolly her mother out of bed and out of her increasingly profound depressions. Clara had the top bedroom in the house at that time – a dormer window on whose ledge she would leave crumbs of bread to encourage birds to land. They became her friends. She named them and talked to them and rejoiced in the tiny fluffy youngsters that appeared each spring.

When she married Henry, she thought her being alone had finally come to an end. Looking back on it now, she can see how wrong she was – how stupid she has been. Her marriage has just been a momentary interruption before she returned to what she now thinks of as her natural state.

She finishes her coffee. It is only lunchtime. She doesn't want to go home yet. The nearest park is St James's so she goes across to it and finds a bench by the water. Ducks wander about on the grass and occasionally squabble noisily with one another over food. A swan sails past stately as a queen. A pelican lands. Clara realises that she is smiling; she loves being surrounded by birds like this. She wishes she had brought some bread and is just considering going to see if she can buy some when a man comes along and asks if she'd mind if he shared the bench with her.

'Not at all,' she replies.

She'd better not go now. He'll be insulted.

'Thank you very much,' he says.

The man is wearing a dark, well-cut suit. Still standing, he slips the jacket off and folds it in two, vertically. Then, holding the result to his chest, he indicates the gap between them.

'You're sure you don't mind?' he asks again, with a smile.

'Not at all,' she says a second time.

She wonders if he wonders whether these are the only words she knows. Just like Virginia, Clara thinks.

The man has a very pale face. Beneath the jacket, he wears a bright white shirt and a dark tie. The jacket is placed on the seat and folded in half a second time. On top of that the man places his hat. Then he sits down. On the front part of the seat, he places a brown paper package that he has been carrying and unwraps it. It contains cut sandwiches made with thick slices of white bread. Then he shakes out a copy of the *Times* and opens it on a particular page, folding it back on itself. He folds it again and then, crossing his knees in what looks to Clara like a precisely synchronised movement, he rests the resulting half page-sized newspaper on his knee. He begins to read and, still with his eyes on the newspaper, gropes for a sandwich, finds one, lifts it up and begins to munch. What is it about men and their newspapers, Clara wonders?

She suddenly becomes aware that she is staring at him. Just as she does, he does too. He turns and sees that she is looking at him. He glances down at his package of sandwiches, then at the newspaper, then at her again. He smiles, slightly sheepishly.

'You can take the man out of his routine,' he says. 'But you can't take his routine out of the man.'

Clara blushes deeply.

'I'm terribly sorry. I really didn't mean to be so rude.'

'Nothing to apologise for,' he says. 'I have to admit it, I'm a man of routine. I come here every day – unless I have to go to one of those silly lunches. I bring my own sandwiches and I save a little at the end for the ducks.'

'No, really,' Clara insists. 'I'm *very* sorry.'

He carries on as if he hasn't heard her.

'Even the filling stays the same – at least for long periods. Currently I'm going through my fine ham and strong mustard phase – compliments of my local grocer, Mr Adams.'

She wonders if he's trying to embarrass her even more than she is.

'I'm sorry,' she says again, and looks away hurriedly.

She wishes she had a paper or something she could bury herself in, hide behind. She is terribly embarrassed. She had better leave and sits forward as a prelude to getting up.

'Think nothing further of it,' he replies.

Then he adds, 'It's a beautiful place here, isn't it – especially on days like today.'

She looks at him again. She reckons him to be about her age or possibly a little older. He has brown hair, grey-green eyes and a fine nose. He has turned ever so slightly towards her. His eyes are bright but she thinks his complexion is so pale as to be almost grey and unhealthy.

'It is. It's a lovely place,' she says. 'I love the birds. I should have brought some food for them.'

She feels herself sit back – almost as if her body decided by itself, without any command from her.

'So you're not a regular then?'

'No,' she smiles. 'But you are?'

'I am. I work in the Foreign Office – over there.'

He indicates with a leftward movement of his head.

'It sounds important.'

'More so than it is. Though it'll probably hot up over the next few weeks.'

'You mean the business with the Archduke.'

It is only because she remembers seeing something on a newspaper seller's poster as she made her way here. She's bluffing. She doesn't really know anything about this. But she remembers one time, when she and Henry were courting, how in a moment of self-analysis and exceptional honesty, she said to him, 'I pretend to know much more than I do.' She is never that honest with Henry now. Now, she keeps all that kind of thing to herself.

'Oh, you know about it?'

He sounds surprised.

'Of course. I *do* read the papers, you know.'

She's really pushing it now. But it's his turn to apologise.

'I'm sorry,' he says. 'I didn't mean it like that. It's just that I find a lot of people don't know – or maybe it's that they don't want to know – what's going on in the world. They're happy to eat and sleep and just get on with it.'

'So what do you think will happen?' she asks. 'About the Archduke, I mean.'

Whatever she learns, she'll try out on Henry tonight. He'll be surprised – and mystified. She won't tell him where it came from though. Maybe she'll just say the same thing to him – 'I *do* read the papers, you know.'

'Too soon to say,' the man from the Foreign Office says. 'There are all kinds of possibilities. None of them are particularly good, and some are much worse than others. Perhaps the most optimistic one says that there'll be a small war in the Balkans.'

Then he adds, 'Again.'

'Oh dear,' she says.

Then, trying to show off the one piece of knowledge she *does* have, she says, 'So you know Sir Edward Grey?'

'He's my boss's boss.'

'What's he like?'

'You're not related to him, are you?' he asks.

What a strange question, she thinks.

'No,' Clara says. 'I'm not related to him.'

'He's the sweetest man. Likes fishing. Very keen birdwatcher.'

Then he adds, 'Birds. Yes, he likes birds. A bit like yourself, actually. But he's not keen on foreigners, though.'

She smiles. She isn't sure whether the man from the Foreign Office is being serious.

'No?' she asks.

She thinks it's a good response.

But all he replies is, 'No.'

Clara isn't quite sure what to say next. She doesn't want to make a fool of herself.

'It doesn't sound like the best qualification to be a Foreign Secretary.'

'No indeed,' he says. 'I once heard him say at a meeting something to the effect of foreign statesmen ought to receive their education at an English public school.'

Clara is smiling but the man from the Foreign Office's face is deadpan. She still can't tell what this is all about. The man is silent for a few moments and then says, 'And he's not that fond of foreign travel, either.'

Clara feels like bursting out laughing but she doesn't know if her companion is being serious or pulling her leg or what he's about. Maybe he's one of these people who've worked in the same place for so long that he's forgotten what the world outside is like and can only talk about where he works. Henry will be like that one day, she thinks. Maybe he is now.

To the man from the Foreign Office, Clara simply says, 'No?' hoping the direction of the conversation will become clearer.

'No. To the best of my knowledge, apart from a non-stop journey through the Continent long ago on his way to India, and a brief state visit to Paris in the retinue of King George V – he has never visited Europe.'

Clara can't help herself any longer and starts to laugh. This is all too ridiculous. There is a terrible moment when she thinks she has gotten this all wrong and that she has grievously insulted the man from the Foreign Office. But then his deadpan expression becomes a smile. He seems to be enjoying the fact that he made her laugh. And she is indeed laughing. For some reason, she finds this desperately funny, so much so that her eyes start to water.

She fumbles in her bag for her handkerchief. The man from the Foreign Office continues to enjoy her reaction. She finds the hankie and dabs at her eyes. Finally she manages to get her laughter under control.

But she is bursting to add a comment of her own, even if she knows it will cause her to erupt again. The man from the Foreign Office seems to be looking at her expectantly. It's as if he knows she has something to say. Finally, almost of their own accord, the words escape from her and slip out.

'We're in good hands so.'

Now it's the turn of the man from the Foreign Office to laugh. He does – a soft, warm chuckle. He has a nice laugh.

'Indeed,' he says dryly.

Clara dabs her eyes again and thinks it's safe to return the hankie to her bag. She's not sure what to say next and so she opts for changing the subject.

'I'm sorry,' she says. 'I'm keeping you from your lunch.'

'Not at all,' he replies. 'Nice to have somebody sensible to speak with.'

She's very taken with his use of the word 'sensible.'

'Is all of that true?' she asks, knowing she risks plunging back into another bout of laughter. 'About Sir Edward Grey, I mean.'

He nods.

'I'm afraid so.'

The laughter is there again, at the door, knocking, wanting to get in. *The Pickwick Papers* all over again. She manages to contain it. Eventually she is able to say, 'Oh dear.'

'Oh dear, indeed,' he agrees. 'Anyway, I should probably be getting back.'

Three of the four sandwiches lie uneaten in the package.

'What about your sandwiches?' asks Clara.

'I'll save the rest until later. I think we may be working late tonight. Oh, that is – unless you'd like them? They're very good. Even if I do say so myself.'

It's Clara's turn to be embarrassed again.

'No, I didn't mean it like that.'

'I know you didn't,' he says. 'But they *are* good.'

'I'm sure they are but no thank you. Save them for later. If you're working late you'll need something. Or if you don't want them, I'm sure the ducks won't say no.'

He smiles at this thought. Then he proceeds to re-wrap the package, stands up and extends a hand.

'Can I say what a pleasure it's been Mrs—?'

'Jordan. Clara Jordan.'

'Mrs Jordan.'

He bows ever so slightly as she takes his proffered hand.

'James Walters. I hope I shall have the pleasure again some day.'

'The pleasure was all mine, Mr Walters.'

And then he is gone, his back quickly disappearing amongst all the others who have been taking their lunch in the park and are now returning to work.

She sits there for a long time after he is gone. Birds continue to fly and swim and run, to waddle around importantly, to land and take off. People come and go.

Why did she tell him her maiden name? She *never* does that. She has been Clara Kenton ever since she got married. What made her do that?

And she suddenly has the strangest feeling. It is as though all of this – the grassy lawns, the water, the blue sky, the paths, the drenching sun, the birds and the people – it is as though all of it has ceased to be real. Rather, it is like it has all become a sort of backdrop to a play or an opera. And she has the feeling that, amidst all of this, she is the only thing that is real. And if that is true, if that is really true, then she is truly and utterly alone – in all the world.

She has felt loneliness before – but never like this. Looking around, it is as though everything else is on the other side of a sheet of glass. Only she is on this side. It is a horrible feeling which prompts her to stand up and seek to escape from this place.

She begins to walk back towards the gate. But the feeling refuses to leave her. Rather, it intensifies. It isn't just that the people are a backdrop now – they are ghosts. Brightly coloured or bathed in sunlight they may be, but they are still ghosts. Nothing is real or substantial any more. Except her – and she is like a wraith who has entered this strange world and now is destined to wander it for ever.

She walks more and more quickly as though she is trying to outstrip this sensation, but she can't. It won't go away. She had intended to get the omnibus home but now she just wants to hide from all of this. She hurries down the steps into the Tube station. But it is the descent into Hades and the platform, with its scattered people, the ante-room to hell. The trip on the train is like a voyage of the damned. People stare vacantly ahead and, even though she emerges into sunlight at the end of her journey, this terrible feeling persists.

When she arrives home, the girls run to meet her. Clara gives them their presents. Mrs Parsons tells her what good girls they have been. But it is as if Clara is wondering who these people are.

Later she goes through the motions of making tea. Henry comes home, kisses her and sits down at the table with the girls. He opens the *Evening Standard* and begins reading. Part way through, he lowers it and, with a 'by the way,' mentions something about the firm having a management meeting on the last day of every month and that he will have to go. She thinks he says something about having to 'stay up in town.' The girls became fractious and normally it is she who reins in their high spirits, but tonight Henry has to do it. Even Ursula notices there is something out of the ordinary because she asks, 'Is everything alright, Mummy?'

'I'm just tired, darling,' Clara says automatically.

Later, after the girls have been put to bed, Clara claims that she has a headache and goes to bed herself. It is still light. Eventually she dozes, but wakes later to find that it is dark. A black, velvety light fills the room. But then she hears Henry on the stairs and he comes in. She pretends to be asleep. He doesn't turn the light on but draws the curtains. He says, 'How's the head, darling?'

She knows he knows she's not asleep.

'Still there,' she says, at length. 'I'm sure it'll be gone in the morning.'

'What do you think caused it?' he asks.

She hears him taking off his trousers.

'Maybe I just got too much sun,' she says.

When he returns from the bathroom, he gets in beside her. She is lying on her side with her back to his side of the bed. He comes across and lies up against her, passing an arm around her and taking one of her breasts in the palm of his hand. He is aroused. *It's not the weekend, is it?* Clara wonders.

'Why don't we dine out next Saturday?' he asks. 'We could go to the Criterion.'

Normally, she says, 'That would be lovely' automatically. This time she says nothing.

'What do you say?' he says, giving her breast a slight squeeze.

'We'll see,' she replies.

He does nothing for several moments. Then, as if he's made a decision, he takes his hand away and rolls onto his own side. They go to sleep with their backs to each other.

Earlier, in the House of Commons, Sir Edward Grey expressed the deep sympathy of the government with the Emperor of Austria in the tragic loss that had befallen him. As it happens, the Emperor didn't actually *like* his nephew that much but diplomatic niceties have to be maintained. 'There is not a Foreign Minister in Europe,' Sir Edward said, 'who does not know what a great support the life of the Emperor of Austria has been, and continues to be, to the cause of peace in Europe.' Sir Edward then went on to talk about tolls on the Panama Canal and how the German Baghdad Railway project would terminate at Basra.

Now, dear reader, is probably as good a time as any to tell you about mobilisation. Mobilisation was central to the Group of Death. Mobilisation was how each of the teams in the Group of Death would get their soldiers into battle. It worked like this: Say you were a soldier or a reservist in any of the armies. If your country went to war then you would become aware of this because posters would appear in cities, towns and villages ordering mobilisation. In France, for example, the posters would read:

Armée de Terre et Armée de Mer.
ORDRE DE MOBILISATION GÉNÉRALE.

In Russia, red notices would be posted up all over the country. Beside each red notice would be a white one. This would inform you that you would be paid a sum of money for your clothes when you exchanged them for a uniform. This sum would vary from five roubles down to fifteen kopeks, depending on the state of your clothes.

It was also possible that you might receive a mobilisation notice through the mail, though this was more likely in some countries than in others. In France, even in remote country districts, it was almost certain that the postman would appear carrying a letter. (One supposes these things are possible in a country where – still – about half the people work for the government.) In Russia, where the exact population was unknown, it was more likely to be posters followed by recruiting officers to ensure that those who were called up went.

Whatever happened, once you became aware that mobilisation had been announced, you would be under orders to proceed at once to a certain military barracks. There you would be outfitted in your uniform, given all your equipment and join your unit. After that you would proceed to a designated railway station at a designated date and time to catch a designated train to a station near the front. From there you would follow certain roads at certain times, in concert with all the other units, to get to your fighting position. All the support services, equipment and so on would be similarly deployed.

The Germans (of course) had taken this a stage further with the Von Schlieffen Plan. The Von Schlieffen Plan was Germany's plan to defeat France in six weeks. (After that it intended to go on and beat Russia.) The Von Schlieffen Plan demanded that four armies consisting of 840,000 men should be passed through a narrow gap, eighty miles wide, in Germany's western frontier. If these crowded armies did not keep moving forward then utter chaos would prevail. As a result the plan laid down what every soldier would do, from the day mobilisation was ordered, until victory in the West was achieved and the German Army was marching down the Champs Élysée.

As you can imagine, mobilisation was horrendously complex – particularly in the days before computers and spreadsheets and project management software. For instance, when it eventually happened, Germany would use *eleven thousand* trains for its mobilisation. France used seven thousand. The Von Schlieffen Plan had taken nine years to complete. The French plan – the so-called Plan XVII – evolved through a series of revisions between 1898 and 1913. The Russian plan was known as Mobilisation Schedule No. 19.

Since these plans were so complicated, each country had only one of them. You can see why this would be so. Since the plans were so complex and had taken so long to prepare, the notion that there might be a subsidiary plan or a series of such plans to mobilise different sections of the army in different scenarios just proved to be too far beyond anybody's ability.

And therein lay the problem. There was only one tiny flaw in each of these plans, as Edmund Blackadder might have said. It wasn't so much that they were bollocks – though you perhaps could have argued that. The problem was that the plans were all-or-nothing plans. Either an army mobilised completely or it couldn't mobilise at all. There was no such thing as partial mobilisation.

Anyway, how could you do a partial mobilisation? How could you mobilise part of your army? Which part? And how would you decide? By geography? That you would mobilise parts of your army to meet threats against certain parts of your borders or to attack particular parts of other people's borders? By the magnitude of the threat? Some other way? No, that wasn't going to work. And so the plans of all the contestants in the Group of Death remained all-or-nothing plans.

And in the case of the German Army, it didn't just mobilise men to a sort of battle station. No, the German plan caused war in that it delivered men and units into warfare – fighting. In other words, partway through the German mobilisation plan, men began firing guns at the enemy.

Mobilisation as it would be practised by the contestants in the Group of Death was something that people would come to regret.

Chapter 11
Monday 29 June 1914

The reason I told you about mobilisation at the end of the last chapter, my trusty reader, is that at number 2 Ballhausplatz on the morning of the 29th of June, Berchtold is the first of the managers in the Group of Death to run into this problem. He wants to just send *some* troops to Serbia – to teach the Serbs a lesson. Can't we just have a *small* war, Berchtold asks.

Not possible, explains Conrad, the Head of the Army. You can't do partial mobilisation. If you do, then the whole mobilisation system gets thrown out. Reservists arrive at their depots and find no units to absorb them, train schedules get dislocated and so on. No, it has to be the full thing or nothing.

I may have given the impression, dear reader, that Clara's husband Henry is something of a boring old stick in the mud. If I have, I must apologise. I have done him something of a disservice because, whatever about at home, in work nothing could be further from the truth.

In these pre-computer days, Henry's insurance company runs on paper. And so the stationary over which Henry presides is quite literally the lifeblood of the organisation. That is why any interruption in its supply would have been so catastrophic for both the company and for Henry's career. That is also why, even though now he has somebody who handles much of the administrative detail of ordering the paper, dealing with invoices and so on, Henry still likes to visit all the departments to get their requirements. In addition he will often sometimes hand deliver stationary to the particular department himself. In doing this he gets to chat to both those departments' managers and their staff. He is very popular with the staff in particular, and this is how he came to meet Mary in New Policies.

In looks Mary is not unlike Clara. She has the same blonde hair and willowy figure, but she is taller than Henry's wife. Mary has a very pretty face and is also younger than Clara. At twenty-nine, she is the same age as Henry. Henry has noticed that some people just look bitter. You can tell without knowing them or speaking to them that they lead bitter lives. If that is one end of a spectrum, then Mary lies at the opposite end. Her face always looks like it is ready to break into a smile. For Henry, this just adds to her prettiness. When Henry visits a particular department, he finds himself drawn almost automatically to the prettiest girl. Indeed, if he was ever asked to, he could name the prettiest girl in each department. Mary is far and away the prettiest girl in New Policies and is probably amongst the top three lookers in the whole place.

Mary was only a few days in New Policies when Henry found a reason to speak to her. He arrived there one day looking for Mr Partridge, the department head. Not seeing him in his glass-walled office, Henry headed in Mary's direction and inquired as to his whereabouts. She smiled and told him, and from that moment on, Henry had to admit to himself that he was captivated. He began to walk by New Policies to catch a glimpse of her. He would chat with her if he met her in the corridor. This, in turn, quickly became compliments about her hair or what she was wearing. 'You're looking particularly nice today,' Henry might say. So then it was only a matter of time before Henry contrived to be walking out the front entrance of the building when Mary was going for lunch. He invited her for a sandwich and she accepted.

Sitting across the table from her, he had time to study her face. She really was quite beautiful. Her hair was a bit on the thin side but she had perfect skin and fine, white teeth. She reminded him a lot of Clara when they had first begun to go together. However, one of the things Henry liked about Mary was that she seemed to find everything he said interesting. She asked lots of questions about his job and his home life and his opinions about things. She seemed interested in the world – or at least, his part of it.

Henry remembered that Clara has been like that once, but that was a long time ago.

Mary seemed to enjoy being with him. She appeared to be particularly taken by the fact that he was a manager. Henry probably had to admit that she wasn't as intelligent or as well read as Clara, but since she seemed happy to let him do most of the talking, that didn't seem to be a problem.

And Henry liked the fact that Mary turned heads. When he was with her he saw both men and women looking at her – and him. Yet she didn't appear arrogant about her looks. Indeed she seemed to accept them as being the most natural thing in the world.

The lunches became a regular thing. Henry limited them to a couple of times a week since he didn't want people to start talking. And anyway, he couldn't afford any more than that, since he was the one who paid for all the lunches. In fairness to her, she had offered to pay for every other one but Henry had said that he wouldn't hear of it. What kind of gentleman would he be if he allowed the lady to pay? So after several more offers, Mary stopped asking. Which Henry started to feel slightly resentful about once it came time to pay. But then he told himself that he had just enjoyed the company of a beautiful girl who hung on his every word and that it would be churlish not to pay the small cost of a couple of cups of tea, some sandwiches and the occasional cake on Fridays.

Henry found it easy to make Mary laugh. She says that this is one of the things she likes about him. But in fact, this is also one of the things he likes about her. She laughs at his jokes. She is a good audience.

But there is one other thing about Mary. The more time Henry spends with her, the more he finds himself feeling very aroused in her presence. If she touches his arm, for instance, as she occasionally does when he tells a joke or says something funny, he feels himself stirring. He has only ever seen her hands, her neck and her face but he finds himself spending long periods of time – especially travelling to and from work – wondering what the rest of her is like. Her breasts are bigger than Clara's – he can see that from the shape of her dress. He wonders what it would be like to hold her breasts, to cup them in his hands, to kiss them, to squeeze them, to tug at her nipples with his teeth.

And then he pictures himself undressing her completely, as he once used to do with Clara. (Now she does it herself.) He sees himself slipping Mary's knickers down around her knees and her stepping out of them. He wonders about the colour and texture of her hair down there. What would it be like to touch it, to run the back of his fingers across it? And then he wonders what the sensation would be if he were to enter her. He believes her to be a virgin. She has told him that she was going to get married about five years ago but then the man threw her over.

And so, one day over lunch, Henry makes his move.

'I say, I hope you don't mind me saying this, but I think you're very beautiful,' is his opener.

He had been hoping that she might reply with something similar from her side, but she merely thanks him for the compliment. He goes again.

'I think if I weren't married, I'd—'

He leaves the sentence unfinished, hoping that she will either finish it for him or respond with something, but this time all she does is smile sweetly and wait for him to finish. When he doesn't, she again doesn't say anything. Instead she cocks her head to one side, her face forming the slightest of quizzical frowns. The silence expands. Henry realises he's going to have to increase the stakes. He finds himself saying something he really hadn't intended to say.

'I say, I think I'm falling in love with you.'

This time Mary *does* reply.

'And I with you, Henry.'

And then she adds, 'What a pity that you're married.'

'But I feel so attracted to you,' he blurts out.

He regrets it immediately. He hadn't meant to say the 'but.' It makes him sound plaintive, like he is pleading with her. Had he simply said, 'I feel so attracted to you,' it would have sounded commanding, manly. But he thinks he just sounded like a lovelorn schoolboy.

If she notices this, she doesn't say so. Instead, she makes his day.

'What would you like to do?' she asks simply.

And so they arrange it. Henry will say that he has to stay up in town for a management meeting. He will also book a room in a hotel. The date is fixed for the day after tomorrow, Wednesday, the first of July.

Chapter 12
Tuesday 30 June 1914

Next morning when Clara wakes, the feeling – or whatever it was – is gone. But she feels groggy – as though she has had too much wine.

'So you remember what I said last evening?' asks Henry at breakfast.

'Last evening?'

She remembers very little about last evening. She doesn't *want* to remember. Henry is irritated. He begins to speak as though he were speaking to a child.

'The management meeting. Once a month. On the first of the month. Because I'm a manager, I have to go now.'

'Oh yes, yes. Sorry, sorry,' she says hurriedly.

There is suddenly a smell of burnt toast. Clara rushes to the grill and pulls out the tray. The toast is salvageable. Henry won't eat it but she will. She puts on fresh for him and stands over the sink, scraping the blackened bread. While the toast drama was going on, Henry went silent, but now he resumes.

'Yes. The meeting will be after work. It will last several hours and, after that, the partners take us managers to dinner. Apparently it's tradition. So, rather than trying to come home at that late hour, I'm going to stay in the little hotel nearby. I told you all this last night.'

'Yes, of course you did, dear. I'm sorry. That headache quite knocked me out. Is the hotel frightfully expensive?' she asks and then instantly knows that she has said the wrong thing.

Henry's irritation flares.

'I've found the cheapest one I could that isn't a flea pit,' he says. 'I have to do these things, you know. It's not like I'll be enjoying myself.

This is work, just as what I do during normal office hours is work. If I'm going to get ahead, I have to go to things like this.'

'Yes, I know. Of course you do, dear,' Clara replies, retrieving two slices of perfectly golden toast and putting them on Henry's plate. That seems to mollify him. He snaps his paper back up and carries on reading.

Because she doesn't want that horrible feeling of yesterday to return, Clara keeps busy. She gets Ursula off to school. This is the last week of term so she'll have her daughter at home from next week onwards. That'll be nice. Clara has a long list of things she wants to get done in the house. She gives some jobs to Mrs Parsons and takes the rest herself. Virginia goes for her nap.

As she works, Clara goes over, what is for her, familiar ground. It is where she tries to understand, tries to analyse yet again, when and why Henry changed. She has pretty much dismissed all of the usual reasons. When she was pregnant with Ursula? No. Unless she's very much mistaken, he found her very attractive then. Her normally petite frame had become more 'voluptuous,' according to Henry. Her breasts had become much bigger and used to drive Henry wild. After Ursula was born? Not then either – her breasts had been swollen with milk and she remembers … no, she doesn't want to think about him doing things like that now. When he got his promotion? She shakes her head. (She actually finds herself shaking her head.) It happened long before that.

She concludes that there are two separate things. First, there is sex, and while he still wants it as much as ever, somewhere along the way the fun went out of it for her. He stopped caring about her, being as generous to her as she was to him. When did *that* happen? Was it when she was nursing the girls and sleep became her first priority? He would want sex, he would get his business done and she, who was already exhausted after the day and possibly previous night, just wanted to sleep. Soon it became a pattern and it is one that has continued. And while there was a time when they might have talked about this, the notion that they would discuss a subject so intimate now seems almost laughable.

Because that is the other thing. She remembers how, while they were courting, he seemed to value her opinion, ask her for advice, discuss problems at work. That went almost immediately after they got married. Yes, it did. She has been over this ground before and of this she is almost certain. Now he sometimes speaks to her in a tone that one would never use with say, a tradesman or anybody, really.

She sighs. Is this what happens? Is this where all marriages lead and end up?

She suddenly thinks of the man from the Foreign Office. James. She never looked to see whether he had a wedding ring or not. She has a vague sense that he didn't but she can't be sure. But she has a strong conviction that he *is* married, that it was his wife who made those sandwiches.

She starts to wonder what *his* marriage is like. Clara pictures a beautiful wife, adored by her husband. Beautiful children. Probably two – one of each, a boy and a girl. The perfect family. Clara imagines them at the dinner table talking about the murder of the Archduke and what it means. A few years ago, all of these things interested Clara. Somewhere along the way, since she had nobody to discuss them with, she stopped reading about them or caring.

Which brings her to the place where she usually ends up – that all of this is actually a problem with herself and not with Henry at all. If she was that kind of wife – James from the Foreign Office's wife – then Henry would be different too.

She knows she should think more on this. She knows that what she should now do – really, if she really wanted to tackle this problem – would be to sit down with a cup of tea, some paper and make a list. A list of ways that she could be more *that* kind of wife. A James-in-the-Foreign-Office's kind of wife. But she is busy. There's lots to do.

Now, she knows that this is just an excuse – an excuse that she is using to stop herself from facing some difficult realities and facts about her character. But as soon as this idea registers, as soon as she is washed ashore on this Island of Possible Self-Discovery, the tide lifts her again and carries her back out to the Sea of More Pleasant Things.

Clara thinks back to the short conversation she had yesterday with James. (He has become 'James' now, rather than 'the man from the Foreign Office.') It was the one bright spot in an otherwise dull and grey day. She wonders why this was. Was it because it was so unexpected? A surprise? Something out of the ordinary? Was that all this was in the end? Was it nothing more than that she found her life a little dull? Actually, she realises, her life must be *very* dull indeed if something as insignificant as this could affect her as it did yesterday.

But if her life is dull she has to remind herself again how fortunate she is. There are people who are lucky to eat one meal of bad food a day, she knows that. But does this mean, then, that all of life is just a struggle – harder or not so – as circumstances dictate until eventually you die? Yes, there will be moments of happiness but they'll be isolated and fleeting.

Yesterday was such a moment – with James. Those few minutes she spent with him were funny and happy and joyful. But, she told herself, she's had many moments like that – with the girls. Many moments when they would do or say something and she would know how blessed she was to have them in her life. But all her moments were to do with the children. There seemed to be none which were about Clara herself. But yesterday had been about her. Yesterday she had established some kind of link with another human being who wasn't one of her children. It had felt so good.

Later she goes out to shop for dinner, wondering if she can repeat the experience. She buys meat but the butcher is distracted by a conversation with his wife about an invoice and so only pays half attention to Clara. As she walks home through the leafy sunshine, she wonders if her problem is that she just thinks too much – spends too much time inside her own head instead of just getting on with things as Henry and most people seem to do. What was it James said yesterday? 'Most people seem to be happy just to eat and sleep and get on with it.' Couldn't she just try to be like that?

It suddenly occurs to her that she should find out what is happening about the business in Sarajevo. With a tiny smile she pictures James in the park with his sandwiches and newspaper. Usually she never buys a newspaper, instead waiting for Henry to bring home the *Evening Standard*. Now, though, on an impulse, she turns back and goes into the newsagents, buying a copy of the *Times*. It is something she never does. And whereas she is known by name in all of the other shops, the newsagent, while polite, doesn't recognise her at all. She folds the paper and hides it in her shopping bag under the various parcels. She will read it after Mrs Parsons has gone home and before Henry comes in. Then she must hide it – she will bury it in the pile of papers that will be used to light fires when autumn comes.

As she turns the bend and sees her home a few hundred yards away, she is suddenly aware again of that feeling from yesterday. It hasn't taken her over like before. But it is as though it is lurking behind a curtain ready to jump and ambush her. Is she the only person in the world who feels like this? She can see how people who live by themselves could be lonely, but how is it possible when you live with three other people? She feels like she is going to cry. What is wrong with her?

Later, when she eventually sits down in the garden with a glass of lemonade and her newspaper, she finds that there is not much in it. The general feeling in Germany seems to be that, while a terrible tragedy had taken place, politically, little or nothing had changed. In Russia the view is that the dead Archduke was no friend of Russia and that any effect on the relations between Austria and Russia would be favourable rather than not. Despite the sunshine, her feelings of earlier return. It really *is* a grey world where even awful things like this have little or no effect. Things just go on. It seems to be the fate of everybody, the great and the humble.

She folds the paper, takes it into the pantry and hides it deep down in the pile.

In Vienna, the debate continues. Berchtold suggests demanding that Serbia disbands anti-Austrian societies and relieves certain officials of their responsibilities. Conrad continues to push for the use of force.

Meanwhile, that same evening in Sarajevo, the Archduke's funeral begins. He and his wife have lain in state in the Konak, the same building where he died, surrounded by flowers and lit candles. Officers of the Austrian Army stand guard – what a pity they hadn't done so two days earlier. Then, after a short service performed by the

Archbishop of Sarajevo, the coffins are sealed and carried by non-commissioned officers and men of the 84th Infantry Regiment to two waiting hearses.

Accompanied by infantry, cavalry, clergy, the suites of the Archduke and Duchess and representatives of the military and civil authorities, the funeral cars make the journey to the railway station through streets lined with troops. (Sounds of stable doors being closed after horses have bolted.) Here the coffins are placed on a special train which leaves shortly after 7:00 p.m. for Metkovitch. As the train leaves the station, volleys are fired by the troops lining the streets, the band plays the Austrian national anthem and the guns of the fortress of Vratza thunder a salute.

From St Petersburg, the Tsar sends a message of condolence to Vienna.

In Berlin, Der Kaiser announces that he will be going to Vienna for the Archduke's funeral.

Chapter 13
Wednesday 1 July 1914

The train carrying the bodies of the Archduke and his wife arrives at Metkovitch at 6 a.m. that morning. From the train the coffins are carried by sailors to the Admiralty yacht *Dalmat*. Then, preceded by a torpedo-boat, the yacht steams down the River Narenta, at the mouth of which an Austrian battleship is lying. A salute of nineteen guns is fired as the *Dalmat* comes alongside. After the coffins have been placed on the quarterdeck, which has been transformed into a chapel, the vessel weighs anchor and, with flags at half-mast, it sets a course northwards for Trieste.

In the House of Commons, impressive tributes are paid to the memory of the late Archduke and his wife.

In St Petersburg, the view is not quite so cosy. The general opinion is that the Archduke brought the misfortune on himself since – in life – he had been very anti-Serbian, anti-Russian – in fact, anti-all things Slavic.

In Vienna, it's decided that there's going to be a criminal inquiry into the assassination. Berchtold tells Conrad that Emperor Franz Joseph wants to wait for the results of the inquiry. So too do both the Austrian and Hungarian Prime Ministers, who are opposed to war. They believe that the criminal inquiry will provide a basis for a proper course of action.

Conrad continues to push for war and, in the end, it is his view that prevails. Serbia has to be taught a lesson – and quickly. There must be some military action but Berchtold insists that it must be a small, self-contained, localised war. He also tells the other Austrian leaders that they should take their holidays, just as they had planned to do, 'to prevent any disquiet' about what has been decided.

In Berlin, newspapers began to suggest that a match against Serbia is now definitely on the cards – 'Germanism,' they say, needs to make a stand. Some writers suggest that it is really Russia that is the team to beat. If you're wondering why they're saying this, perplexed reader, then I probably need to tell you about the issue of *alliances* in the Group of Death. No – don't tense up. Not another boring history lesson. Relax – it'll be painless.

There is at least one way that this Group of Death differs from a conventional one. In an ordinary Group of Death all of the teams are independent and just play on their own behalf. Not so in our Group of Death. In our Group of Death, some of the teams have formed alliances, so that, in fact, there are two camps. Germany and Austria form one camp, one alliance, while Britain, France, Russia form the other. Now, how are you going to remember this, dear reader, on top of all the other things you're having to get used to?

Well, if you can just remember that Germany and Austria are allies, then you should be okay. Germany and Austria have a historical closeness. Remember that one of the acts preceding the Second World War was that Hitler annexed Austria to Germany on the basis that they were essentially one country anyway. So – Germany and Austria – allies in the Group of Death. And everybody else allied on the opposing side.

This is also the reason, I hope you can now see, why Germany's Von Schlieffen Plan is about defeating France first and then Russia. France and Russia are allies. From Germany's point of view, they 'surround' Germany – France to the west, Russia to the east. Hence the Von Schlieffen Plan.

So now this is where the alliances start to come into play. Austria wants to play against Serbia – and give them a good hiding for what they've done to the Archduke. Austria reckons this will be no big deal. On form, a match between Austria and Serbia would be a bit like a match between Real Madrid and Scunthorpe United (with all due respect). But because of the Britain/France/Russia alliance and because Russia backs Serbia, if Austria plays against Serbia, Russia will want to support its ally (Serbia) and so play the Austrians as well. And for the Austrians, that would be a horse of a whole different kettle of fish, as the (two) sayings go.

If Austria is going to end up having to play Russia, it (Austria) is going to need help. And there's only one place it can turn to for help. It must turn to its one ally in the Group of Death – it must turn to Germany. The Austrians need to phone a friend. So now, before anybody does anything else, Austria needs to check if the Germans are onside. And for that they need to ask the German manager. Berchtold is going to have to check with the big boys. He's going to have to check *mit* Der Kaiser.

Clara wakes with an idea. She will go back to St James's Park. This sensation began there. Maybe she has to go back there to clear it, to end it.

She will have to work this out carefully. This is Wednesday. On Friday, Ursula will be on her school holidays. Clara has been looking forward to having the two girls around for the summer – and of course, there is their holiday in August in Devon – but now, suddenly she realises that the girls are going to be an obstacle to returning to St James's Park.

She knows she has to go back to the park by herself. With the girls she won't be able to clear whatever has to be cleared. And anyway, what if that terrible sensation comes over her again? Or something worse. No, she has to be by herself. So she will have to find a day when she can do that.

In theory, she could choose any day. All she has to do is to leave the girls with Mrs Parsons. But in reality, this won't work. There are two problems. The first is that the girls will protest. She told them that the three of them would go into town. Their protests she could probably deal with, but their protests plus the fact of her going into town by herself for a second time is sure to attract comment from Henry. It isn't that she never goes into town alone, but it is probably a once-a-month occurrence. For it to happen twice in as many weeks would be sure to excite his curiosity. It isn't that she feels she is doing anything wrong. It's just that this is a part of her life, a piece of herself, really, that she wants to keep to herself. She's entitled to some privacy after all – even if she is married.

So she certainly can't go again this week – that means it will have to be next. She looks at the little diary she keeps in her handbag. In it she keeps notes of birthdays, school holidays, when her periods start and stop (she uses a little code for that, so that only she can understand it), whenever she takes any kind of medicines or cures and any domestic things that she feels need to be recorded.

Monday is the sixth. She will take the girls into town on Monday. She unscrews the cap of the fountain pen that her father bought her when she first began to work in the shop. In the space for Monday, in blue ink, she writes slowly 'Town – girls,' dotting the 'i' thoughtfully. Clara likes her handwriting. It is the kind that people remark on. She likes the *act* of writing. The words aren't just symbols on a page. They are people, ideas, incidents in her life.

Then, in the space for Thursday, she writes, 'Town – just me.' She considers this for a moment. Then she crosses out the 'just,' considers it again and smiles.

Henry is staying up in town tonight, so she will tell the girls tomorrow when he is back and they are all together at teatime. There will be a big, excited fuss about it. In the midst of all that she will mention that she intends to go into town herself later in the week on Thursday. If Henry raises an eyebrow or questions it in any way, she will say that Monday is for the girls – to buy some clothes for their holidays. On Thursday she will be buying some holiday things herself and also some 'women things.' That will probably be enough to end the matter.

That night, Henry does indeed stay in town. After work, just as they have arranged, he and Mary leave the office separately and then meet at the Bank Twopenny Tube station. They go from there and get off at British Museum, walking to the hotel that Henry booked yesterday. Henry carries a small bag with a fresh shirt and collar and his shaving tackle in it. Mary brings a small weekend case. She tells Henry that somebody at the office asked her what she was doing and where she was going.

'And what did you reply?' he asks anxiously.

'I told them I was staying overnight at my sister's house.'

Henry had worried that he would be nervous about the whole undertaking but he finds that he is not. On the crowded train, the two of them sit side by side, thighs pressed together and once again, Henry finds himself aroused. Every time he turns to look at Mary, she smiles that beautiful smile of hers. On one of these occasions, he reaches across, takes her hand and squeezes it.

They have a drink at the hotel and eat dinner. Henry would happily have skipped eating but Mary says she is hungry and so she must be because she clears her plate and orders dessert. Eventually they make their way up to the room.

I know that at this point, dear reader, you might have felt that the book merited a sex scene – and indeed, that you as the reader, deserved one. I have some sympathy with your point of view. You have sat through a certain amount of exposition of dull historical facts and, while I have tried my best to make them interesting and memorable – or at least not boring – there's certainly nothing like a sex scene to get the pages turning.

However, it's equally true that there are far more bad sex scenes ever written than good ones. And remember too, that the book started out with a sex scene, so you can't be feeling too hard done by at this stage. And so, my frustrated reader, you will have to settle for what I suppose could be described as a summary of the action. It goes like this:

Henry and Mary spend a passionate night. They get so little sleep that it will be remarked on to both of them the next day. Mary is an enthusiastic and generous lover, and Henry has two orgasms during their night together. Mary has one and then pretends to have three more, telling Henry what an amazing lover he is. Henry is surprised to find that she is not a virgin after all but he obviously cannot say anything about this to her. Where would he begin? What would he say? No, even though he wonders about it while she dozes, he eventually has to put it out of his head. In the morning, he wakes to find her up and looking at him.

'I love you,' she says simply, and with these words, Henry hopes that this will have been the first night of many to come.

Chapter 14
Thursday 2 July 1914

This morning Der Kaiser abandons his plans to go to Vienna for the Archduke's funeral 'owing to a slight indisposition.' The newspapers report that he has a touch of lumbago after his morning ride. (It certainly has nothing to do with his upcoming boating holiday.) Instead he gives audiences as usual and is in thoroughly good form. There can only be one reason – matters nautical. On Monday, he will be heading for the sea yet again, this time for his annual cruise in the Baltic.

Another man who has things nautical on his mind is the Russian manager, Tsar Nicholas. That night he embarks on the Imperial yacht *Pole Star* – he has a couple of yachts – to witness manoeuvres by Admiral Beatty's British fleet.

Also that night, in Vienna, while the moon is still high in the sky, the bodies of the Archduke and Duchess arrive from Trieste. Through lamp-lit streets, the funeral cars are escorted from the station to the Hofburg Chapel by Court officials and an imperial bodyguard of cavalry.

Meanwhile, at number 2 Ballhausplatz, Count Alexander Hoyos, Berchtold's *chef de cabinet* is chosen to take a letter to Berlin to Der Kaiser seeking his support for the actions Austria is about to take.

'Damn it all, Clara – some of us have to work tomorrow. If you can't sleep at least maybe you could let the rest of us get some.'

Clara has been tossing and turning since she went to bed. She had hoped that Henry was asleep. He came home looking terribly tired and very grumpy, hardly acknowledging her when she announced she would be going into town next Thursday. He went to bed early and was deeply asleep when she came up. But now he sounds like he's wide awake.

'I'm sorry, darling,' she says appeasingly. 'I don't know what's wrong with me. I'll go downstairs and leave you alone. Maybe if I read I'll get sleepy.'

Henry says nothing. She puts on her royal blue dressing gown with the flowers down the front, goes downstairs through the kitchen and opens the back door.

It is a warm night – she thinks it might actually be warmer outside the house than in. She looks for the moon but remembers that she had seen it earlier, just before closing the curtains. It was setting then, about to disappear behind the roofs of the houses, gibbous with a cheesy light.

Thoughts of the moon suddenly remind her of paintings she once saw. It was during their honeymoon. They had gone to Yorkshire and happened upon an art gallery. Was it in Leeds? She thought that maybe it was. What was the artist's name again? Grimes? No – Grimshaw. Atkinson Grimshaw. She remembers a suburban lane with a wall on one side, bare trees, welcoming yellow light in windows and the moon watching down. A hooded woman walks alone along the pavement bathed in the moonlight. Was she going towards one of the lighted houses? Or leaving it? Or did the houses have nothing to do with her? It was ambiguous.

As soon as Clara saw that painting, she thought, 'I am that woman.' She remembers she gazed at that one painting for ages until Henry came and asked if she was ready to go. Had she had the money that day she would have bought it, but it was so far beyond her reach.

She steps out of her slippers and walks down the cool stone steps onto the dewy grass. It is cold on her feet but refreshingly so. She listens to the night sounds. A dog barks. A door closes. Somebody who sounds drunk shouts and then goes silent.

Yes, she reflects as she stands in the warm velvety air, she is that woman – trapped, just as the woman in the painting is trapped, held there for all eternity.

Chapter 15
Friday 3 July 1914

As Clara prepares breakfast, she can only marvel at the effect a good night's sleep can have. She hears Henry upstairs in the bathroom. He's whistling. She can't remember when he last did that at this time of day. Her astonishment continues over breakfast. Henry leaves his newspaper unopened on the table as he chats with the two girls about what they might like to do during the weekend. (Henry has to work Saturday mornings but after that the rest of the weekend is free.) When he heads out the door, instead of the normal peck on the cheek or no kiss at all because he is 'in a hurry,' he kisses her, a long, slow, lingering kiss. As she closes the front door behind him, Clara shakes her head.

In Vienna, the bodies of the Archduke and Duchess lie in State for the day and the public is allowed to file past. In the afternoon, a funeral service is held. At ten that night the coffins are taken to the Western Railway Station. From there they go to Poechlaren and then across the Danube by ferry to Artstetten Castle, the summer seat of the Archduke's family. Meanwhile, in the streets of Vienna, Austrian supporters clamour for a match against Serbia.

In Berlin, the German kit for the Group of Death is proving to be a problem. The new field service uniforms of the German Army are deemed to be unsatisfactory in both texture and colour. It is decided that the grey tunic material will have to be made in a different shade. In addition, all of the players, both officers and men, will have grey trousers. These can be worn both in peacetime and in war; in other words both on and off the field. Patterns of the new cloth will be ready in a month.

Sir Edward Grey goes about his business. To be honest, his main preoccupation at the moment is not a matter of foreign policy at all but rather a personal one. His eyesight is deteriorating. He finds it increasingly difficult to follow the ball during games of squash or tennis. More depressing for such a nature lover, he is unable to pick out his favourite star in the sky at night. He is sure that if he could spend more time at the cottage, the relaxation would help a great deal – especially over the summer. He has always found sunlight on water very good for his eyes. And in spite of his loathing of foreign travel, he has thought that maybe it is time he visit a renowned eye specialist in Germany.

That country will indeed loom large in his sights over the next five weeks but not as the cure for his eyesight problem.

The surprises continue for Clara when Henry arrives home that evening. While she is preparing dinner, he comes behind her and puts his arms around her waist, embracing her tightly. He kisses the back of her neck and says, 'I love you, Clara.'

Since he is behind her he can't see the puzzled look on her face.

'I love you too,' she says, her voice managing to sound warmer than she feels.

That night, as soon as Henry gets into bed, he starts to kiss her. It is Friday night. He must be up for work in the morning but he doesn't seem at all concerned about the prospect. She responds as he kneads her breasts through her nightgown. Then he does what is, for Clara, an unbelievably surprising thing. Rather than hoisting up her nightdress and lying on top of her as she has been anticipating, he rolls her over on her side, lifts up her leg and enters her from behind. Henry is very aroused. He is unbelievably hard and drives into her with powerful, deep strokes. It doesn't take long for him to climax, a huge, silent, shuddering spurting.

Nor does it stop there, because once Henry has taken a minute or two for his breathing to return to normal, he begins to stroke her vulva with his finger trying to find a way in. He does and begins to stroke her soaking vagina. Clara is really not in the mood for this and after Henry has worked away for a few minutes with no tangible result, she finds his finger slowing until finally it stops. He has fallen asleep.

Later Clara falls asleep and has a dream. She sees a painting similar to the one she saw in Leeds, but the scene is different. It is after rain. The cobbles of the road and flagstones of the pavement are wet and slick. There are bare winter trees and a full moon. The funereal light from the moon illuminates the scene as bright as day, but as cold as the grave. All the house windows are dark – there are no comforting yellow squares of light.

The woman – and Clara feels that it is she – walks not on the pavement, but in the roadway. This act conveys a sense of her suffering some great distress as though she is disoriented and unaware of where she is going. As well as that, the figure of the woman is very small in comparison to the rest of the painting – the wide road, the vast night sky, the great dark mass of the house. The road is long and curves at the end to disappear round a bend. The scene looks as though it belongs in the grey land of the dead.

Chapter 16
Saturday 4 July 1914

On Saturday morning the Archduke and Duchess's remains are finally laid to rest in the family vault at Artstatten Castle. Now that these formalities are finally out of the way, the Group of Death can really begin.

It is the weekend. With relief Sir Edward Grey heads for his cottage.

Chapter 17
Sunday 5 July 1914

Following diplomatic protocol, Count Hoyos gives the Austrian letter to Count Szogeny, the Austrian Ambassador in Berlin. Szogeny in turn gives it to Der Kaiser over lunch. In it the Austrians say that the assassination has been traced to a plot organised by the Serbian government. In its concluding passage the letter says that there can be no reconciliation between Austria and Serbia, and that Serbia must be eliminated as a political power-factor in the Balkans. In other words, Austria wants to play Serbia.

The Austrians absolutely don't want a Group of Death. What the Austrians want to do is to launch a quick war on Serbia while Europe is on its summer holidays. In other words, they want to play an unfriendly, as we have said. The war would kick off and be all over before any of Russia, France or Britain could complain and the Austrians could chalk up a victory for themselves. The Austrians ask for Der Kaiser's support for this idea. Specifically, what the Austrians want is that Der Kaiser will use his influence to make sure that none of the other big teams muscle in on this minor match.

Der Kaiser is in a good mood in anticipation of his boating holiday. He is conscious of the fact that Austria is really Germany's only friend. Russia, France and Britain all band together. Der Kaiser is mindful too that it is a fellow Emperor that has been killed. He visited the late Archduke and Sophie only a few weeks previously so he feels a sense of personal loss, which makes him quite decisive. The murderers of Emperors should be discouraged and one should support one's friends.

There shouldn't be a problem, is his analysis. The Tsar – Nicky, Der Kaiser's cousin – is hardly going to come down on the Serbian side. If he did, he would essentially be saying that he supported the killing of Emperors. If one went down that road, where would it end? (The Tsar, along with his family, will find out the answer to that question on a July night in just over three years' time.) As well as that, the Germans do not believe the Russians are ready for the Group of Death. They lack the artillery; their strategic railway system is far from complete. To be perfectly honest, they can hardly manage in peacetime – never mind conduct a war.

While stressing that he has yet to consult his Chancellor, Bethmann Hollweg, Der Kaiser is of the opinion that Austria should deal swiftly and firmly with Serbia and that any such action would have Germany's support.

During a walk in the park at Potsdam with the Chancellor, Der Kaiser makes up his mind. But just to be on the safe side, he summons a meeting of his top advisors. Der Kaiser explains that this Austrian ultimatum to Serbia might have serious consequences. Is the team ready – even if it has to play Russia? They are all agreed – Germany is ready. Indeed no harm would be done, is the general feeling, if they actually ended up in a match against Russia.

General Falkenhayn, the Minister of War, when asked if he is ready, clicks his heels, brings his hand smartly to his helmet and replies, 'Completely, Your Majesty.' The German Army has always been of the view that it will have to play the mighty Russia someday. In 1912, Russia announced its 'Great Military Programme' scheduled to be finished in 1917 and which involved building a railway network through Poland to mobilise its army more quickly. The German Army has long been in favour of a pre-emptive strike on Russia, a so-called 'preventive war.' It is keen to play Russia now while the latter is still in its current state of (not very good) preparedness.

Just to be completely on the safe side, Der Kaiser checks with representatives of big business. Are they prepared for a match against Russia? Give us two weeks, they reply – to sell our foreign securities.

Reassured by all of this, Der Kaiser can – with a clear conscience – give a gesture of solidarity to the Austrian team. The meeting agrees that what Austria does about Serbia is its own affair, but that whatever it does it can be sure of Germany's support if Russia intervenes. Bethmann Hollweg is instructed to pass this message on to the Austrian Ambassador.

The meeting that Der Kaiser has just chaired is probably typical of many meetings that take place these days. It's probably true to say that many of today's workers spend a lot of their time at meetings. Maybe this is true of you, my hardworking reader. If that is the case, then you will know that some meetings are incredibly important and useful. However, most meetings are rubbish. They're crap. I think it's true to say that the recently ended Der Kaiser's meeting falls into this category.

The thinking of the great men who attend Der Kaiser's meeting is not particularly clear. For instance, none of them knows exactly what demands Austria is going to place on Serbia and, therefore, what they are actually supporting. General Falkenhayn believes that the Austrians won't actually follow through on their tough talk at all and that the whole thing will fizzle out. Another view is that there will be a war but it will be a localised one between Austria and Serbia. Russia will stay out, is the general feeling, since its rearmament programme is not complete, and anyway, a war would probably just trigger civil unrest and revolution in Russia.

Der Kaiser has a more personal view: that his cousin and Russian manager, the Tsar, can't condone the murder of Emperors and so won't go to war (or can be persuaded from doing so) for that reason.

Finally, there is the sense that if there is going to have to be a war with Russia then now is the ideal time.

Great men.

Important men.

Having meetings.

Making decisions.

God help us.

Sir Edward Grey must return to London this evening but he has time to go 'a short trail.' It has been a day of brilliant light with a gorgeous, azure sky. There are still a lot of roses around the cottage but many things are over. Lime flower is out and he hears a family of great tits. Other than that, very few other birds sing. In the relative silence the hum of bees is loud. It is the song of midsummer at its height. The honeysuckle on the east side of the cottage has come into a very fine bloom for a second time.

Chapter 18
Monday 6 July 1914

A t quarter past nine that morning, Der Kaiser, refreshed and strengthened, eyes gleaming at the thought of being rocked gently by the waves tonight, heads off northwards for another cruise. The sea is calling. Der Kaiser states privately that he is going on his planned holiday 'in order not to alarm world opinion.' He leaves Berlin by train and arrives in Kiel that afternoon. There, he proceeds onto the Imperial yacht *Hohenzollern* for his annual yachting trip along the Norwegian coast.

Behind in Berlin, Bethmann Hollweg sends a telegram to the aging and partially deaf Austrian Ambassador, Szogeny. Couched in the usual diplomatic language, the final two paragraphs read:

Finally, as far as concerns Serbia, His Majesty, of course, cannot interfere in the dispute now going on between Austria-Hungary and that country, as it is a matter not within his competence.

The Emperor Francis Joseph may, however, rest assured that His Majesty will faithfully stand by Austria-Hungary, as is required by the obligations of his alliance and of his ancient friendship.

Szogeny passes this information on to Count Hoyos who promptly returns to Vienna carrying what will quickly become known as the 'blank cheque.' Hoyos's message to his people at number 2 Ballhausplatz is unequivocal. Germany will cover Austria even if Russia wants to get involved. Austria can count on Germany's full support even if grave European complications ensue. Germany will do everything in its power, including war, to support Austria. Austria ought to march at once against Serbia.

Clara goes into town with her girls. She is tempted to suggest that they take a walk in St James's Park but, in the end, thinks better of it. If they ended up bumping into James, then Henry would only hear about it and there is no point in that. She buys swimsuits and other odds and ends for the girls for their holiday. They have lunch in an ABC.

Henry spends the day wondering how soon he'll be able to spend another night with Mary. If he had expected to feel guilty after betraying his wife, then he is pleased to find that nothing could be further from the truth. He is happy and is enjoying the fine summer weather and feels it is good to be alive. He feels cocksure – with the emphasis on 'cock,' he jokes privately to himself.

Of course he has no long-term plans with Mary. Actually, he hasn't really thought about how the future might involve her at all. And if he were asked, if you happened to meet him at, say, the train station and he got to talking about all of this, and he opened up to you – which it's quite possible he would do, given that he feels a real urge to brag to someone about his conquest of Mary – he would probably paint a picture of life continuing on as normal at home with Clara and the girls.

'And what about Mary?' you might ask. Then Henry would go into quite a long (-winded) explanation of how lots of men, 'particularly in this modern age,' have mistresses. Hadn't the late King Edward set the fashion, having had a succession of them all his life? And the vision that Henry would unfold – if he was pressed – would be of life going on as usual in Horn Lane and Mary – or somebody – as a dalliance to sweeten things and spice up his life. He works hard after all. He provides well for his family. He is a good husband and father. He doesn't drink or smoke to excess or gamble on the horses. Doesn't he deserve this one small pleasure?

At the Foreign Office, Sir Edward Grey has a meeting with the German Ambassador. The Ambassador warns that a dangerous situation has developed in the Balkans. He asks Sir Edward to use his influence to advise moderation in Russia in case Austria, as now seems likely, demands some form of satisfaction from Serbia.

Grey replies that he feels that cooperation between Britain and Germany should be able to resolve any dispute between Austria and Serbia. He believes 'that a peaceful solution can be reached … that the German government are in a peaceful mood and that they are very anxious to be on good terms with England.'

Chapter 19
Tuesday 7 July 1914

Now that Austria has decided to play Serbia it needs an excuse to start the game. Its Council of Ministers debates what to do next. Berchtold, who up until recently had been reluctant to play in the Group of Death at all, now pushes for a surprise attack on Serbia. However, others feel that it would be better if it were made to appear that Serbia caused the war – a sort of legal basis for the war (remember weapons of mass destruction in Iraq?). They feel that this can be achieved by placing harsh demands on Serbia which it will find difficult or impossible to meet.

The Hungarian Prime Minister is a lone voice against war. He argues that any attack on Serbia will, 'as far as can humanly be foreseen, lead to an intervention by Russia and hence, a world war.' (This, alert reader, I'm sure you have worked out, is because of the alliances, France will weigh in on the side of Russia and subsequently, then, Britain on the side of France.)

However, his protestations go unheeded. All except the Hungarian Prime Minister finally agree that Austria should present an ultimatum to Serbia which is so outrageous in its demands that no self-respecting country could possibly accept it. Over the next few days these demands will be drafted.

Chapter 20
Wednesday 8 July 1914

Henry wakes in the dark hours before dawn, aware that he may have a problem. Or rather, there is a potential problem he wants to forestall and avoid having. Until this moment the significance of what Mary told him about her first almost-marriage and the man who threw her over has never really occurred to him. At the time she told him, Henry was genuinely (if briefly) saddened for her and said that the man must have been a bad egg. But now it hits him like an express train. How did he miss it, given how obvious it must have been? Mary wants to get married.

Now of course she knows that he is married. Henry has made no secret of this. But what if she starts pressuring him to leave Clara? Or worse still, threatens to tell Clara about her dalliance with Henry. He suddenly remembers a question she asked the night they slept together. 'What would she say if she found out?' Mary had asked. At the time Henry had thought Mary was just being triumphalist – delighted to have gotten one over on some other woman. Henry had answered the question truthfully – Clara's anger would be biblical. But now he suspects the question could have had a whole other meaning.

Now he's wide awake. Mary could tell Clara quite easily. Find the records of Henry's insurance in the files and then write Clara a letter. Or worse still, visit the house. Of course, Henry would poo poo the whole thing. He imagines himself doing exactly this now. The scene in the kitchen as Clara holds the letter, accusing him angrily. She doesn't often get angry – the last time must have been several years ago – but she has a terrifying temper when she does.

Henry would explain that there's a woman in work who has become infatuated with him. That a fellow threw her over – nice touch this, he feels – and that since then she has been a bit unhinged. For some reason he now finds himself on the receiving end of her lunacy.

So having rehearsed this scene a few times, Henry feels he'd be able to manage that eventuality should it occur. Now he returns to what he feels is the more pressing problem and the more likely possibility – that Mary will start pushing him to leave Clara. And clearly he has no intention of doing this. He needs to make this point to Mary. He needs to show her – lest she be in any doubt – what her position is, where she fits into the scheme of things. She is his mistress, God damn it. And now he feels himself getting angry at her. He is prepared to buy her lunches and dinners and treat her to nights in hotels. He may even – and now that he has thought of it, he knows he will pretty much have to – buy her presents on her birthday and at Christmas. Jewellery and the like. But that is as far as it goes. And if she doesn't like that – if she can't be satisfied with that – then she can lump it. There are plenty more fish in the sea.

But he realises that he needs to be – what's that word that the partners are always using at the management meetings? – proactive. Yes, proactive. He needs to do something before this issue grows and develops into something. He needs to show Mary her place in the world – well, in his world anyway. He needs to show her and, if necessary, keep reminding her, that he is happily married. And he knows just how to start. With this all resolved, Henry suddenly falls asleep again until the alarm clock's call drags him back into the world.

As Clara stands at the grill waiting for the toast to brown, she feels bathed in happiness. This was the phrase she wrote in her diary this morning while everyone else was still asleep. It is only one more day until she gets to go to town by herself. Hopefully, she will meet James from the Foreign Office again, but even if she doesn't, she is still excited about her day.

'I was wondering if you'd like to meet for lunch tomorrow,' Henry suddenly says, breaking in on her reverie.

Later, Henry is pleased with himself as he rides the omnibus to work. He sits on the open top deck. He has allowed himself plenty of time so he won't be late and here he can enjoy the sunshine. The phrase 'free as a bird' circles in his brain. He will meet Clara for lunch tomorrow. Admittedly she didn't seem all that overjoyed when he asked her, but never mind that. The important thing is that today he will make a point of saying to Mary that he can't go to lunch with her tomorrow because he has to meet 'the wife.' As well as Friday, Thursday has always been one of their more popular days for lunch – the working week more than half over, 'downhill to the weekend' as Mary often says. By not going with her tomorrow, he hopes he will be making a very definite point.

Another man making a very definite point is Der Kaiser. In Vienna, Berchtold receives a message from His Majesty. The message declares that Der Kaiser expects Austria to play Serbia and that Germany would not understand if the present opportunity was allowed to go by without a blow being struck.

Sir Edward Grey meets with the French Ambassador and tells him that Britain and France will have to do everything in their power to calm the Russians. Paul Cambon, the Ambassador, warmly agrees.

Later, Sir Edward tells the Russian Ambassador that it is crucial that the Russians not give the Germans any reason to believe that some kind of military action is being planned against them.

Grey often thinks that really, in a perfect world, he would be able to bring all of the Foreign Ministers to London. There he would sit them down, rather like a headmaster with a particularly troublesome class, and they would sort everything out. He would go through their grievances one by one, asking each side in turn to give their side of the story. Then he would adjudicate, give a judgment, both sides would shake hands and that would be that. How simple it would all be. He could be Foreign Secretary on three days a week and spend the rest of his time at the cottage. Europe would be at peace.

Instead he has to work through these ambassadors. He has to interpret whether or not they are dealing in good faith. And even if they are – and Grey thinks he has good, honest relations with most of them – can the same be said of their governments? Have the ambassadors been told the full story? The Tsar is weak and the Kaiser is mad, so who knows what goes on in those places. It is all impossibly complex. No wonder his sight has been affected. For this job he really needs the eyesight of an eagle, poised high over the continent and able to see down, not just into the courts of Europe but into the hearts of men.

Chapter 21
Thursday 9 July 1914

Finally Thursday has arrived. But it is not the Thursday which Clara had been anticipating with such eagerness. She has arranged to meet Henry at one o'clock. There is an ABC near his office but for some reason he suggests a different one to her. Happily, it is nearer to St James's Park. She wonders if she can make the lunch a short one so that she will still have time to get to the park. She dresses in her favourite going-into-town-in-sunny-weather clothes – a light white blouse and a long fawn coloured skirt. She wears the same hat she wore last week. The girls and Mrs Parsons see her off from the front door. Lewis, the sixteen-year-old boy next door, who is mowing the small square of grass in the front garden, calls, 'Good morning, Mrs Kenton,' to her.

As the train rattles in towards the city centre it occurs to her that the original reason for her trip into London seems to have disappeared. She has felt none of that lonely gloom for several days – ever since the weekend, really. Today, even though she must meet Henry and may not get to see James from the Foreign Office, she feels relatively happy. She wonders if that episode last week was just about boredom with her life and it has all passed now that she is doing a few new and different things. Maybe she should make this a regular occurrence.

Henry is on his way up the stairs to New Claims when he sees Mary, a flight above, coming down. She looks radiant. She is wearing fresh lipstick so that his eyes are drawn to her lips. His body remembers what it was like to kiss them. They stop on a landing and he smells her perfume. The memory of it arouses him. He recalls the sensation the first time he entered her. How tight she was. How good it felt as he rode her and then climaxed inside her.

'Good morning, Mr Kenton,' she says.

It is standard practice for juniors to call managers 'Mister' but Mary often does it when she and Henry are alone. It is a sort of private joke between them. She did it when they were making love and for some reason, Henry found it very erotic. This morning, though, he gets straight down to business.

'Ah, Miss Graham, I'd been hoping to bump into you.'

Lowering his voice, he continues, 'I'm afraid I'm not going to be able to have lunch with you today. I've got to meet the wife. Something about buying things for the family holiday in Devon in August.'

Henry had been rehearsing what he would say from the time he left the omnibus and began his short walk to the office. That bit about the family holiday only occurred to him on the spur of the moment but he is pleased with it. He feels that his short speech succeeded in giving Mary a double reminder of his marital status and also how long term that was likely to be.

If he had been expecting her to be upset or disappointed or sulky, he is taken by surprise when she is none of these things. Instead, she says, 'I had been hoping to bump into you too, Mr Kenton. Don't worry about lunch. There'll always be another time. No, what I wanted to tell you was that my sister, you know the one I visited last week when I stayed up in town. Well, it turns out she's ill and I'm afraid I'm going to have to stay up in town again tonight to be with her.'

Mary fixes him with her eyes and Henry understands. His mind begins to race so that he forgets to say anything.

'Well, you could say you were sorry to hear of her indisposition,' says Mary, and it's only the uncertainty about whether she is teasing him that snaps Henry back to the here and now.

'Of course,' he says hastily. 'Of course, I'm very sorry to hear she's not well. Please give her my best wishes.'

'You could always give them yourself,' Mary says and then with an 'Anyway, I'd better go and get those files or they'll be wondering what's happened to me. Please excuse me, Mr Kenton,' she steps past him and continues on her way down the stairs.

Henry is already waiting outside the ABC when Clara sees him. He hasn't yet seen her. He takes out his watch and checks it. Clara wonders anxiously if she is late. Then he sees her. He seems stressed.

'I hope I haven't kept you waiting,' she says, wondering whether he's going to be grumpy and ruin their lunch.

'No, not at all,' he replies, kissing her cheek even though Clara doesn't really proffer it. 'No, it's just that, well, something's come up. The partners aren't happy with the figures for the first half of the year – they only just became available this morning, you see. So they've called a special management meeting for this evening. I'm going to have to stay over again. And as for lunch…'

He tails off.

'But you have no things,' says Clara.

It occurs to her how accommodating she always is. Henry has ruined her whole day and yet she is still trying to make sure that things run smoothly for him. Is she a good wife? Or a fool?

'I was wondering if you could buy me some while you're out shopping. I can use the same shirt probably, so just a collar and a razor. Here, let me give you some money.'

Henry takes his wallet from his inside jacket pocket and extracts a red and white ten shilling note.

'That should be enough,' he says. 'But if there's any left over, you be sure to spend it on yourself. And have them parcelled discretely, won't you? You could drop them in at the reception desk. I can pick them up there. You're a darling.'

Henry kisses her again, says that he really must dash and then does exactly that. Clara is left standing there. She is suddenly overjoyed. If she hurries she can get to St James's Park and James from the Foreign Office should still be there. After that she can get Henry's things and do some of the shopping that she's meant to be doing anyway.

She guesses that it must be about half past one when she passes the milk stall at the Spring Gardens end of St James's Park, with its two tethered cows that supply the milk. There is a long queue of thirsty customers. Clara hopes she is not too late. She buys a bag of breadcrumbs for the birds and then heads in the direction of the seat she occupied last week. While she is still a way off, she sees that James is already there – eating a sandwich and reading the paper.

'Hello again,' she says, as she reaches the seat.

He looks up. There is a moment when he doesn't recognise her and then his face breaks into a warm smile. He stands up, holding the paper in one hand and a half-eaten sandwich in the other.

'Why, Mrs Jordan, what a pleasure to see you again.'

Hastily, he puts everything into his left hand so that he can extend his right. She takes it and he invites her to sit down. The parcel of sandwiches and a half-drunk bottle of lemonade are on the seat.

'Here as always,' he says with a smile of pretend weariness.

'You haven't had to travel to the Balkans to sort them all out then?' she asks.

He laughs.

'No indeed. It looks like on this occasion they might actually do that for themselves. *And* without a war.'

'That's a blessing,' she says.

'Mrs Jordan – have you eaten lunch? Would you care to share my sandwiches?'

'No thank you.'

'No, please, I insist. Or would you care for something else besides ham and mustard?'

He jumps up as she says that, no, she likes ham and mustard.

'And permit me to get you something to drink. Lemonade?'

Clara's protests are ignored. Going over to a nearby vendor, he returns a few minutes later with a second bottle.

'Now please,' he says. 'Do eat up. If you like ham and mustard, you won't eat better.'

She takes one of the sandwiches and bites into it. It *is* very good. The bread thick but airy, the meat exploding with flavour and the mustard so fiery that it seems to flare down her nostrils. Her eyes water.

'Good Lord,' exclaims James, who sees the effect on her. 'I'd forgotten. I rather like mustard.'

Clara is unable to speak for a moment and takes a drink from the lemonade bottle.

'You do, don't you?' she laughs, when she has swallowed.

His face is suddenly anxious.

'Please – shall I get you something else?'

'No, really, it's a magnificent sandwich.'

'You're not just saying that?'

She shakes her head, again unable to speak as the heat flames again in her nose.

'I've never heard a sandwich described as magnificent before,' he says. 'Do you like food, Mrs Jordan?'

Clara thinks that it's the oddest question. She has never really thought about it, but now that he's asked it, she realises that she *does* like food. Ever since those days when Clara's mother took to her bed, and Clara, aged nine, had to come home from school and prepare meals for her brother and her father, she has enjoyed everything about it.

She quickly worked out how to choose good produce in the shop or the market. She found a notebook her mother had with recipes written in it from *her* mother. Clara studied the copy of *Mrs Beeton's* and found things to cook. She found the preparation – washing, peeling, slicing, chopping, stirring – strangely calming, especially if her mother was going through one of her bouts and her father was smouldering with suppressed resentment. And she enjoyed it when it all came together, as the smells and sounds of cooking filled the air. There was something uncomplicated about it all – in comparison to life in her house, which seemed very complicated indeed.

'Yes, I do like food,' she replies.

'It's life really, isn't it?' he says. 'At least that's what the Italians think. Or is it the French?'

'Have you been to those countries, Mr Walters?'

'Please, please – you must call me James.'

'James,' she says. 'And you must call me Clara.'

'Clara. Delighted,' he replies, before biting into a sandwich. 'Yes, I have. Well, I suppose somebody has to do it since our Sir Edward doesn't like to. Fact is though, I *love* travelling.'

Clara notes the 'I'. She sees now, too, that he isn't wearing a wedding ring.

'Perhaps you should be our Foreign Secretary.'

'If love of travel were the only qualification, I'd already have the job.'

'I'm afraid I've never been to any of those places,' she says. 'I've never been outside England.'

'Don't think it matters, my dear Mrs Jo … Clara. Once you step outside your door in the morning, you're travelling. At least that's the way I like to think about it.'

Clara thinks it is an extraordinarily beautiful way to think about it. And now she sees an opening.

'And do your family like travelling as much as you do?' she asks.

They are sitting on the bench turned towards each other, but now James looks into her eyes.

'I'm afraid there is no family. I have no children and my wife and I divorced several years ago.'

'I'm so sorry,' she says. 'I shouldn't have pried.'

'Think nothing of it. You could hardly have known.'

Clara isn't in the least sorry that she pried, and after this response she intends to pry some more.

'So you live alone now?' she asks innocently.

'I do. I have a little two bedroomed terraced house that suits my needs. One of the nice things about my divorce from the former Mrs Walters is that, whatever else we argued about, we never had any disputes about money. The result is that we now both live in houses with which we are relatively happy.'

'So your divorce was amicable?' asks Clara, astonished at her own daring.

'You could say that. However, you could equally argue that if it was that amicable there would have been no divorce in the first place. And you, Clara. You have a husband? Children?'

'One and two,' says Clara, pleased at her little joke.

'Probably better than the other way round,' he says, smiling. Then he adds, 'So you must live in a busy house?'

'That would be the understatement of the century. I rarely get time to myself. That's why coming here is so nice.'

Then, realising, that he could have misunderstood what she said, she adds, 'Not that I mean I want to be here by myself. It's … It's nice to have some grown-up company.'

And then worried that this could be open to further misinterpretation, she adds even more hastily, 'Not that my husband isn't.'

Clara realises she is blushing. If he notices, James says nothing. He is on a different track.

'It's not good to be alone,' he says, almost to himself. 'But then I also like my own company – and solitude, time to think. How to reconcile the two? Now that would be a happy marriage, I suspect – where one could have both things. What do you think, Clara?'

'I think it would be a very happy marriage indeed,' she replies. 'For certain types of people.'

'Wisest words I've heard all day,' James says.

The conversation goes on to other things. For his holidays, James is going walking in some part of France that Clara has never heard of. Picardy. He mentions a river. 'The somm' it sounds like. He describes the landscape and she imagines him walking under a blue sky over chalky pathways that cross rolling green hills, thinking who-knows-what thoughts. She pictures him stopping at some out-of-the-way French country restaurant or inn. The French are meant to have such great food. She tells him about Devon. She hopes that she will find some time for herself down there. She wonders (but doesn't say) whether it would be too much to ask that Henry take the girls for a day so she could go off by herself. After all, they're his children too.

They finish their sandwiches. Clara thinks James is like no other man she has ever encountered before. She senses that he lives a rich interior life, just as she does. Clara doesn't know what to say or do next. The only thing she does know is that she doesn't want this to be the last time she speaks to this man.

'I suppose I should be getting back,' he says.

He stands up and shakes crumbs from his lap. Then he takes up the paper that the sandwiches had been wrapped in and does the same. Some birds notice and began waddling eagerly in his direction.

'I shall be in town again next week,' says Clara. 'On Thursday again. If you were going to be here, I could bring the sandwiches.'

He looks at her and she isn't quite sure what she sees in his eyes. Perhaps it is curiosity. Or surprise?

'I should like that very much.'

They shake hands and separate. As Clara walks away, she admits to herself that she came here today, not to banish some feeling or other, but rather for this conversation. She came to see James. And now she has arranged to see him again.

What does she want from this? Where is she hoping it might lead? A once-a-week rendezvous between a divorced man and a married woman? Could she ever imagine inviting him home to meet the rest of the family? Of course not. The notion is laughable. Would she ever bring Henry with her to one of these assignations? She knows the answer to that too.

A funny thought comes into her head. Where will they meet when the weather isn't so fine? A tea shop? A restaurant? The reception area of a hotel? It doesn't matter. All that matters for now is that she will see him again next Thursday.

Clara buys Henry's things and drops them off at the reception desk of his office. As she wends her way home, she feels like there is a little flame burning inside her. There is something new in her life. Part of her wants this little flame to flare into life, whatever that might mean or consist of. But she thinks it's more likely it will go out. Maybe when the fine weather ends that will happen. But for today she is much happier than she has been in a long time.

The Permanent Under-Secretary of State at the Foreign Office tells Sir Edward Grey, 'I have my doubts as to whether Austria will take any action of a serious character and I expect the storm will blow over.'

Sir Edward is like almost all politicians that one comes across – today every bit as much as a century ago. It is very difficult to get a straight answer from him. The situation that has begun to develop now will eventually become known as 'The July Crisis.' What it needs at this stage, early in July is to be nipped in the bud. And Sir Edward is perhaps the only man in Europe capable of doing exactly that.

What's needed now is for Sir Edward to say to the German Ambassador that, if Germany were to make any threatening moves or menaces towards either France or Russia, Britain's allies, Britain would come crashing down on Germany like a ton of bricks. Just that. Unequivocal. No shilly shallying or carefully worded phrases or diplomatic language. And for the Ambassador to pass that on verbatim to his masters.

But not for nothing is he referred to as a diplomat, his trade as diplomacy. At a meeting he tells the German Ambassador that England wishes 'to preserve an absolutely free hand so that in the event of continental complications she might be able to act according to her judgement.' He explains that various naval and military conversations have taken place between Britain and her allies since 1906 but these do not constitute agreements which impose any binding obligations whatsoever.

Maybe this is the first time, dear reader, that you've heard World War I described as a 'continental complication.' If it helps at all, in Ireland, World War II is known as 'The Emergency.'

In Paris, the French are also looking at their kit and considering a change. In the Chamber, the Minister of War states that it was the English in the Transvaal who first realised the danger of bright uniforms and had substituted khaki. In the Balkan War, the Bulgarians and Serbs did the same. The French have been carrying out experiments with different kinds of clothing. At 1,500 yards, the old cloth is as visible as the new is at 550 yards. A change will have to be authorised at once. This is because it will take four and a half to five years for sufficient amounts of cloth to be made available for the whole army. (This is the time it has taken the Germans to make a similar change.) It is stated that aesthetic considerations should not matter. What matters is giving the soldiers a uniform which strengthens their morale and augments their confidence and fighting capacity.

The measure is approved.

Chapter 22
Friday 10 July 1914

Henry wakes. He is in an unfamiliar bed. He is also naked and it takes him a few moments to remember where he is. The hotel room. He is lying on his side with his back to Mary, who is also naked. He hears her snoring softly. He rolls over and looks at her. She tends to sleep with her head pushed back exposing her throat, but even with that and her mouth open and the snoring, he thinks she looks beautiful. He remembers that he no longer feels this way about Clara whenever he sees her asleep – even though he once did.

He recalls his lovemaking with Mary last night. It was every bit as exciting as the first time. In fact, if anything, even more so. It took him longer to climax, which extended the pleasure. She told him again what a marvellous lover he was. He checks his watch. He still has half an hour before he needs to get up, so he begins to tease her nipples with his mouth. He lays his finger along the line of her vulva and he feels her respond, moving her thighs slightly apart. He is about to ease his finger into her when, still with her eyes closed, she says sleepily, 'Wouldn't it be nice if we could wake up like this every day?'

Henry has become extra alert to any statements like this. He continues what he is doing and responds with, 'Maybe then the excitement would go out of it. It would just become like all the other miserable marriages we know.'

'I don't think so,' Mary says, opening her legs even wider. 'Not with you, Henry.'

And really, there's nothing he can say in response to that.

Clara wakes feeling desperately unhappy. That little flame of joy which burned inside her up to the time she went to bed last night has well and truly gone out. Whatever she may have wanted it to flare into – and she has been deliberately vague about that – she knows that it will actually lead to nothing. In a year's time she will be surprised if she remembers the details of it or even that it happened at all.

She goes downstairs in her dressing gown. It is early. Now that it is the school holidays, both the girls are in bed. She will leave them there until they wake. She is glad that Henry is not here. She goes out into the sunny pool of the garden. It gives her no joy. She doesn't want today. She doesn't want to live through another day that is part of an endless rosary of empty days. She doesn't want the succession of dozens of pointless activities that will make up today and tomorrow and the next day.

What is she doing here anyway in this house in London? Was it God that put her here? And if so, for what? She isn't sure she believes in God. Instead it seems to her that this is all an accident. There is that enormous family tree of people who came before her – she has photographs of some of them in a box in the sitting room – parents and grandparents and so on before that. All of them – from what she has seen anyway or been told – seem to have lived lives of greater or lesser unhappiness or hardship. And now, here she is doing the same. There is no grand plan, no God, no heaven. There are just accidents of birth and lives lived in loneliness.

Later she lies in the bath and sponges herself all over. She thinks she has a nice body. She is not tall, has blonde hair and small breasts. The fact that she has had two children is obvious but not unpleasantly or disgustingly so. She takes care of her body, eats well and just uses very small amounts of makeup.

When she was younger she dreamed of marrying some man who would worship her. He would wake up every day and tell her how much he loved her. She would be excited at the prospect of his coming home in the evening. Their lives would be blissful.

As a girl, she had wanted a man who would adore her body, like she thought Anthony must have adored Cleopatra's or Romeo, Juliet's. She has never spoken of this, of course. Not to anybody, not to Henry, not even when they were courting. She hasn't written it in the series of diaries she has kept since she was a girl – in case somebody should find it. But it hasn't stopped her thinking of it, fantasising about it. She dreams of a man who would kneel before her and bury his face in her belly and tell her how beautiful she is.

How stupid and girlish that seems now. She doesn't even know why she takes care of her body any more. Henry just sees it as something to empty himself into. She wonders if he will notice as it gets older and starts to sag or look worn. She thinks not. At some stage she assumes he will no longer look for sex from her. What he will do then, she prefers not to think about.

Der Kaiser receives a dispatch from the German Ambassador in Vienna. In it he explains what the Austrians are trying to do, putting their unacceptable demands to Serbia so as to make it look that Serbia is responsible for an outbreak of war. Der Kaiser is becoming impatient. In the margins of the Ambassador's dispatch, he scribbles angrily, 'They've had enough time for this.'

Chapter 23
Saturday 11 July 1914

The German Foreign Office cables Der Kaiser asking if they should – as is usual – send a telegram to King Peter of Serbia congratulating him on his birthday. 'Blasted fools,' Der Kaiser thinks irritably. Patiently, he replies, 'As Vienna has so far inaugurated no action of any sort against Belgrade, the omission of the customary telegram would be too noticeable and might be the cause of premature uneasiness. It should be sent.'

In the afternoon, Sir Edward makes for Hampshire and arrives towards evening. On arrival, he clips some of the roses and puts them in a vase in the living room of the cottage. Then he walks down to the river. Everywhere flowers are heavy with honey. He hears the distinct and clear song of a nightingale. He feels the peace of the place soaking into him.

Chapter 24
Sunday 12 July 1914

Clara wakes from another dream. It is a dream so vivid that she feels she must get up straight away and write it down before it is lost. She hurries downstairs and takes her diary from her handbag. This is what she writes.

I had a dream about a statue in a park. It was a very beautiful statue. A woman, naked like a Greek goddess. She was leaning her right elbow on the horizontal branch of a tree with the result that she leaned back slightly, pushing her tummy and groin forward. Her hair was tied up and the statue was smooth, giving the impression that her skin was perfect. In her left hand, which hung by her side, she held a large flower and a bunch of grapes. The woman was perfectly proportioned. But it was the expression on her face that was the most enigmatic. Despite the fact that she was naked she had a look on her face as though she was somewhere else.

Sometimes I feel like that woman. I know it is probably disgraceful to say it but I sometimes feel like I would like to strip off all my clothes and stand there like that, displaying myself and not caring.

In my dream, I was that woman. I was somehow the statue. It was like I was trapped inside it. The statue was in an out-of-the-way corner of a park. Very few people visited that corner or stopped to look at it. In the morning the sun would rise and would touch the statue's face first before gradually working its way down the body, bathing it in red light. Then the day would go on, people would pass, some would look at it, but they were unaware that it was me. They thought it was just a statue.

Night was the worst time. The sun would set, the sky would go deep blue, the moon would rise and the cold would settle on the park. In winter there would be frost or snow. It was so cold; so far away from the warm south where the flower and the bunch of grapes had come from. And I was all alone. In the whole world.

And then, after a few minutes' thought, she adds, *I have so much love to give – and this is love that will never see the light of day now. Love that will go wasted.*

Henry spends most of the weekend racking his brains to come up with another reason to stay in town one night this coming week. In the end he settles for the ongoing story of the company's poor performance in the first half of the year. He'll tell Clara that there is going to be yet another management meeting to try to work out ways of improving sales. (In reality, of course, there is no such problem. Sales are up on last year and this business with the Archduke seems to be causing some positive ripples in the insurance market.) Henry thinks he can get one, possibly two more weeks out of this story before he has to find another one. But he is sure he'll be able to find something else. In the meantime, this will more than do. He will tell Clara at breakfast tomorrow, saying that he's sorry he forgot to mention it earlier.

In Berlin, everyone in the German government wants to see Austria play Serbia, and they bridle at the continuing delay and Austria's apparent indecisiveness. The Germans feel that there will never be a better time to play Russia, and indeed France, if they have to. They are also convinced that the British don't want to be in the Group of Death at all.

Finally, the Austrian demands to Serbia are ready, but then the Austrians say that they don't want to give them to the Serbs until the French President's visit to Russia is over. Even though Der Kaiser is annoyed that the ultimatum will now be presented so late in July, this is probably pretty sensible on the part of the Austrians. If the French and Russian managers were actually together when mighty Austria dropped its ultimatum on tiny Serbia, they would be far more likely to goad each other into some rash action, such as both declaring war on Austria. Austria just wants to play its walkover against Serbia and then go home. It really has no wish to play in the Group of Death.

Chapter 25
Monday 13 July 1914

Henry tracks Mary down to the filing room. Here, between two long racks of dusty files, he tells her that he can get away again one night this week. All she has to do is name which one suits her best. Instead of the delight he expected to see on her face, Henry is dismayed when she frowns and says, 'I'm not sure I'll be able to meet you any night this week, Mr Kenton.' He wasn't expecting her to call him 'Mr Kenton' either.

'Why not?' Henry blurts out, and regrets it at once, since yet again he sounds like a disappointed schoolboy.

'I just don't think it's a good idea,' says Mary. 'I thought you liked my company, but now it's clear to me that you just want to be bedding me all the time.'

'It's not that, Mary. You know it isn't. I—'

Henry wants to say 'care for you very much' but he has already told Mary numerous times that he loves her. Apart from that first time, all the other times he has been inside her when he has said this, but he realises there is no going back now. 'Love you,' he finishes, after a pause that he knows has ruined the effect of the declaration.

'I don't just want to be your whore,' says Mary, and Henry almost flinches at her use of the word.

'You're not,' Henry blusters. 'You know you're not … you're not … *that.*'

'So what am I then?'

'You're a woman I love—'

'A whore,' she interrupts, saying the word even more vehemently. Then, softening her tone a little, she adds, 'At least that's what it feels like to me.'

There is a silence. Henry doesn't know what to say. Then Mary fills it by saying, 'I want so much more than that. I love you, Henry.'

The use of his first name makes Henry feel that Mary's attitude is perhaps softening a little. But then she says something that is truly alarming.

'I might want to have your child. Have you thought of that?'

Despite his alarm, Henry dodges that last sentence.

'And I love you,' he says. 'That's why I want us to be together. You know it isn't easy for me—'

Then Henry realises that he has uttered completely the wrong thing, as Mary says, almost with a snarl, 'Then make it easy for yourself.'

When you're in a hole, stop digging, the saying goes. Henry keeps digging.

'What do you mean?' he foolishly asks.

Mary tells him.

In Vienna, the Austrian investigation into the assassination of the Archduke has delivered bad news to the Austrian manager, Berchtold. Their report concludes (quite incorrectly): 'There is nothing to prove or even to suppose that the Serbian government is accessory to the inducement for the crime, its preparations or the furnishing of weapons. On the contrary, there are reasons to believe that this is altogether out of the question.'

The report depresses the Austrian manager beyond belief.

Henry stands alone in the aisle between the two sets of files where Mary has left him. On the one hand he just wants to be done with her. It's all become far too complicated. Leave it now. Find somebody else less demanding. But on the other hand, he can't get certain pictures of her out of his head. (All of these pictures involve her in a state of partial or full undress.) And he can't bear the thought of her being with some other man. He wants her. And he thinks it's not just for her body and for sex. As far as he can tell, he wants *her*. He wants the happiness and laughter and fun they have when they are together. How colourless his life would be if he went back to things as they were. And he can think of no other woman in the entire company, or indeed that he can remember ever having met or seen, whom he finds as attractive as her.

He tries to find her that afternoon, but is unable to. Eventually, when he asks in New Business (and gets an odd look from the girl he asks in the process), he's told that she's gone home, that she wasn't feeling very well. Henry feels bad that he seems to have been the cause of this. He wouldn't have wanted to hurt her for anything. But he also knows where he wants this to end up – married to Clara with Mary on the side. Certainly he could never imagine not being married to Clara, or telling her that he was leaving her or having to tell the children. This means that it is inevitable that there will come a time where he has to say goodbye to Mary and let her go. Either that or she'll have to accept that he is, and will remain, a married man. He could tell her this now and risk losing her. Or he could string her along and wait.

Henry makes his decision.

Chapter 26
Tuesday 14 July 1914

More and more of the managers are taking to the sea as the month progresses. The Tsar is no exception. Along with members of the Imperial family, he leaves for a yachting cruise in Finnish waters.

In Vienna, Conrad, the Austrian Army commander, does something very unexpected. You'll remember, dear reader, that up until now Conrad was the man who was most anxiously pushing for war. But now that it is almost upon him, he dithers. He points out to Berchtold that much of the army is on leave, helping to bring in the harvest. (It's obviously important that that the Austrian players should be well fed if there were to be a Group of Death.) If these men's leave is cancelled now, it will alert the other powers to Austria's intentions. Most of the soldiers are scheduled to return on July 21st or 22nd and so, really, July 23rd is the earliest date that would suit the army.

Surprising, don't you think, coming from the man who had been so hawkish up until now. But again, we have an answer, and once again it is about a widower and a married woman.

Conrad's wife, Vilma, died of stomach cancer in 1905. Vilma was eight years younger than Conrad and he had always thought that he would die before her. Her passing devastated him. 'I depended on this woman with all passion of the heart and of the mind,' he wrote. 'The entire harmony of my existence, all of my striving, every interest rested upon only her.' Vilma's death pushed Conrad into a gloominess that invaded every corner of his life. He would suffer bouts of deep depression. Shortly after her death, he even suffered severe abdominal pains which made him wonder whether he too had stomach cancer. (An army doctor would go on to give him a clean bill of health.)

So this was Conrad on the evening of 20 January 1907, when he attended a dinner party at the home of a certain Baron Kalchberg. Amongst the gathering he spotted Gina von Reininghaus, a woman whom Conrad had met seven years earlier at the Kalchebrg's Trieste home. Later they found themselves seated beside one another at dinner. Gina would later recall that Conrad spent the whole evening talking about his late wife. After dinner, Gina played the piano accompanying Captain Franz Putz, a gifted singer and, as it happened, Conrad's *aide-de-camp*. Gina and Putz had such fun that she invited him to visit her at her house. Loyally, Putz asked if he might also bring his boss.

So began a routine where, every sixth day, Conrad would visit Gina at her home at Opergasse 8, next to the Vienna Opera. Two months later, at the end of a visit to Gina, Conrad declared in a private moment that he had 'only one thought: that you should become my wife.'

There was only one problem with this suggestion. Gina was already married – to wealthy industrialist Hans von Reininghaus.

When Gina recovered from the shock, she told Conrad that such a thing was out of the question. At twenty-eight, she was barely half his age. As well as that, she had six children by her husband, the youngest of whom was barely a year old.

Not to be put off by this, Conrad asked her again in May, saying that if she turned him down, he would never ask again. She did, saying that she couldn't leave her children, but this didn't deter Conrad. As we have seen, he believed in the doctrine of the offensive – relentless attacks with no concern for the moral or emotional casualties. For her part, Gina told him how her marriage to Hans had become loveless and how she hoped that, one day, he would agree to a divorce.

Gina would eventually get her divorce and she and Conrad would end up marrying in 1915. Long before that, though, she had become his mistress. With Gina, Conrad was like a lovesick schoolboy. When they were apart, he would write her letters every day. In a personal book that he called the *Diary of My Woes*, he wrote much longer entries in the form of letters, never mailed and dripping with unrequited love. In short, when Conrad should have been thinking about his job as head of Austria's Army, he was instead mooning over Gina.

And so, as his lovesick commander in chief gloomily relays the news of the Austrian Army's readiness – or lack of it – Berchtold knows that the Germans are not going to be pleased about this. But it can't be helped. The plan now is to deliver the ultimatum to the Serbs on July 23rd with a forty-eight hour deadline, expiring on the 25th.

Even though it is only Tuesday, Henry asks Mary to lunch and she accepts. Once they are seated and have ordered, he tells her that last night he told Clara he wanted a divorce. Mary looks into his eyes and for several moments Henry can see the uncertainty there. Can she believe him? She isn't sure. She begins to ask questions. How did Clara react? Did she cry? What about the children? What's going to happen next? And most importantly of all, when is it going to happen?

Henry has prepared well for all of this. He didn't sleep very well last night, and during his waking hours he imagined in great detail what it would have been like if he *had* told Clara that he wanted a divorce. Henry can see that Mary's questions stem from a combination of several different factors. Partly, just like a policeman, she wants to verify that his story is true. She is looking for inconsistencies; she wants to see if he slips up. But Henry's picture of the tormented scene with Clara is quite perfect, ending as it does with, 'I think it must have been about four o'clock. I was exhausted from talking and from her crying. I just had to go to bed.' And in response to the unspoken question that hangs in the air after this statement, Henry adds, 'She didn't go to bed. She was asleep on the couch when I got up.'

Several times, as Henry unfolds his story, Mary reaches across and takes his hand and squeezes it. She says things like, 'How awful' or 'It must have been a nightmare for you.' After one of these interjections, Henry manages to slip in that he and Clara won't be saying anything to the children about any of this until '*at least* after their summer holiday in August.' He sees a momentary wave of displeasure cross Mary's face as he says this, but she knows better than to say anything. Henry was ready for her if she had and was intending to snap angrily at her, saying something like, 'Have you no pity – not even for the children?' In the event, this little piece of drama proves unnecessary.

Apart from checking his story, Henry thinks he can also detect both satisfaction and pity in Mary's demeanour; satisfaction in that she has been the victor in this contest for Henry and pity for Clara. In fact, Mary actually says, 'The poor woman' or 'The poor thing' a number of times.

When Henry feels that they have spent sufficiently long on this, he suddenly checks the time and announces that he must be getting back. He had decided earlier that he wouldn't give Mary any time to respond. Rather, he would let her mull it over at her leisure. And this she seems to do because, before he goes home, she asks him if he could stay up in town on Thursday night, the day after tomorrow. Henry is delighted at such a quick turnaround, as he sees it, and agrees on the spot. But he is also surprised to find that he has the faintest sensation of wishing that she hadn't come back to him at all and that he had just gone home to Clara and the children.

Chapter 27
Wednesday 15 July 1914

In France, a row has broken out about the state of preparedness of the French team. In the senate, Charles Humbert, senator for the Meuse, has declared that in spite of the vast and increasing sums being spent on the army – the heavy artillery, the forts on the Eastern frontier, the stores of war *materiel*, boots, uniforms, shells, as well as the transport, bridges and wireless equipment – it is very much inferior to that of Germany. Monsieur Humbert claims that when the German wireless station at Metz is transmitting, the French station at Verdun goes on the blink. But it's the issue of the boots that really makes the headlines. Humbert claims that the French Army doesn't have enough boots and that soldiers will be going into action with one pair of boots and *a single* spare boot.

The Minister for War, while accepting the substance of the charges, insists that rapid progress is being made to remedy these deficiencies. Large sums have already been spent on reinforcing the field artillery and the machine gun sections. With regard to fortress artillery, there are plans to replace the older model guns with two hundred 115-millimetre guns by the end of 1915 or the beginning of 1916. Also by the end of 1915, the stock of shells will have been trebled. By the end of 1917, it is intended that two hundred howitzers will have strengthened the artillery. As for heavy field artillery, the older types of guns are being modernised and new types are being manufactured or are undergoing trials. New wireless installations are on order for the frontier forts.

Also today, at 11:30 in the morning, Raymond Poincaré, the French manager and his Prime Minister leave the Gare du Nord for

Dunkirk on the presidential train. The plan is to, early the following morning, board the battleship *France* to travel to Russia. The visit has been arranged for quite some time but now, with the situation that has been unfolding since Sarajevo, it has added urgency. The purpose of the visit is simple: Poincaré wants to make sure his ally will stand fast whatever Austria does.

Late that night Henry wakes up intensely annoyed. He had gone to bed early so as to get a good night's sleep and be ready for not much sleep with Mary on Thursday night. But now, with the alarm clock reading just after midnight, he is wide awake. Clara is asleep beside him, her blonde hair scattered on the pillow, back to him, the bedclothes pulled protectively up around her shoulder. Henry is awake because he has just thought of something else that could upset the whole apple cart.

When he went to bed, all was right with the world. He had been in good form, played with the girls for a while until Clara took them off to get them ready for bed. He had kissed her goodnight and was in bed by ten. Before he drifted off, his survey of his life seemed quite satisfactory. The situation with Mary was stabilised until after the summer. It would be September before she might start to become annoying again, with her talk of his leaving Clara. Maybe then Henry would have to end it all, but in the meantime there were two months of enjoyment and pleasure to look forward to. Clara and the girls were looking forward to the holiday and were busily and excitedly making preparations. The little world that revolved around him – at least, this was the way he saw it – was just as it should be. But the thing that has woken him up, that actually has him sweating, is that it has suddenly occurred to him that Mary could become – by accident or by design – pregnant.

Up until now, this has been an issue of no concern to Henry. Essentially he assumed that Mary was taking care of it. And despite the fact that they have done some extraordinarily intimate things, this is not something that Henry feels he could ask her about. He would be too embarrassed. Yes, he has had his face in places that he would have thought no woman would allow, but no, this is not a subject he could ever imagine himself discussing with Mary.

And he realises now that this has been a big mistake and that he is going to have to. Because she could be pregnant at this very minute. This was the thought that catapulted him from sleep, with the phrase, 'I might want to have your child' ringing in his brain.

Now it has to be said that that Henry has absolutely no *rational* reason for thinking that Mary might be pregnant. It isn't that she has said something about a missed period, for example – or anything at all. But he is suddenly overwhelmed by the question, 'What if she became pregnant?' Or worse still, what if she pretended to be pregnant to try and snare him? He believes she would be quite capable of doing this. Mary could not be described as a weak woman, some kind of wilting violet. Henry has a sense – from her lovemaking, if from nothing else – that when Mary sets her mind on something, she will go all out to achieve it. So what if she did suddenly announce she was pregnant? Henry needs to make it clear to her what would happen if she ever did. And he needs to do it quickly.

Chapter 28
Thursday 16 July 1914

Finally Thursday arrives. Clara has been racking her brains to work out how she will be able to make sandwiches for her lunch with James. Either the girls or Mrs Parsons will see. And even if she manages to somehow find a way to do it without their being aware, there is still the problem of taking a package of sandwiches out of the house without them seeing it. In the end she decides she won't be able to make any – she will have to buy them. This bothers her greatly. Firstly, she feels guilty about spending some of the housekeeping money – some of Henry's hard-earned money – on lunch with … well, another man. She quickly puts that idea out of her head. But there is also the fact – and in her mind, this is really the more significant reason – she wanted the sandwiches to be made with her own hands. She wanted to show him what she was capable of, her skills in the kitchen – even with something as simple as a sandwich. But in the end, she accepts that it is not to be and that that will just have to wait for another time.

At first she doesn't see James when she arrives, and for several seconds she feels her world crumbling. She is on the brink of tears. But then she sees him walking towards her and waving. It just turns out that their usual seat was taken and he has found the next one along. Clara heaves a huge sigh of relief.

'So how is everything in Europe today?' she asks as she sits down, placing the paper bag containing the sandwiches and drinks on the bench.

'Oh, more of the same. The Austrians are huffing and puffing against Serbia. The Germans are pretending they're not really interested in the revelations about the state of the French Army. I assume you saw that?'

Clara nods even though it's not true. For the last few days, she has been unable to concentrate on anything, except the thought of her lunch today. Every time she sat down to read a paper or a book, she found that the words made no sense to her. Eventually she gave up trying.

'And in Paris,' James concludes. 'The Socialists are suggesting that if there was a general strike there couldn't be any war since nobody would turn up.'

He folds the paper and puts it down.

'Actually, not a bad idea that. Not sure it would work in practice but a good idea nonetheless. Now, what have we here?'

Clara began to unwrap the sandwiches.

'Ham and mustard – as you ordered,' she says, looking into his eyes.

He smiles.

'I'm afraid I didn't get a chance to make them myself, so I bought them.'

'They look delicious.'

They begin to eat and, almost immediately, Clara finds that an awkward silence has descended between them. James seems to be waiting for her to continue the conversation. But the only thing she can think of to say is the question she has been dying to ask ever since last Thursday.

'I've been thinking all week about your wife – what you told me about being divorced,' she says, gazing out at the water, crowded with birds. 'Can I ask – I hope you don't mind – please tell me if it's none of my business. How did you decide? How did you know when you couldn't go on?'

There is no response and Clara wonders whether she has gone too far. One of the things she likes about James is that conversation is so easy between them, but has she been too impertinent in raising this now? Suddenly alarmed, she turns, an apology starting to form on her lips. She is fearful now that this might be the end of it all and that is something she really could not bear.

He lowers his sandwich and places it back on the open brown paper in which it came. Then he turns to face her.

'Like all couples, we loved each other – initially, at least. But as I found out, she was angry at her father – for what I never found out, though I had my suspicions. The result was that rather, than take it out on him, she took it out on me.'

'How?' asks Clara, puzzled. 'How did she do that?'

'The anger she should have directed at him she directed at me. From her point of view he was an impossible target, I was an easy one. And so our relationship became like a war with a battle followed by a period of calm followed by another battle. One day I woke up and found that I had been dreaming about the Hundred Years' War. It wasn't that I had a particular interest in that period. I had learned about it at school but other than that—'

He shrugs.

'But then I remember I was on the way to work. I had come out of the Tube and was walking down Whitehall when it came back to me. The Hundred Years' War. I thought, Yes, that's what my marriage will be.'

He smiled faintly.

'That was the moment. That was the moment when I knew. I told her the same night that I wanted a divorce.'

'Was it awful?'

'It's not for the faint hearted,' he says. 'It was easier because we didn't have any children. If we had, I don't think I'd have had the courage to go through with it.'

'How long were you married?'

'Four years. And now, this year, divorced four.'

There is a pause and then he asks, 'Why are you asking me this?'

It is the question that she probably knew was coming. She is relieved and terrified at the same time. She takes a deep breath.

'Because I'm really unhappy in my marriage. And you're the only person I know, the only person I've ever met, who has had a divorce. I suppose I wanted to find out about it.'

There, she has said it.

'It would not be easy,' he says.

Afterwards, many times afterwards, Clara will replay this conversation in her head. She will come to appreciate – though it will take quite some time – the significance of how James responded to her question. 'It would not be easy.' The implication, of course, being that she had already decided to go through with it. And a further implication that he approved of her course of action. And further implications still that he would support her and help her. And most importantly of all, that he would be waiting for her at the end. In short, he wanted her to do this.

'I didn't think it would be,' she says and she finds that her voice has dropped almost to a whisper.

'It's far easier for a man than for a woman. You would have to have grounds – adultery, cruelty, something like that. You would have to prove it.'

'Am I correct in saying that any property I had before the marriage would be mine after a divorce?'

'You are well informed.'

'We have an encyclopaedia at home.'

'Ah. I'm no lawyer, but yes, I believe that is the case. Your children – they're young, I assume.'

She detects a faint compliment in the question. She nods.

'Six and fifteen months.'

He winces.

'I believe you would be entitled to custody of your children. But depending on how your husband reacted, it could be a fearful battle. I'm hardly one to advise about divorce but it could be a long and cruel road if you chose to go down it.'

'Longer and more cruel than the one I am on at the moment?'

She too has put down her sandwich and her hands lie in her lap. Now he reaches across and lays his hand gently on hers.

'Only you can answer that, my dear friend.'

Clara suddenly feels that she needs to be by herself.

'I should probably go,' she says, standing up.

'I didn't mean to upset you,' he says, looking alarmed.

'No, it's not you. It's nothing … I just need to think.'

'Of course.'

'Thank you,' she says. 'I'm sorry I haven't been such good company today.'

'Do you mind if say something to you?'

She looks at him. He takes both her hands and looks into her eyes.

'We don't know each other very well, we've only spoken a handful of times. But I want you to know –if you decided to go ahead – I would give you all the support I could in any ways that I could. I have friends … contacts. I know people.'

'You're very kind,' she says, and she knows her eyes are starting to mist.

Then she turns away, gets up and begins to thread her way through the crowd on the busy path. She feels like she needs to run but, of course, she can't in the skirt she is wearing. And anyway, what would people think?

She has just reached a point where several paths intersect when she feels a hand on her shoulder. She jumps. Her first thought is that it is Henry. She looks round.

It is James.

'I'm sorry,' he says. 'I didn't mean to startle you. It's just … I meant to tell you that I have booked holidays for the next couple of weeks.'

Her heart sinks. Here it is. The one person in the world who seems to value her in any way, the one person she could talk to about any of this, is about to go out of her life.

'You may remember I mentioned that I was intending to go to France.'

Why is he telling her all of this? He seems nervous.

'You see … that is to say, I *had* booked them. The holidays, I mean. But what with the situation in Europe, I thought it might be better for me to defer my holidays for now. Just in case anything happens, you know.'

What does any of this have to do with her? She wishes he would let her go. She is afraid she is going to burst into tears and she can't do that in public. And not in front of him.

'Well, you see, I thought – if you wanted to – I could *still* take next Thursday off and we could spend it together. Or at least as much of it as you could … whatever time you could spare. Or any day, really. It doesn't have to be Thursday if some other day—'

Clara sees that James *is* nervous. He's gabbling a bit. Realisation dawns. She smiles – a smile that feels weary and full of relief.

'I'd like that very much.'

'So whatever time suits you,' he says.

'I could be here for eleven. Or maybe a little earlier.'

'Perfect. Usual spot?'

'Usual spot.'

'I'll see you then,' he says, and then, leaning forward, he kisses her on the cheek.

She is so taken aback by this unexpected gesture that all she can do is to stand there while he raises his hat and then, turning around, walks off.

In St Petersburg, a report is received from the Russian Ambassador in Vienna. In it he states that, 'Information reaches me that the Austro-Hungarian government at the conclusion of the inquiry intends to make certain demands on Belgrade … It would seem to me desirable that at the present moment, before a final decision on the matter, the Vienna Cabinet should be informed how Russia would react to the fact of Austria's presenting demands to Serbia such as would be unacceptable to the dignity of that state.'

The Austrian Ambassador in St Petersburg is asked about this. He tells the Russians that Austria is not planning on any measure that might cause a war in the Balkans. The Russians take no further action.

Clara lies in bed unable to sleep. She tosses and turns and is glad that Henry is staying up in town. He would be terribly annoyed if he was here and she was doing what she is doing now. She can't imagine what the process of asking him for a divorce would be like. She knows he would be angry and that he would try to make it as difficult as possible for her. And she daren't think about Ursula and Virginia – not yet. So instead of dwelling on how nightmarish all that might be, she tries to imagine life afterwards.

Assuming it is true that she would be able to keep the house then she would be here afterwards with just the children. The poor girls – how awful it would be for them. And Clara would have to find a way of earning money. She doubts Henry would give her any. Does the law require him to? She doesn't know. But even if it does, she knows he would try to ensure that it would be the least amount he could get away with. Where could she work? Working in a stationary shop is the only thing she has ever known. And even if she could get a job, who would mind the children while she worked? She wouldn't be able to afford Mrs Parsons. And even if she could, and Mrs Parsons was minding them all day, would that mean that she would, in effect, become their mother?

Almost without realising it, Clara puts her hand to her forehead. This is all too much. She can't go through with any of this.

At exactly the same time, Mary lies post-coitus in the crook of Henry's arm. Their room is in darkness, Henry having put out the bedside lamp shortly after they had both climaxed – Mary genuinely so on this occasion. It was a bit of a struggle for Henry to get there tonight, since he had other things on his mind. But Mary coaxed him along, gripping his cock and eventually jerking it savagely all the while saying lewd things to him like a prostitute, until eventually he splashed all over her hand. He would dearly love to sleep now, as he is exhausted, but he cannot let another moment go by without them having this discussion.

'You do take precautions, don't you?' he says, lying on his back and trying to make it sound like he is speaking to the darkness.

'Precautions?'

The fake innocence really irks him.

'Against becoming pregnant, of course.'

'You wouldn't like me to have your baby?' the innocent voice continues.

'Not until you and I are together,' he says, and he thinks this is a pretty good rejoinder. And he is happy that he said 'together' rather than 'married.'

He wants to hear her say, 'Of course I take precautions. Don't you worry about any of that.' Instead, what he hears is, 'And what would you do if I did become pregnant?' She pauses – for effect, he thinks. 'Before we were *together*, I mean.'

'I couldn't afford another child at the moment.' Henry had decided – after a lot of thought – that this was probably the best argument to advance. He hopes this will be the end of it, but she is relentless.

'So you'd want me to not have the baby?'

'That would be your decision.' Henry speaks to the darkness again.

He thinks that this is another really good riposte and he waits to see what she will say in response to this. There is a long pause and then Mary extracts herself from Henry's embrace. She turns her back to him and moves away to the edge of the bed. Henry doesn't know what the morning with her will bring. Maybe she will have had time to consider this and will have absorbed it. Maybe she'll still be angry with him. Maybe this will be the end of it. Henry finds he doesn't actually care. He feels she has pushed him around quite a bit up until now, but with this he's been able to strike back. It's a good feeling; a satisfying feeling. He's pleased. The talk has had the desired effect. She knows where she stands. He turns his back to her as well and goes to sleep.

Chapter 29
Friday 17 July 1914

Henry is pleased to find that Mary wakes in good humour. Indeed she is awake first, kisses him from sleeping and repeatedly calls him 'darling' as they dress and get ready to leave – separately – for work. The talk last night has had the desired effect. Henry is whistling as he leaves the hotel.

Berchtold, the Austrian manager, is feeling the pressure. What if Serbia accepts the terms of his ultimatum? This would really be an own goal for his team. While it would be a diplomatic success, Austria – and by implication, Berchtold – would be seen as weak and no longer capable of vigorous, decisive action. Its powerful ally Germany, in particular, would take a dim view of this.

Berchtold's unhappiness continues. His mood isn't improved when the Austrian team's Quartermaster General reports cheerfully that he can 'move at a moment's notice.' 'We in the General Staff are ready,' he continues. 'There is nothing more for us to do at this juncture'; thereby reminding Berchtold – as if he needed reminding – that the ball is firmly is his court.

Clara finds herself thinking a lot about James. He seems so happy even though he has no wife. He gives the impression of being … well, sort of self-contained, like he doesn't need anybody else. Or if it's not that exactly, that he is at least happy in his own skin – content to be himself.

She imagines him waking in the morning in his house. Does he have a woman who comes in and does for him? Clara assumes he must, even though he hasn't mentioned her. Does she make the sandwiches or does James make them himself? And cooking – does he cook? Clara has a feeling that he does. It is one of the things she must ask him.

She imagines him to be very good at what he does and highly respected in his job. She assumes he has a great deal of responsibility and many friends whom he meets to discuss the matters of the day. Or maybe he prefers to stay home and read. She pictures him in a sort of study cum library surrounded by books. Then, at weekends, she pictures him walking in the countryside, stopping at some wayside pub.

She has a sense that he enjoys everything. Whether the sun shines or it rains; whether he sits outside bathed in sunshine drinking a pint of beer or pulls in close to a roaring fire, sipping whisky; whether he is concerned with great events at work or feeding the ducks in St James's Park, she has the feeling that he is content. Even though he lives alone, he doesn't seem lonely. He enjoys being by himself or with other people. He seems to find pleasure in every day; in just being alive.

Now, Clara realises that she knows very little about James and that a lot of this is just her imagination and may not have much basis in reality. Yet she has a very strong feeling – indeed, for her it is pretty much a certainty – that this is what he is like.

And how different all that is from Clara. She is so discontented. And even as she thinks this, she feels guilty – again reminding herself of all that she has to be thankful for. But there seems to be some kind of central core missing from her life – a core that James appears to possess. Or is it just an attitude? If she approached each day as he seems to, and if she could take pleasure in all of the little things that made up the day, could she find some of his contentment?

And then she remembers with a shock that she once had that contentment. When she worked in her father's shop, before she met Henry, she *did* have that contentment. The James she is describing, that she pictures – that was the way *she* was before she got married. That's why it seems so familiar and also why she is so certain about it. It is because she knows this feeling herself. She was once like this. But where and how did she lose it?

Clearly it was when she married Henry. In the same way that he took on the role of what he thought a husband should be, she too took on a role – the dutiful wife. She wanted to be the perfect wife for him. But in doing so, she lost something. She lost that very core of herself that she recognises in James. And now she wonders if it's possible to get it back and, if so, how? Or is it lost forever?

Chapter 30
Saturday 18 July 1914

Mary finishes work at lunchtime and goes home to the house she shares with two other women. Her housemates want to go and do something. Get out and enjoy the fine weather. Go to a park, lie in the sun. All three of them are in their twenties, single and unspoken for. Mary is the eldest. The biggest concern all three of them have – though none of them ever talks about it – is that they will be left on the shelf. So the urge to go out and 'do something' is actually an unspoken wish that today they will meet the man of their dreams. Or if not that, then at least some man.

Most of the time, Mary goes with them on these Saturday afternoons. All three work and so, on Saturdays, all three have been paid. They will perhaps buy an item or two of new clothing because all three of them love pretty things. Especially in fine weather, they will stroll in the park, eat ice cream, perhaps flirt with some men. They will have tea in a restaurant and often go to a music hall show in the evening. But today, Mary tells them that she's not feeling very well – 'usual complaint,' she tells them – and so they go off without her. In reality, there is nothing wrong with Mary; she feels absolutely fine. But there is something she must do.

Mary is, more than anything else, a realist. She wasn't always like this. Looking back to the time when she nearly got married, before the man threw her over, she sees how starry-eyed she was. She was in love and just got swept away with the whole thing; she thought it would be always like that. After it was over she spent a long time thinking about what a fool she had been, but she is past that now.

Now she understands that nobody is perfect. She sees how love and marriage are about settling; about saying to oneself that this is as good as it is going to get. Of course, she wouldn't settle for any old thing. A man who drank or beat her or never washed – there are some things that she just couldn't countenance. But in Henry she feels she has found most of the things that would enable her to settle.

To begin with, he has a good secure job and she has the impression that he is reasonably highly regarded in the company. She thinks he will see further promotion in the years ahead. (This high regard is not necessarily shared by some of Mary's workmates – not that they know anything about her relationship with him. While most are indifferent to Henry, she has heard one or two make disparaging remarks about him. They think he gives women the glad eye and that he touches a bit too much for a married man. They reckon 'he puts it about' and that they 'wouldn't fancy being his wife.')

Mary knows that, just as with all men, there is not a lot she can do about Henry's fidelity. But she feels that if she keeps him interested in the sex then he should not have too much reason to want to look elsewhere. He is not a bad lover, though nowhere near as good as the fellow who nearly married her. But Mary flatters him and pretends when she has to and that seems to keep everything in the garden rosy.

Mary really would like to have a child, with Henry as the father. But at the moment she is being careful not to. It would be far too risky to play that game – to become pregnant and then to try to force him to marry her. She is certain that he would do what most men would do – pretend to have no knowledge of it and drop her like a hot potato.

But while this is a risk she is not prepared to run, there is another that she is. And it is this that has kept her indoors on this glorious Saturday of hot sun and blue skies and London parks buzzing with people, carefree for a few hours at least.

She is pretty sure that Henry was not telling the truth when he said that he had told his wife he wanted a divorce. But whether he is or not, time is running on and things are moving too slowly for Mary. She suspects that, given the chance, Henry will delay and delay and it could be years before he leaves his wife – that is, if he leaves her at all. So Mary is going to see what she can do to accelerate the process. She is going to try to force the issue. She is conscious that this could all go terribly wrong. But she is prepared for that. If it does, she will just have to start again and go and find somebody else. And if what she is proposing to do works, then she will have finally reached that happy place that has eluded both her and her housemates up until now.

Mary sits at the heavy living room table. Outside the sky is blue above the slated roofs and chimney pots of the houses opposite. However, the room feels cool. It is as though the net curtains draw the heat and passion from the day outside. In front of her are some sheets of paper that she took from work earlier. She dips her pen in the glass inkwell and begins to write.

As Mary is busily writing, Sir Edward Grey is heading to Hampshire after a fairly uneventful week. He arrives, sheds his jacket and tie and decides he will go a long trail. There has been very little rain this month and the lawn that leads down to the river is getting brown.

As usual, it is the birds he is most conscious of as he rambles. The older ones are moulting now, the younger ones spreading about and discovering the world for themselves. The river and lakes are full of broods of water hens, coots, dabchicks and ducks. A couple of weeks ago he spotted a cuckoo's egg in a reed warbler's nest and this nest now contains a solitary young bird growing feathers. He looks forward to a good day's fishing tomorrow.

Clara is in bed and trying to quiet her racing mind so that she can hopefully fall asleep. She has been through all the things she must do tomorrow and decided upon the food she will cook for each meal. Normally, like a sentry who completes one section of the perimeter he is patrolling before moving on to the next, she would move on to worrying – about the girls, about Henry, about herself. How she hates that she does this but there never seems to be anything else to think about after she is finished with the next day's practicalities. Except that tonight there is. Her mind turns to James.

What is he doing now, she wonders? It is close to midnight so she assumes he is asleep. She wonders what he wears in bed. Pyjamas? An old-fashioned night gown? Or maybe nothing at all. Clara has often thought that she would like to sleep like that – especially when there are clean sheets on the bed. In winter it would be like being an animal sheltering from the elements, hibernating in a cave. In summer, on those really hot nights, she could throw the bedclothes off and let the moonlight bathe her body.

She is all alone in the world. Of course, everybody is alone, everybody lives their own life, is born, does whatever they are going to do and then dies. But everyone else doesn't seem to think of themselves as being alone. They are parts of families, they are relatives or friends of other people, they are parents of children, they are in clubs or work together. For heaven's sake, she lives in a house with three other souls. Two of them are her children, sprung from her body. And yet she feels so utterly alone.

If she asked Henry – which she wouldn't, of course – if he was alone, she knows he wouldn't really understand what she meant. And if he probed a bit – which he wouldn't because he doesn't particularly care – and she managed to explain what she meant, he would say that he has her and the children and his extended family and his workmates. He might expound that 'no man is an island' and that we all live our lives in a web of links to other people.

Why can she not feel this way? She is the woman in the Atkinson Grimshaw painting walking down the moonlit suburban lane, alone, utterly alone. She tries to picture it now but this time she is *in* the picture. She sees the slick cobbles beneath her feet. Her shoes tread soundlessly on the stones. She is aware that one of her shoes is leaking so that the foot of her stocking is damp and soggy. She carries a basket on her hip. What was in the basket in the painting, Clara could never remember. She wonders whether it was intended to be a baby and that this perhaps accounted for the woman's disorientation. Tonight Clara doesn't want it to be a baby and so it becomes some laundry instead. She is returning it to the big house. It is how she earns her living, washing and ironing for the people in fine houses.

She reaches the white door in the wall and turns the latch. It is open and she steps onto a flagstone path through wild, overgrown gardens that lead her to the house. She comes to the back door and, once again, finds it unlocked. Inside, the house is a maze of passageways but she seems to know her way. She is conscious that whenever she has to make a decision about which way to go, she chooses a route that takes her upwards. As though in a dream she finds herself sometimes on the servants' stairs and sometimes on the main stairs of the house. From the outside she didn't remember the house being so high, but her journey upwards seems interminable. Finally, she emerges through a door onto a corridor and walks to a particular bedroom. She enters and at last is able to put down her basket.

There is a large four-poster bed in the room and to one side of that is a door that she knows leads to the bathroom. She begins to undress and throws her clothes on the carefully made-up bed. She is going to take a bath.

Chapter 31
Sunday 19 July 1914

As we have seen, after receiving their assurances from Der Kaiser, the Austrian team went into serious preparation for the match in Belgrade. These preparations centred on devising that ultimatum to the Serbs, which they would be unable to accept. Working steadily, by 19 July the ultimatum is ready.

The Austrians make ten demands on the Serbs. They are to suppress publications which incite hatred and contempt of the Austrian monarchy. They must dissolve any anti-Austrian societies. In schools, teaching anything that foments anti-Austrian feeling is to be forbidden. Any officers in the armed forces thought to be anti-Austrian are to be removed – *and Austria is to be granted the right to provide the names of such officers*. Serbia must also allow the Austrian government to assist in the suppression of anti-Austrian elements in Serbia. And this is just the beginning. It gets worse.

Serbia is to begin a judicial inquiry into the assassination of 28 June and, again, elements of the Austrian government must be allowed to participate in the investigation. Serbia must arrest two named officers which, Austria has already decided, were implicated in the plot. Serbia must stop illicit arms traffic across its borders and arrest the border officials who assisted the Sarajevo assassins. (One assumes that Austria has also already decided who these people are.) Serbia is to explain why certain highly placed Serbian officials at home and abroad have expressed anti-Austrian sentiments. And finally, Serbia must notify Austria without delay that these measures have been carried out.

As Winston Churchill will say, upon hearing the terms of the ultimatum, 'it seemed absolutely impossible that any State in the world could accept it, or that any acceptance, however abject, would satisfy the aggressor.'

Meanwhile, Der Kaiser's team is considering a friendly against England. Recently the Royal Navy visited Kiel and now the Germans are thinking of sending the Third Squadron of its navy to visit a British port. The squadron will return from Norwegian waters on 8 August and the visit will be confirmed after that. There are also unconfirmed reports that Der Kaiser's son, the Crown Prince, also known rather unkindly as 'Little Willy,' will visit England.

In Germany, Jagow, the German Foreign Minister, publishes a note in the semi-official *North German Gazette* warning other powers 'that the settlement of differences which may arise between Austria-Hungary and Serbia should remain localised.' When Jagow is asked by the French Ambassador to Germany how he knows about the contents of the Austrian ultimatum, as he has revealed in the *North German Gazette*, he pretends to be ignorant of it.

The British Embassy in Berlin reports, 'We do not know the facts. The German government clearly do know. They know what the Austrian government is going to demand … and I think we may say with some assurance that they have expressed approval of those demands and promised support should dangerous complications ensure … the German government do not believe that there is any danger of war.'

Clara has taken a long time over her imaginary bath in the Atkinson Grimshaw house. Last night she fell asleep as she began to discard her clothes on the bed. Tonight, she resumes her fantasy, beginning again out on the wide suburban lane and coming in through the gate. She fills out more details now. It is the end of summer – maybe September, Clara's favourite month, when it is still really summer but the first sadness of autumn is starting to appear. She had been afraid that, if she returned to the fantasy too often, she would not be able to recover the original feeling it had for her. But it is as though the picture has a force that draws her in and everything feels just as good as it did the first time.

The moon is full and so she can see that the foliage in the garden is wild as though it has passed the whole summer completely untended. Once again she enters the house via the back door and spends an age climbing up through the house. She realises now that her slow progress is about deliberately delaying her arrival at the bedroom. But she eventually gets there, opens the door and begins to undress. Even though it is September, the room is warm, as a yellow and red fire crackles in the grate. The door into the bathroom is ajar. Yellow candlelight flickers inside and there is the sound of water running and the heavy, damp thud of the bath filling. The air beyond the bathroom door is hazy with steam and smells of water.

Clara, now naked, pads from the bedroom into the bathroom. The bathroom is warm too and has its own fire. She crosses warm wooden floorboards and deep, furry rugs. In the gauzy air of the bathroom she climbs into the bath where the almost unbearably hot water envelopes her body.

Clara falls asleep at this point but wakes some time later. She is in bed, with Henry, wearing a nightdress but in her mind she is in the bath in the Atkinson Grimshaw house. The water has cooled and she gets out, finding a huge, hot towel close by – just like the smaller ones that she always has ready for the girls when they have baths. Clara has never seen such big towels – didn't know that such things existed. She wraps one around herself and comes from the bathroom where she knows a man will be waiting. She wants it to be James but not just yet and so for now, it is an unknown man. Not that he is a stranger. Rather, a man that she just hasn't put a name and a face to.

The man kneels at her feet and parts the towel. He kisses her belly just below her navel and then starts to move his lips gradually downwards. She put her fingers in his hair and gently pushes down on the top of his head.

Chapter 32
Monday 20 July 1914

The day starts badly for Raymond Poincaré, the manager of the French team, on the first day proper of his state visit to Russia. As the battleship *France*, steaming along at 15 knots and commanded by an admiral of the fleet, approaches the harbour at Kronstadt, it accidentally rams a Russian tug that is towing a frigate. The incident wakes Poincaré in his cabin. It is not an auspicious start.

Things perk up, however. Around lunchtime, as the ship steams into Kronstadt, naval vessels and other craft, decorated with bunting, sail out to welcome the visitors. The imperial launch pulls alongside to transfer Poincaré to the Tsar's yacht *Alexandria*. Artillery salutes rumble across the Gulf of Finland. National anthems are played.

There is (rather startlingly high definition) British Pathé footage of the visit. It shows lots of cars and carriages, men in their best uniforms, women in white summer dresses with big hats. There is plenty of saluting and Monsieur Poincaré raises his top hat several times. Flags wave in the summer breeze. There are Cossacks with swords and tall furry hats. The Russian Army stages a march past. The weather appears to be of that incredible, pre-war, last-summer-of-innocence quality that we know (or feel we know) so well.

Everything is neat and tidy. There is a feeling that the Russians are really trying their best. This isn't really their thing, you feel – they'd much rather be celebrating in a different way – but they're trying. And as for the Tsar, the Russian manager, you get the impression that he'd much rather be doing something else entirely. But still, they're doing their best.

With President Poincaré, you get the sense that he'd much rather be back in France – or at least back *on* the *France*. There, the food and wine would be more familiar – not to mention, better. In France he would know that his team was a *real* team as opposed to this one. The Russians are putting on a brave show – God love them, he knows they are and full marks to them. But really, I mean, really – if it comes to it, if it ever comes to there being a Group of Death, what will they really be capable of? Surely they will just field countless armies of untrained, badly armed and poorly led peasants; poor, luckless souls, conscripts who will be scythed down in their droves because their generals have no real idea about how to conduct a war.

But this is not Poincaré's problem. In fact, for him, these countless millions are a good thing because they are the keys to France's defence. As long as the Russians threaten Germany in the east and he treats the Germans with 'firmness' (by which he really means intransigence) then France's security is assured. The threat to Germany of a war on two fronts, east and west, will always be guaranteed to make the Germans see sense.

Der Kaiser is on the yacht *Hohenzollern*, anchored at Balholm in Norway. Matters nautical are also on the mind of the German government. The government informs the directors of both the Norddeutscher Lloyd and the Hamburg America Line shipping companies that Austria will soon present an ultimatum that may cause a general European war, and that they should start withdrawing their ships from foreign waters back to Germany at once. That same day, the German Navy is ordered to start concentrating the High Seas Fleet. On the Vienna, Berlin and Paris stock exchanges, there is a continual demand for gold bars. In the end, so that all of this activity can take place and complete, another four days are allowed before the ultimatum is delivered.

Because of the Austrian delay in writing the ultimatum, the element of surprise that Germany had counted upon in the war against Serbia is lost. Instead, the strategy of 'localisation' is adopted. This means that when the Austro-Serbian war begins, Germany will pressure other powers not to become involved.

The postman usually delivers the post before Henry goes to work and so it is this morning. During term time, when they hear the postman at the letterbox, one of the girls will ask Henry if they can go and retrieve the mail. He allocates the job evenly from one to the other, sometimes – if he is in a good mood – making a bit of a show out of it, pretending to try to remember who did it last time. If he's in an especially good mood, he can keep this going for all of breakfast time and work the girls up into a frenzy of excitement and anticipation and false starts. 'Let me think now,' he'll say. Or, 'I'm sure it was Ursula who did it yesterday,' knowing full well that it wasn't. Or, 'You'll have to be very, very quiet while I try to remember,' until the girls, unable to contain themselves any longer, will be squealing with delight. It can be quite a performance and Clara is always glad to see everybody so happy.

This morning, though, it being the school holidays, the girls are still in bed and fast asleep. Clara hears the letters being pushed through the letterbox and she gets up from the table to go and fetch them. Usually they are all for Henry. On those odd occasions when there is one for her, he will always ask her whom it's from. If she can't tell from the writing on the envelope, he'll get her to open it and tell him. It is something that really annoys Clara so that this morning, when she finds that there is a letter addressed to her in a hand she doesn't recognise, she is intrigued. While still out in the hall, she slips the letter into the pocket of her apron. She will read it after Henry has gone to work.

Once that happens she pours some fresh tea and takes the letter out of her pocket. It occurs to her for a moment that it might be from James – how exciting that would be, but she remembers that she has never given him her address. He could find it out, she supposes, working where he works and knowing who he knows. Whoever it's from, the confident handwriting in dark blue ink is unfamiliar her. It is a woman's hand, Clara thinks. She slits the envelope open with her breakfast knife. The single page of ordinary writing paper is folded in two. She opens it and reads.

Her first reaction is that she must have opened someone else's letter by mistake – that it has been wrongly delivered to her. She checks the envelope again but there is no mistake. It is her name and address with the word 'Personal' written on it. So she reads the letter again. It is only two sentences.

'Dear Mrs Kenton, This is to let you know that your husband is carrying on an affair with another woman. I thought you should know.'

It's signed, 'A well-wisher.'

Clara puts the letter down on the oilcloth of the kitchen table. Then she pushes it right across the table as though to distance herself from its message. She stands up, goes to the window and looks out into the back garden. She finds that she is hugging herself. She feels as though some kind of monster has invaded the room. By looking out into the normality of the garden, she hopes that somehow it will go away. She doesn't know how long she stands like this, looking but not seeing. However, when she turns, the letter is still there on the table.

She picks it up again and reads it, just in case she had somehow mistaken its meaning. When it's clear that she hasn't, she throws it back down.

It is what she has feared all along. The thing she has wondered about, spent all those nights worrying about, has at last happened. Her normal, humdrum life is over. She has entered a new and strange and terrible world.

She sits back down in her chair and phrases begin to form in her mind. The things she is going to say to Henry when he comes home. But her mind quickly jumps from this to the fact that while he has been having sex with her, he has also been doing it with somebody else. She thinks of his cock inside that other woman, whoever she is, and then coming home and putting it into her.

Then she starts to wonder who this woman is. What does she look like? What do she and Henry talk about when they're not in bed fucking? What does she have that Clara doesn't have? Clara is angry. She has always been a good wife. She has given him sex whenever he wanted it, borne him two beautiful children, fed him well – his stomach is a testament to that. She has kept a neat home and put up with all his moods and foibles. She has been careful with the housekeeping money, rarely spending anything on herself. Is this the thanks she gets?

By now, Clara is crying. Tears are streaming down her face and she can hardly see, her eyes are so wet. She gets up from the chair and takes a couple of steps but finds that she is unable to stand. She crumples onto the linoleum floor, her skirt pooling around her. She buries her face in her hands and begins to keen. What has she done to deserve this? Why has her life ended up in such a shambles? All she wanted was to meet a man who would love her – love her, as she loves – with everything, body and soul, heart and mind. Was this too much to ask?

Clara has no idea how much time goes by, but eventually her keening stops though she continues to cry. She wonders where tears come from. Is there a limitless supply? Can the body eventually run out of tears? And if it did, would that mean that all the water was gone from your body? And would that mean you would be dead? Maybe she will just cry herself to death.

She needs to get some air. With the help of a chair she pulls herself to her feet and goes out into the garden. She leans against her father's tree and stretches her arms around it as though she would embrace it. She presses the skin of her cheek into the hard crust of the trunk until it hurts. What is she to do? Oh God, what is she to do?

Then it occurs to her that the letter is false. It is somebody just trying to hurt her. But who? She knows so few people. And she can't imagine why anybody would want to hurt her. To the best of her knowledge, she has never done anything to anybody that would make them feel like that towards her. She doesn't think she has any enemies.

'Mummy, Mummy. Where are you?'

Clara hears the voice as though from a long way off. It sounds like the voice of a child lost in a forest, in those fairy stories she used to read when she was young. She pulls away from the tree and turns round, hastily dabbing at her eyes with her sleeve. Ursula is standing in the frame of the back door. Clara knows she must look a sight.

'What's wrong, Mummy?'

'Oh nothing, darling,' Clara manages to say airily. 'I was just chopping onions.'

'Oh, there's Mrs Parsons,' says Ursula and disappears back through the kitchen.

Clara had forgotten about Mrs Parsons and, oh Jesus, the letter is still on the table. Clara hurries into the kitchen and retrieves it, stuffing it into her apron pocket. She needs to go to the bathroom and compose herself. She hurries through the hall, brushing past Mrs Parsons who is coming through to the kitchen.

'Alright, Mrs Kenton?' It is what Mrs Parsons always says but this morning Clara notices a tiny note of alarm in the housekeeper's voice.

'Oh yes, thank you,' says Clara.

She wants to say more, to offer some kind of excuse, but she realises that if she says anything else she will burst into tears again and she's not sure she'll ever be able to stop. She hurries upstairs and locks herself in the bathroom. She would happily stay there all day but before long, Virginia is knocking on the door wanting to get in. Clara feels like a trapped animal. Dear sweet God, is there no place she can find some peace? She looks in the mirror. Her face is beetroot red and around her eyes is swollen.

'I'll let you in now, darling,' she calls.

Clara splashes cooling water in her face and hurriedly dabs it dry with a towel. Then she opens the door, lets Virginia in and goes out to face the world.

As she comes into the kitchen, Mrs Parsons says, 'Sit down there now, Mrs Kenton, and I'll pour a nice cup of tea.'

Clara does as she's told.

'The girls have taken their breakfast outside,' says Mrs Parsons.

She places the cup of tea on the table in front of Clara, saying, 'There now, that's the stuff to give the troops. Now you stay there and enjoy your tea. I'm just going to start in the living room. It's a lovely day again today, Mrs Kenton. We've lots to be thankful for with this fine weather, don't we?'

It's a rhetorical question – Mrs Parsons isn't expecting or doesn't need an answer. She continues as she is wont to do.

'And your beautiful home and your two gorgeous little girls. Yes, we've lots to be thankful for.'

And with this, Mrs Parsons picks up the wooden box of polish and cloths and goes off to the living room. Moments later,

Clara hears her softly singing some song or other as she works. Clara is struck by the fact that Mrs Parsons never mentioned Henry.

Somehow Clara gets through the rest of the morning and into the afternoon. In her head she goes over what she is going to say to Henry when he comes in. She will get the girls to bed and then she'll go at it. She anticipates the moment she will do this with a mixture of longing and dread. She is not even sure she'll be able to act normally when he comes in at six. By mid-afternoon, her head is crowded with the words and phrases and sentences she is planning to use. They are like arrows in a quiver, just waiting to be fired off.

She and Mrs Parsons take an afternoon cup of tea together, as they normally do, but Clara hears nothing of what Mrs Parsons says. Her voice is like a fly buzzing around a room as Clara enacts, in her head, the scene that is going to play out this evening.

But then, just after she hears a bell tolling what she thinks may be five o'clock, a thought slips into Clara's mind like somebody squeezing onto an over-crowded Tube train. It is something James said.

'You would have to have grounds – adultery, cruelty, something like that.'

Adultery. Adultery. What a strange word. Adult-ery. Something adults do. It's certainly that. But this word, 'adultery,' stops her in her tracks. 'You would have to have grounds,' was what James said. And now, with what appears to her to be quite unbelievable timing, she *has* grounds. What she might do with those grounds, with this adultery, she is not at all clear, but she doesn't want to do the wrong thing. Should she visit a solicitor? Should she ask James? No, she shouldn't draw him into this monstrous entanglement which has now suddenly invaded her life. What should she do? Stop – that's for certain. Think about it. Take her time. Her father had his 'twenty-four hour rule.' 'Just sleep on it, lass,' he would say. 'It'll look different in the morning.' And this is what she decides to do.

When Henry comes in, Clara finds herself looking at a different person than the one who went out this morning. Of course, he looks the same. His clothes and hair are a bit rumpled after the day and his face is tired, but whereas this morning, the man she saw off to work was her devoted husband, she now finds herself looking at a philanderer. (What a wonderful word. She loves that word. Philanderer. Philanderer. She says it over and over to herself.) And instead of the slightly pompous but quite powerful man who takes her out on Saturdays and then fucks her afterwards, she now sees a short, plump, not especially attractive man.

He comes in and she finds herself watching him as though he were an actor on stage. When he picks up the paper and shakes it out to read it, she feels like laughing. It is like watching a man playing a self-important ass in a theatre production. She knows his secret. She knows his dirty little secret so that any time he speaks or makes some kind of pronouncement, a little voice in her head keeps repeating, 'I know your secret. I know *all* about you.'

She is conscious, too, that there was a power he used to have which has quite disappeared. And it is this loss of power that intrigues her most. Because if she feels that his power has gone, hers has increased. It's almost as if his has transferred to her. Right now, as she sits across him at the table, she feels that there is nothing she could not do. Yes, she may be dependent on him financially but she feels that with this power, she could divorce him, get a job, start a new life, anything. And wait until he takes her out on Saturday night. Everything is going to be different from now on. Everything.

Earlier that same day, Mary finds an excuse to go by Henry's office. He likes to work with the door open – 'be able to see what's going on,' he once told her – and he is there now, his head down, writing. Mary stops at the door and clears her throat. He looks up. She smiles and makes a tiny wave at him. He smiles back. She looks around, sees there is nobody on the corridor, blows him a kiss and hurries on. The letter obviously arrived after he left home.

With seven deliveries a day in Metropolitan London, Mary knows her letter will arrive some time on Monday. She knows now that it will be only when Henry gets home that he will find out that his wife knows about his affair. (Mary always thinks of Clara as 'his wife'; she can never think of her as being 'Clara.') When Mary planned this, she wondered whether Henry's wife would tell him how she found out. Would she show him the note?

Mary knew it didn't matter. She has disguised her writing, sloping it very far backwards where she normally writes with it sloped slightly forwards. So all Henry will know is that his wife has found out. Mary will not be in the picture at all. Henry may have his suspicions but she'll be able to act wide-eyed and innocent of any involvement in it.

What will happen next? Will she throw him out? Mary has already checked in the company's files and she knows that Henry has no mortgage on the house. So, she reckons he would be able to afford to rent himself a small place. Would she then move in with him? She wondered about this but decided against it. She is going to wait until he gets divorced and then they can marry. Only then will she move in. She has a strong sense that Henry doesn't like being alone and that, if he found himself in that situation, he would want to get out of it as quickly as possible.

There is a danger, of course, that Henry tells his wife that he doesn't care how she feels and that he is just going to go on with his affair. But according to Henry, his wife is a bitch a lot of the time and so Mary feels that Henry wouldn't be able to tolerate living in the same house as somebody like that, after what he was doing was out in the open. Henry likes things to be just so and this would be a permanent disturbance that Mary feels he just wouldn't be able to tolerate.

So, essentially, Mary is hoping that the forces that will now repel him from his marriage and the attraction his wife provides will be enough to prompt Henry, whom she considers at heart a weak man, to make the move from his wife to her. Tomorrow, Mary should know all.

Chapter 33
Tuesday 21 July 1914

On Tuesday, Mary is so sure she is going to get an early morning visit from a frantic Henry that she goes into work early in case he decides to do the same. However, he is not there when she arrives and it is after eleven before she can contrive to walk by his office. He is there as yesterday, working contentedly away. Seeing her, he calls her in and asks if she would like to have lunch on Friday. He also asks when they can be together again. He doesn't think he can use the 'special meeting' excuse again this week, but maybe next? Would that suit her? She tells him that lunch on Friday would be fine and any day next week that suits him. She walks out quite nonplussed.

But she is baffled. The letter *must* have arrived, Mary reasons, so obviously the bitch hasn't told him yet. Maybe she doesn't believe the letter and has thrown it away or burned it. Maybe the bitch believes that her precious Henry would never do something as underhand as that. Or maybe – and Mary decides this is more likely – the wife is in shock and needs another day or two before she can confront Henry.

With this calming thought, Mary decides that, if nothing happens in the meantime, she will wait until they have their lunch on Friday.

In St Petersburg, there are rumours that Austria is planning a match against Serbia and that this is being done with Der Kaiser's blessing.

In Berlin, the German government tells both the French Ambassador and the Russian *chargé d'affairs* that it has no knowledge of Austrian policy towards Serbia.

In Vienna, Berchtold continues to push for haste in getting the game under way. Suppose Serbia offers compensation for what happened to the Archduke, he argues. (They might do this under pressure from France and Russia, for example.) Then all pretext for war would disappear. Berchtold's depression deepens and his anxiety grows.

When Clara wakes on Tuesday, she is desolate. She remembers that she was crying silently during the night. As she leaves the room to go downstairs and begin Henry's breakfast, all of the things she felt yesterday about the shift of power seem to be gone. She feels tiny and doesn't know how she is going to deal with this vast problem.

When Henry arrives in the kitchen she feels subservient and mouse-like. It as though she is some kind of house servant – like they would have in the Atkinson Grimshaw house. She is somebody to be ordered about with no rights and no feelings. Rather than join him at the breakfast table she stands at the sink staring out the window. If he notices he says nothing, continuing to read his paper. She is relieved when he kisses her on the cheek she automatically proffers, and departs.

She knows she will have to start to think rationally about this but almost immediately, the girls are down and Mrs Parsons is fussing around. Dear God, could she not just get a little time by herself? The day passes and Clara is in bed when she can finally turn her mind, uninterrupted, to the problem.

She is tempted to just ignore all of this. How easy that would be. She could carry on as though nothing has happened. Lots of men, especially upper-class ones, have wives and mistresses. Maybe this is a sign that she and Henry have gone up in the world. She laughs a silent, bitter laugh at this.

Ignoring it would be the easy thing to do. Just go on as if nothing has happened. Get used to being one of these kinds of wives. She is sure that London is full of them. But she can't imagine the thought of having sex with him ever again. The notion that they would come in from a Saturday night dinner and that he would be inside her is unspeakable. She can't imagine sitting through a dinner in a restaurant with him, never mind lying under him while he fucks her.

But Clara is angry – angry that it is no decision of hers that has brought her to this point, other than the original one to marry Henry. He has made all the decisions and now she has to bear the consequences. If she ignores this, he goes scot free and that is not something she is prepared to countenance. When the time comes, she will make decisions and then he'll know all about it.

Part of her wants to confront him straight away. Part of her wants to wake him now and tell him that she knows all about his bit on the side. She wants to be biblically angry with him – as she can be. She would like to punch him and kick him and spit in his face and call him every vile name she can think of. She wants to say all the things she has kept pent up these last few years and command him to stop.

But command him to stop? The damage is done. She knows that once he's tasted the forbidden fruit, he's not going to stop. She would have thought that the difficult part – if it was difficult at all for him – was deciding to be unfaithful in the first place. After that, it will just be a question of how many times. Even before she married Henry, he was always a bit of a man to flirt. She just saw it as something innocent – that he was popular, good with people, got on with them. She felt proud to be the one he had chosen. Now she knows that some of Henry's brains are in his trousers. Maybe most of them.

If she isn't going to ignore it, and she isn't going to tell him to stop, then she must divorce him – and now, it appears, she has 'grounds.' What will that be like? What is the law? Would she have any money if she did that? Or a roof over her head? And what about the girls? Clara has made her bed; maybe now she has to lie in it. It isn't fair that the girls should suffer for decisions that Clara has made.

And the worst part is that she will be a divorced woman. It'll be a scandal whatever happens. She's heard of women – they are almost always of the upper classes – who divorce and just carry on as though nothing had happened. She knows it won't be like that for her.

She needs to go and see a solicitor. But who? Where? How does one begin something like this? And without Henry knowing?

She must talk to James. He will know a solicitor – and he said he would help her. But did he actually mean it? And even if he did, surely he doesn't know what it's actually going to mean now that she has become involved in this whole sordid business. James won't want to know her once he understands what she is engaged in. If she has been starting to imagine a life with James, he won't want to know her as a divorced woman – even though he's divorced himself.

Ignore it, tell Henry to stop, divorce. These are her three choices. But in reality, she has only two. The middle one is no option at all. So this is what it comes down to. Live out the rest of her life like this or destroy everything – her home, the girls' happiness, everything – and see what happens then. The prospect makes her feel physically sick.

Chapter 34
Wednesday 22 July 1914

Clara wakes very early after a few hours of restless sleep. Her first thought is how she wishes that all of this were a dream. How gorgeous it would be just to have woken up and found it was another long summer's day and that she had nothing more pressing on her mind than to find things to entertain the girls and keep them amused.

She needs to do something. She can't just wait about while things happen to her. She doesn't know what it is but she has to take some action. Now that she's had a second night to let it sink in, she is more convinced than ever she should not say anything to Henry. Her knowing his secret gives her some advantage, some kind of power. She's just not sure what this power is or how best to use it. But she believes it will eventually become clear to her.

She is meeting James tomorrow. She is going to tell him everything. She will tell him what is happening and see whether he is with her or not. Ghastly business or not, she must find out if she has an ally. And if he doesn't want to get involved and walks out of her life, so be it. She will do this on her own.

In Berlin, it is reported that the rumours of Austria wanting to play Serbia have been greatly exaggerated. It is true that Austria will be delivering a diplomatic note to Serbia in which it will request that some actions be taken with regard to the recent killing of the Archduke. But this note will be 'courteous' and will not place any time limit on the Serbians to reply. Any reports of Austrian mobilisation, it is declared, are pure invention.

It is evening, and now that Clara has decided to tell James, she is somewhat at peace. The girls are asleep, Henry is downstairs reading and Clara has some time to herself. She selects the clothes she is going to wear tomorrow. First is her best underwear. She wonders about this. Obviously James isn't going to see it but the thought of these pretty garments against her skin excites her in a way that she cannot really explain. She chooses a skirt the colour of cornflowers, a white blouse, then her white hat with a blue ribbon the same colour as the skirt.

She is eager to go to bed, to get the next few hours over with so that she can meet him. And she is eager for another reason – she wants to continue the Atkinson Grimshaw fantasy. Ordinarily, she would go downstairs and wish Henry goodnight. Now she just thinks, 'fuck him.' He's going to be seeing a great deal more changed behaviour on her part in the near future. And he's not going to like it. Or understand it. And that will be the best bit. She can feel her power again and she is starting to get a vague sense of where it will take her.

Her fantasy has evolved even further. It's now becoming a story. It begins as it always does on the wet, suburban lane with the bend at the end and the wall on one side. Previously, Clara went voluntarily through the door in the wall, but now somebody – an unseen man – abducts her, throwing a coat or cloak over her head and then encircling her with arms as strong as leather straps. She is pulled into the house and taken down to the basement. Here she finds a handful of other young women – Clara seems to be the oldest. When she asks why they are being kept there, she is told, 'For the master's pleasure.'

Later she and the other women are taken upstairs to the master's study. Once again, Clara doesn't put a face or a name on the man. The women are made to strip and while the others are reluctant and wail and resist, so that they have to be beaten with a riding crop, Clara takes off her clothes haughtily, disdainfully. She is made to lie on her back on a table and has to open her legs while the master looks at her, touches her, strokes her, probes her. Then she has to bend over while he examines her hole. Clara is selected as the one the master wants. Then she is made to go down on all fours on a deep rug in front of a roaring log fire, while the master enters her from behind. All the other women have to watch while this is going on and Clara finds herself becoming wet at the idea of having an audience. She brings herself quickly to an orgasm and then falls deeply asleep.

However, she wakes after only a couple of hours and is instantly wide awake. She realises how far off balance this information about Henry has thrown her. Her thinking has been completely cockeyed. Normally, when she is faced with any problem, Clara is a clear thinker, but with this, up until now, her mind has been a jumbled up mess.

This thing that has just happened to her may be the biggest calamity of her life. However, it may also be that she has been handed a second chance at happiness. To get her thinking clear, she knows exactly where she has to start. What does she want?

She doesn't think her little list is too much to ask for. First, she wants a home where she can feel happy and not alone. Now this 'not alone' business is not as simple as it sounds. There is a part of her that likes to be alone. In her marriage with Henry it seems like the only time she can have this is now, when she is lying in bed, thinking about the future or playing out her little fantasies. So she wants to be able to have that. She wants to sometimes be Clara Jordan, as she was before she was married – to do the things that girl used to do. Read books. Go out by herself. Have a little money. Meet the friends she had, all of whom seem to have drifted away in the intervening years.

But then she also wants a man to cherish her. He will have his own life, as James does, and then they will have a life together. She imagines the four of them going to France together, one little, happy family. Could they do that next year? Could it happen so soon? She imagines them in a little country inn on the bank of that river, the 'somm.' A steep thatched roof. Are the roofs thatched in that part of France? The girls sharing a room and she and James in the room beside them. Could the girls get used to that – that James wasn't their real father but he was acting as their father? Could they ever accept that? It is so far beyond what is normal. Her father, much as she loved him, would be shocked that she is thinking along these lines.

And she also wants that man to love her body. Desire it. Want to touch it and lick it and caress it and yes, to fuck it. And she wants a man's body that she can do the same to. She thinks that James has a handsome face. He is taller than Henry by several inches and from what she can see his body is slim – certainly slimmer than Henry's even though James is older.

What would it be like if she were married to him? Would he be a good father to the girls? A step-father. The words sound strange. She thinks he would be. She could imagine him being very loving towards them. But what if he wasn't and he lived a sort of life of his own separate from her and the girls? Clara sees that her only real course is that of divorce. To stay with Henry while he carries on with this other woman would just condemn her to a lifetime of misery. If she takes the path of divorce, it's possible – just possible – that the result will be that she will be handed a second chance at happiness. She believes that pursuing this course will exact a terrible price from her. If she is to go through with all this, she wants to be sure about what is waiting for her at the end, what all this suffering might lead to and whether it would be worth it.

Henry. Her mind suddenly catapults back to the man who lies beside her. Those nights he has spent away, he has spent fucking another woman – putting his cock into her and riding her. It is an image she can't get out of her mind. Clara feels disgusted and finds herself moving away from Henry so that she is right over on the edge of the bed. It is here that she falls back asleep.

Chapter 35
Thursday 23 July 1914

July 23rd dawns, the day the Austrians are due to play the Serbs. The whole of the German military and political leadership ostentatiously go on holiday. All along Germany has been egging Austria on, while at the same time trying to deny all knowledge of what its ally is doing. The holiday thing is part of that. Germany's game plan now goes like this:

As soon as Austria presents its ultimatum, the Germans will do a big diplomatic push with the other teams – Russia, France, Britain – with the intention of localising the war. The Germans intend to say that the Austrian action has taken them completely by surprise. They will point out the fact that Der Kaiser is on his boating holiday and that eminent men like the Minister for War and the Chief of the Grand General Staff are on leave.

In London, Clara is in the kitchen when Henry comes down. He is dressed – all he has to do is put on his jacket – and carries his newspaper. Ordinarily, Clara would have made tea and allowed it enough time to reach just the strength he likes. When she heard him coming down the stairs she would have started his toast under the grill. This morning she has done neither of these things. As he comes into the kitchen with a cheery, 'Morning, my dear,' Clara doesn't respond and instead just walks out. She goes upstairs in the direction from which Henry just came, goes into their bedroom and sits on the edge of the bed, looking vacantly out the window.

Henry is quite nonplussed by this. His first thought is to go after Clara, saying, 'What about my tea and toast?' But something tells him that this mightn't be the best thing to do. He makes some tea himself.

Then he tries to light the grill but realises that he doesn't actually know how to do that. 'Damn it,' he curses. 'Blasted woman.'

Intensely irritated, Henry ends up leaving for work on an empty stomach. When Clara hears the door slam – which it does, shaking the house – she says, 'Fuck him!' aloud.

Today, for President Poincaré, there are more salutes, more anthems and, at last, the visit is complete. His final words to the Tsar are, 'This time, we must hold firm.' Then the President's warship sets course for Stockholm. 'Thank God that's over,' Poincaré thinks.

Behind him, in St Petersburg, the Russian Foreign Minister tells the German Ambassador that Germany will have to 'reckon with Europe' if she supports an Austrian attack against Serbia.

When Der Kaiser reads the dispatch reporting this conversation, he writes in the margin, 'No! Russia, yes!' So the other part of the German plan is a 'bring it on' with Russia. Germany wants to play one game in the Group of Death – against Russia – and then be declared the winner. But of course you know, clear thinking reader, that the Von Schlieffen Plan doesn't allow for this scenario. Would that everybody else had been as clear thinking.

'There's something I need to discuss with you,' Clara says.

James has hardly had time to raise his hat in greeting her. She has decided it's best this way. Get the whole business done and over with so that if he wants to walk out of her life, he can do it now. Standing – she hasn't heard him when he suggested they find a seat – she tells him what has happened.

'I didn't know whether to tell you or not,' she says, looking into his eyes and trying to gauge his reaction. 'It all seems so ... so sordid and I know it's nothing to do with you and maybe I shouldn't have involved you but I didn't know where else to turn—'

Clara feels herself rapidly losing her composure. She really doesn't want to break down and cry. Things are bad enough.

'Please—' he says, but Clara just keeps going.

'I need to know if I have a friend in you.'

As she hears the words, she knows how plaintive they sound. She imagines that James has lots of friends and here is she without one in the whole world other than this one, this stranger who she has met in a park.

'Please,' he says again, and this time she stops – or, at least, pauses.

'I said that I would help you. I shall – in every way I can. In the short time I've known you, you've become a very dear friend, Clara. You have no idea how much I've looked forward to our day together today. If you would like to meet with a solicitor, I shall arrange it. I shall come with you if you would like that.'

'Oh, yes please, I would,' she gushes. 'That would be too kind of you.'

'It's nothing, my dear Clara,' he says.

At exactly 6:00 p.m. at the Serbian Foreign Office in Belgrade, the team of the mighty Austria lines out against that of tiny Serbia. With a name straight out of light opera, the Austrian minister to Belgrade, Wladimir Baron Giesl von Gieslingen, hands over a note containing the Austrian ultimatum to the Serbs. He tells them that he expects a reply within forty-eight hours. He doesn't tell them that if the Serbian government does not accept all the points of the ultimatum, his orders (from Berchtold) are to sever diplomatic relations and leave the country immediately along with all the embassy personnel.

The Serbs are unable to reply to this early score, and victory in this first leg goes to the Austrians. It is one of the few times the Austrians will win a game in the Group of Death.

The defeated Serbians have to do something before the second leg, which will now be played at the end of the forty-eight hour deadline – in other words, on Saturday 25 July at 6:00 p.m. Nicholas Pasitch, the Serbian Prime Minister and manager of the Serbian team, is on an election tour in the south of the country when the Austrian note arrives. When summoned to return, he does what any sensible man would do in the circumstances – he leaves for a holiday in Greece and has to be pulled off the train to receive the telegram of recall. There is only one thing for it. Just as with Berchtold before him, Nicholas Pasitch also needs to phone a friend.

Pasitch's problems are twofold. First of all, he wonders if he will even have a team. The Serbian harvest isn't in. If he issued the order to mobilise, would the Serbian peasants actually obey it at all? Or would they instead carry on with their harvest, ensuring food for the winter and money to pay their taxes and for wine? In addition, the Serbian team has only 120,000 rifles and no artillery. Gloomily, Pasitch comes to the conclusion that he can only play if Russia backs him. Of course, what this really means is that he will have to do whatever the Russians tell him to do. If they say play then he'll play, if they say don't play, then that's going to be the end of him in the Group of Death. It perhaps makes him wonder why Serbia has a manager at all – since the Russian manager effectively manages both teams.

That night Pasitch asks for Russian support. However, the Russians know they're not fit to play Germany, which could well be what would happen if they decide to support the Serbs. Pasitch's request is refused. He's told to accept the Austrian ultimatum and that, with any luck, international opinion will cause the Austrians to change their minds. Some friend, Pasitch thinks.

At about the same time that Pasitch is gloomily pondering the nature of friendship, Clara is lying in bed replaying one of the nicest days that she has had in a long time. Not that anything dramatic happened. Well, she supposes, telling James all about Henry was dramatic. But after that, they walked around the park for a little. They had lunch in a café. They walked some more and sat in the sun and watched the birds. Clara was somewhat fearful that she would bump into somebody she knew – not that she knows that many people – and so she kept steering them into the less frequented areas of the park. But in the end they met nobody and it was as though time slowed down so that the afternoon seemed to go on and on and on. Before they parted, they exchanged addresses, Clara writing his on the inside back cover of her little diary.

'If there's anything,' he said, 'any kind of emergency, write to me. Say where I should meet you or what I should do, and you can consider it done. Or come to where I live. If there's anything – anything at all.'

'But you know you can't write to *me*,' says Clara anxiously.

'Of course, I know that,' he replies.

More than anything else, Clara believes that James is a man who is considerate, who wouldn't take her for granted as Henry does all the time now. Although that's in the process of coming to an end, she thinks vindictively.

Clara finds that her head is full of James. She is either remembering the events of the afternoon or wondering how she will get through the seven long days before she sees him again. For this is what they have arranged. And James is going to organise a meeting with a solicitor and they will meet again next Thursday for James to tell her when that meeting will be.

Before she falls asleep, Clara recalls the high point of that sunny afternoon where, some time before they arranged to meet again next Thursday, James said to Clara, 'I like you very much, Clara' to which she replied, 'I like *you* very much.'

Late that evening, Grey writes in his diary. 'If war should occur between the four Great Powers, it would result in a complete collapse of European credit and industry; in the present great industrial States, this would produce a state of things worse than 1848, and, irrespective of who might be the victors, many things might be completely swept away.'

Chapter 36
Friday 24 July 1914

The Russian Council of Ministers meets in the afternoon to decide its response to the crisis. They are all agreed that neither the Russian Army nor Navy is ready to play Germany or Austria or anybody else for that matter. But they are also agreed that Russia cannot stand entirely aside. What are they to do?

Sazonov, the Foreign Minister, comes up with an idea. How about if Russia mobilises in the military districts adjacent to Austria? It would show that Russia is supporting its ally, Serbia. At the same time, since there would be no mobilisation along its border with Germany, this would show the Germans that Russia had no warlike intentions towards them. The rest of the Council of Ministers is delighted with this idea. It seems to give them exactly what they want. It's a gesture of support for Serbia but without any firm commitment. It also doesn't raise the diplomatic temperature in a way that might risk a war against Germany.

Of course, you, well-informed reader, know that there is a rather serious problem with Sazonov's suggestion. And as usual, it is Edmund Blackadder who has the best analysis – it *is* bollocks. It's unworkable. You know that partial mobilisation can't work for the reasons that we've explained much earlier in our story. So why does Sazonov not know? Well, I suppose in fairness to him, he's not a military man.

However, there is one man at the Council of Ministers meeting who should know. That is the Russian Chief of Staff, Nikolai Yanushkevitch. But Yanushkevitch is new to the job and is reluctant to contradict the Foreign Minister. As well as that, maybe

Yanushkevitch doesn't actually know that there is a problem with partial mobilisation. He has spent most of his career occupied by administrative duties in the Ministry of War. He has never held a field commission and his command experience is limited to a short period as a company commander. (That and pornography and anti-Semitism, both of which Yanushkevitch has an abiding and active interest in.) It is said that Yanushkevitch owes his promotion mainly to his engaging personality – something which, presumably, Russia's Jews would not agree with.

So for whatever reason, the meeting breaks up under the illusion that a policy of partial mobilisation is possible and an order is issued to that effect.

In England, while people are reading about the Austrian ultimatum in the *Evening Standard*, Sir Edward Grey holds a copy of the document in his hand. He is at a Cabinet meeting attended by, amongst others, Winston Churchill, and they have been discussing a separate issue entirely – the possibility that there might be conflict in Ireland following the partition of that country. In quiet, grave tones Grey reads the document. When he has finished he says that he has 'never before seen one State address to another independent State a document of so formidable a character.'

It has been clear to Grey for many years that Austria wants to play Serbia. In the past he has managed to discourage this with the help of the Germans. He intends to try this approach again, unaware that Der Kaiser has already told the Austrians that they will have his backing. So Grey suggests mediation between Italy, France, Germany and Britain as the best way of stopping an Austro-Serbian war. A conference could be held in London chaired by these four powers to resolve the dispute between Austria and Serbia.

How convenient it would be, Grey has often thought, if these endless silly squabbles in Central and Eastern Europe could be worked on and resolved here in London. The countries could just send their ambassadors – even though they are foreigners, they are men that Grey likes and gets along with – and the problems could be worked through. Then there would be no crises and he could spend his weekends fishing and listening to birds.

Now instead, Grey is going to have to work with the other managers – Poincaré, Der Kaiser, Berchtold, the Tsar. They are distant people whom he hardly knows at all. Now, he will have to try to guess what they were thinking and planning to do. He will have to examine minutely what they say and try to judge whether that is what they really mean. He will have to ask himself whether they were acting in good faith or are scheming.

It is all so complicated. But he takes as his opening position that nobody in their right mind would want to play in the Group of Death. That much, at least, has to be true. So having gained the Cabinet's approval for the intervention by the four powers, Grey looks forward once again to a weekend at the cottage.

It has been an enjoyable day for Der Kaiser on board his yacht the *Hohenzollern*, anchored at Balholm. He receives a dispatch from the German Ambassador in Belgrade saying how sad the Serbian people are at being faced with the choice of either war or national humiliation. Wilhelm writes in the margins of the report: 'Bravo! One would not have believed it of the Viennese!'

In Vienna, the British Ambassador reports, there is wild enthusiasm for a game against the Serbs.

In London, the British Prime Minister Herbert Asquith writes to his friend Venetia Stanley that 'the Austrians are quite the stupidest people in Europe.'

That same day, Henry and Mary go for lunch. By this time, Mary is so full of anger, she feels like a coiled spring. She is angry with Henry because of the way he is stringing her along. She is now firmly convinced that he *hasn't* told his wife that he wants a divorce. And she is angry at that bitch of a wife of his, who is now clearly playing her own game. They have only just left the office and are heading towards the tea shop when Mary says, 'You haven't asked her for a divorce, have you?'

Henry looks at her. There is anger in her face that he has never seen before.

'I told you I have.'

'You're lying.'

'I'm not lying.'

Henry is about to say that he'd rather not go to lunch if Mary's going to be like this, when Mary drops her bombshell.

'She knows you're having an affair.'

'She doesn't,' says Henry. 'She has absolutely no idea.'

'Yes, she does,' says Mary, and she smiles in a distinctly unpleasant kind of way.

"Look, why don't we leave lunch,' says Henry. 'You're obviously not in a mood for it today—'

'She knows because I told her,' says Mary.

Henry stops. She is still wearing a smile that could only be described as malevolent.

'You met her? You don't even know what she looks like.'

'I wrote her a letter, you stupid fool.'

'A letter?' blusters Henry. 'Saying what?'

'Telling her that you were having an affair.'

Henry feels like everything is starting to collapse around him. Just yesterday he was thinking how fine his life was and how right the world was. Now, with this one appalling action, Mary has gone and destroyed everything.

'Get away from me, you vindictive bitch,' says Henry, and with that, he storms off, going he doesn't know where.

After he leaves Mary, Henry finds himself walking down to the Thames. There, he leans on the stone quay wall and looks into the dirty depths of the river. With the summer heat, a strong malodorous scent rises off the green water. For a moment he contemplates suicide. He cannot swim so he could jump in and end it all. That would take all these complications out of his life. It would serve them right, all these women who are hanging off him. But that thought quickly passes. 'Think,' he says to himself, 'think.' And so he does. And by the time he is on his way home, he has the answer.

He catches the omnibus home, sitting upstairs. It is an evening of beautiful summer colours – the azure and gold of the sky, the green of suburban leafiness and the grey and red brick of the buildings.

Clara knows – that much is clear. Yet she hasn't said anything. What game is she playing? After much turmoil as he stood gazing into the Thames earlier on, the answer, when it came to Henry, was simplicity itself. Clara knows but she's not going to say anything. Why then, neither will he. And he will carry on as though nothing has changed. Over the weekend, because he hasn't had time to think about her yet, he will sort out what he wants to do about Mary. But if Clara hasn't said anything, then the chances are she won't. Clara may think she has power over him but, in fact, she has none. Henry is the one with all the power. Over her. And over Mary. Life can go on just as it was – either with Mary, if she wants that, or with someone new. If Mary thought she was playing a trump card, all she's actually done is give away whatever power *she* had.

The bus stops and Henry dismounts. He begins the short walk in the direction of home. Things couldn't have turned out any better if he had planned them.

Chapter 37
Saturday 25 July 1914

In St Petersburg, the Russians are only too aware that the Austrian ultimatum to Serbia means that they – the Russians – might end up in the Group of Death. They aren't keen.

There has been a lot of unrest in Russia recently – workers striking and rioting, mounted Cossacks being sent in to quell disturbances, crowds on the streets. The country is very volatile. The Russians fear that if they end up having to field a team to play the Austrians, there is no telling where this could lead. It might all end in revolution. However, if they do nothing and just let the match between giant Austria and tiny Serbia take place, maybe the Russian people will revolt out of disgust at their weak leaders.

The Russians do what all sensible people do when stuck between a rock and a hard place. They stall. As well as that, while stalling, they try to find a way to wriggle out of the mess they suddenly find themselves in. They ask the Austrians to extend the deadline and ask the British to put in a similar request. They tell the Serbs to give in and just accept all the terms of the ultimatum. They suggest that any outstanding issues can be handled at a peace conference. The Russians ask the Germans to mediate, unaware that the Germans are egging the Austrians on. The Germans say that they knew nothing about all of this and that the Russians should talk directly to the Austrians. The Austrians turn down all the Russian requests.

The Tsar doesn't want to see the match between Austria and Serbia played and assumes Der Kaiser doesn't want it either. The Tsar tries to carry on his normal routine: playing tennis, canoeing with his daughters, having tea with his relatives, meeting various dignitaries.

But he is sick with worry and struggles to remain cheerful. He doesn't want a Group of Death. And he doesn't at all like the idea of being a manager if there *is* a Group of Death.

There is another meeting of the Council of Ministers presided over by the Tsar. At this they make a momentous decision. The Council decides to activate something known as 'Regulation on the Period Preparatory to War of 2 March 1913.' This law governs what should happen in the period prior to mobilisation. It provides for heightened security and readiness at magazines and supply depots. It accelerates the completion of railway repairs and states what readiness checks need to be carried out in all departments. It ensures that covering troops are deployed to positions on threatened fronts. Reservists are recalled to training camps. Troops training at locations remote from their bases are recalled immediately. Three thousand or so officer cadets are promoted to officer rank to bring the officer corps up to wartime strength. Harbours are mined while horses and wagons are assembled.

But this takes place *across the whole of European Russia.*

How will the Germans be able to tell the difference between this and mobilisation proper? Now the Russians have upped the stakes. Now they really are playing with fire.

July 25th is a Saturday and clearly it would be too much to expect Sir Edward Grey not to go fishing. Looking out through his windows at the trees, the lawns and the lake of St James's Park, he is reminded of his cottage, the River Itchen and the many different species of birds that make their nests there. How wonderful it is for little creatures to feel so safe there. The weather is dull, but as Grey has written, 'no day in midsummer can be unrelievedly heavy if there are goldfinches in the garden and ash trees in the field beyond.'

Later he sets off for the country. But before he goes, he formally approves the suggestion that Britain would host a peace conference. This is passed on to all of the interested parties as Grey's car makes its way out through the hot London suburbs that smell of tar.

He is weary after the week. He frets again about his failing eyesight. These days he can barely see after half an hour's reading.

Two months ago, his ophthalmologist advised six months' rest without offering any hope of a cure. Six months' rest – how likely is that in Grey's position? The best he can hope for right now is these restorative weekends – the roses, the river and the trout, now at their fattest and most glittering. And of course, he will be in touch all the time with the Office. Even into the cottage, that refuge of peace and sanity, the snarls and menaces of Europe can penetrate, even there the ambitions and resentments of the dangerous continent can echo.

He arrives there and walks down to Grey's Bridge. He sees a kingfisher on a branch and then, in an instant, it is gone, seeming to leave a blue streak in the air as though it had been painted there. Leaning on the wooden rail, he watches the water flow beneath his feet. It has done so for thousands of years and will continue to do so after they are all gone. How uncomplicated it would be if they all fished – the managers of the five teams. They could sit on the river bank, talk out the problems and bring the solution back with them in time for tea. That would have been the way to sort it out, he thinks, with a tiny smile.

In France, leave is cancelled for all French troops beginning the following day. The majority of French troops in Morocco are ordered to return to France.

The battleship *France* has arrived in Stockholm on the next leg of Poincaré's trip. Despite probable attempts by the Germans to jam communications to the ship, the President has a fair sense of what has been unfolding in the rest of Europe. His approach is unambiguous – firmness is the only way to deal with the Germans. 'Weakness,' he says, 'is always the mother of complications.' His analysis goes like this: The Austrian demands on Serbia are clearly outrageous and unacceptable. So now the decision as to whether there will be peace or war now lies completely outside of his control. It lies with the Germans. If the Germans restrain Austria there will be peace. Otherwise – and Poincaré is quite ready for this eventuality too – it will mean war.

In London, the German Ambassador tells his people in Berlin that they are crazy to try to provoke a war between Austria and Serbia.

He tells them that, despite what they might think, Britain would intervene in a continental war. He pleads with the German government to accept Grey's offer of mediation and the peace conference to resolve the Austro-Serbian dispute.

In Belgrade, the Serbs have gotten wind of Sazonov's partial mobilisation idea. For them, this is good news. It looks as though, if push comes to shove, Serbia will not be left alone by its big friend, Russia. The prospect stiffens the Serbian resolve. Through Saturday, they work on their answer to the Austrian ultimatum. Their changes are sometimes conciliatory, sometimes insolent but, essentially, they have accepted all of the Austrian conditions. The only one they have baulked at is that of admitting Austrian officials to the Serb inquiry.

The Serbs also decide to mobilise the army and to move the government to Nis, a couple of hundred kilometres further from the Austrian border. Pasitch himself delivers the answer to the Austrian legation with five minutes to spare at 5:55 p.m. He then catches the official train to Nis. It is game on – the return leg of Austria versus Serbia.

In the Austrian legation in Belgrade, Baron Giesl von Gieslingen is also anxious to catch a train. He takes a quick look at the Serbian reply and is appalled by what he sees. Essentially, Serbia has accepted all of the Austrian demands. It agrees to suppress all anti-Austrian movements on Serbian soil. It will bring to justice anyone concerned with the murder of the Archduke. Although it cannot agree – what country could? – to Austrians participating in the judicial process, Serbia is willing to submit the whole issue either to the International Tribunal at the Hague, or to the Big Five for adjudication. It is the last thing that the Austrians expected and a huge victory for the underdog Serbs.

But Baron Giesl von Gieslingen has his orders. After reading the document he sees that it is not a complete and utter acceptance of the Austrian terms. He sends back a note – which he had already prepared – announcing that he is leaving Belgrade and that diplomatic relations between Austria and Serbia are now broken off. The code books are already burnt, the luggage packed, the cars are waiting. Baron Giesl von Gieslingen, his wife and staff arrive at Belgrade station in time to catch the 6:30 evening train to Vienna.

Ten minutes later, at the first station beyond the Austrian frontier posts, he telephones the Prime Minister with the news. The Prime Minister in turn passes it on to the Emperor Franz Joseph who is on holiday at Ischl. 'Breaking off diplomatic relations does not necessarily mean war,' Franz Joseph remarks.

Berchtold is also at Ischl but is out for a walk when the news comes. Later that evening he persuades Franz Joseph to sign the order for mobilisation of eight army corps to begin operations against Serbia on the 28th. 'Mobilisation does not mean war,' Berchtold says.

But Berchtold is not a happy dweller in canvas accommodation. His bluff – for bluff it was – supported by, amongst others, Der Kaiser – is starting to go badly wrong. He was told that if Austria showed itself resolute, Serbia would give way.

But it hasn't.

In Acton, Henry and Clara are living what is starting to become a strange life. Clara has adopted the tactic of alternately behaving just as she used to – facilitating Henry's every wish and need – and then not doing that at all. Today, for example, she made sure that he had no clean shirt available, so that he had to re-use yesterday's. When he arrived home there was a faint whiff of stale sweat and cigarette smoke off him. He was clearly very annoyed and had great difficulty keeping it in, but keep it in he managed to do.

Then she asked if they were going out to dinner, it being Saturday night. She actually would have enjoyed it and had planned to order expensive food and wine, where normally she would have been conscious of the prices on the menu and of not upsetting Henry by ordering something too lavish. But Henry claimed to have a headache and so she agreed to leave it until next week, but not before adding, 'It's a pity. I was really looking forward to a night out.'

Tomorrow, Clara has decided she will once again play the part of the old Clara. She will cater to Henry's every whim and anticipate his needs. She will be that pitiable creature that she was only a few days ago. Can it really only be such a short space of time in which such a monumental change has occurred?

For she sees now how lost she had become in the role of Henry's wife. That mousy, subservient creature was never who she really was. And now she has found herself again – the woman who managed her father's stationary business, the mother who bore two beautiful girls, the capable housekeeper who makes the house run like clockwork. Henry has done her such a favour by engaging in his sordid little affair. But this doesn't mean that she isn't going to make sure he regrets it. Oh, how he's going to regret it.

Because if tomorrow she will be the old Clara, on Monday she will be the new, mischievous one. She will find some other thing to do (or not do) that will irritate him. And already her mind is racing with possibilities. They range from the mildly irritating things she has done so far to going into Henry's office and publicly accusing him of infidelity and making a huge scene. She's not sure she would actually do this but she enjoys imagining it and similar scenes as she happily gets through the tasks of the day.

Of all our characters, both in England and abroad, Henry is by far the last to fall asleep on this Saturday night. It is actually dawn on Sunday before he finally slips away, because Henry is seething with anger and resentment. This is not at all the way it was meant to turn out. Clara is deliberately trying to goad him into … into what? Anger? So that she too can become angry and accuse him? He doesn't know. He doesn't know what game she's damn well playing. But he can see she's enjoying herself. God damn it, she's happier than he's seen her in a long time.

And he doesn't even have the consolation of Mary. Nor does he know if he wants such a consolation any longer – at least not with that scheming bitch. They are both scheming bitches. What has he done to deserve this, he asks himself, having these two cunts in his life.

Chapter 38
Sunday 26 July 1914

O ff Balholm in Norway, Der Kaiser's yacht *Hohenzollern* raises anchor and sets course for home. He is still unaware of what the Serbian reply to Austria has been.

At half past nine that morning, Der Kaiser's younger brother Henry, who has been yachting at Cowes, calls in – as one would – to see his cousin King George at Buckingham Palace. (Yes, this is something that we haven't mentioned up until now – but only to avoid any confusion. Not only are Der Kaiser and the Tsar cousins, but both men are also cousins of King George V. If we think of all of this as a family squabble, it should have been possible to sort it all out. But we choose our friends, we don't choose our families – and sometimes family squabbles are notoriously difficult to sort out.)

Anyway, the two royal gentlemen tut tut over the international situation.

'The news is very bad,' says the King. 'It looks like war in Europe. You'd better go back home straight away.'

Henry says he'd like to go down to Eastbourne to see his sister, the Queen of Greece. Then, in the evening, he'll return to Germany. He then asks George bluntly, 'What will England do?'

'We shall try all we can to keep out of this,' says George.

At least that is what Henry *recalls* George saying. And it is this version of events that he will pass on to his brother, Der Kaiser, when he returns to Germany.

George has a slightly different recollection.

'I don't know what we shall do,' he records in his own notes of the conversation. 'We have no quarrel with anyone and I hope we shall remain neutral. But if Germany declares war on Russia and France joins Russia, then I am afraid we shall be dragged into it. But you can be sure that I and my government will do all we can to prevent a European war.'

At the end of the conversation, Henry says, 'Well, if our two countries shall be fighting on opposite sides I trust it will not affect our own personal friendship.'

Henry is then driven to Eastbourne under a cloudy summer sky.

In London, James Walters is at work even though it is Sunday. He too is in ignorance of the Serbian reply and has come in to find out what it is. During the afternoon the news comes in.

Also that afternoon, the German Ambassador strolls over to the Foreign Office. He has a message from the German government, from the Chancellor. The Germans, edgy about what might be happening in the mysterious wastes of Russia, want Grey to use his influence with the Russians to stop them from engaging in any form of mobilisation. The Ambassador finds nobody to talk to at the Foreign Office. Grey is down at his cottage. He is expected to return that evening but nobody knows exactly when. The German Ambassador decides that it can wait until the morning.

Brooding on the problem in Hampshire, Grey has little confidence that his proposal for mediation will be accepted. How he would have liked that Britain, the most powerful nation on the planet, could have acted as a disinterested and sensible arbiter – stepping in to sort out these squabbling European powers. But whether he likes it or not, Britain is now involved. And not just because of the current crisis. There is another reason.

It is Grey who, without telling Parliament, has agreed that the British and French military should have talks about what to do in the event of war. It seemed perfectly sensible at the time. Britain and France were allies. If and when somebody opened up hostilities against them would hardly be the time to begin discussing the best way the two sets of military could work together. But now Grey is starting to find himself in the position of a man who courts a woman for years and discovers that she is thinking in terms of marriage.

Anyway, apart from all that, if the German Army was to suddenly appear on the coast at Calais, if the German Navy were capable of operating out of Boulogne and Calais, then Britain's interests would be threatened. So Britain isn't really an observer or some kind of independent referee – she's a participant. So the question now is how to avoid war breaking out in Europe.

Grey returns to London that evening. Years after, he will write, 'One danger I saw so hideous that it must be avoided and guarded against at every word. It was that France and Russia might face the ordeal of war with Germany, relying upon our support; that this support might not be forthcoming, and that we might then, when it was too late, be held responsible for having let them in for a disastrous war.'

The words are interesting. First we can see that Grey is not focussed on the right problem. If the issue is saving the peace in Europe, why is this not his central concern? He has already moved on to the next problem. The assumption is that the current issue – the peace of Europe – is already lost.

So now, for Grey, the issue had become saving the honour of Britain. What does this phrase actually mean? It is hard to see how it could be interpreted as anything other than saving the honour of Sir Edward Grey. Grey has made or implied certain promises. Now, as he sees it, these will have to be met.

It is a truism that a government must protect its citizens. Where is the protection here? Grey might have argued that there was a long-term threat if Germany should invade France. But at that point no invasion was under way. There had been no Pearl Harbour or invasion of Poland. So in talking of war, there are a group of citizens – in the armed forces, for example – whose protection is suddenly being put to one side.

Now you may argue that it's not the job of the government to protect the army, but the job of the army to protect the government. But does this then mean that certain citizens get no protection?

And anyway, leaving all of this aside, if there was to be a war, then people – whether soldiers or civilians or both – would die. Were Grey's decisions taken in a world we cannot understand now – a world before television where people didn't understand the full horror of war? A world before the two world wars, before the Holocaust? A world where life was cheaper – or at least that certain lives of certain classes were?

One has to wonder what Grey would have chosen had the result been that his beloved ducks and other birds would die.

In Berlin, the French Ambassador is winding up a meeting with the German Foreign Secretary.

'May I speak to you man to man?' asks Jules Cambon, the Ambassador.

Von Jagow, the Foreign Secretary, nods.

'Let me tell you that what you are going to undertake is stupid. You will gain nothing from it and you will risk much loss. France will defend herself a great deal better than you expect. And England, which committed the serious blunder of letting you crush us in 1870, will not do so again. You may be sure of that.'

'You have your information,' replies the Foreign Secretary. 'And we have ours. We are sure of England's neutrality.'

In Paris, the Ministry of War orders the recall of officers on leave. The men will be left for another few days – the harvest needs to be brought in.

In London, Grey has arrived home. Winston Churchill, First Lord of the Admiralty, finds him there. Churchill explains that the British fleet, concentrated in the Channel for the review at Spithead, is going to be kept there and not ordered to disperse back to its home ports. Will it help the situation – or not – to state this publicly?

Grey has no doubt. Stating it publicly will have a steadying effect on Europe. Churchill goes back to the Admiralty and drafts a communiqué accordingly.

Berchtold does indeed reject Grey's offer of mediation, writing that if localisation of the war with Serbia isn't possible, then they'll be counting 'with gratitude' on Germany's support 'if a struggle against another adversary is forced upon us.'

The Russians also reject Grey's offer of mediation, saying that the proposed conference would be 'too unwieldy' and that they would prefer direct talks with the Austrians.

Back in the Foreign Office, Grey tells his officials that he believes a compromise solution can be worked out if Germany and Britain work together. Not all of his people are convinced, feeling that the Germans may not be dealing with the crisis in good faith. One of them, Nicolson, warns Grey that, in his opinion, 'Berlin is playing with us.' But Grey rejects this, believing that Germany is interested in stopping a general war.

Clara finds Henry upstairs checking that he has a clean shirt for tomorrow. Later on she sees him polishing his shoes, something that she used to do. And her day is complete when she catches him in the kitchen, lighting the grill. 'I thought I smelt gas,' he says limply, as his cheeks glow a beetroot colour.

Henry spends another restless night wondering if he can't at least get part of his problem sorted out. He decides he is going to take no action with Mary. Whether she stays or goes is going to be entirely up to her. Either way, he doesn't mind. He tells himself this but, in fact, he'll be sorry to lose her. He gets aroused just thinking about her. But he can't let his penis rule his life, he tells himself. ('Any more,' he might have added if he was being completely honest with himself.) So he is going to see what Monday brings with Mary. If she comes crawling to him, then he'll take her back. And if not, then he'll find somebody else.

It is on this note that Henry falls asleep only to wake just over an hour later realising that he hasn't dealt with the problem at all. The problem is not Mary, though she is something of a problem. The problem is that his marriage with Clara is in ruins. And she is now playing him like a fish. How long does she intend this to continue? It could go on for years. No. God, no. He couldn't tolerate that.

He must have it out with her. Make up some story, confess his wrongdoing and tell her that it will never happen again. No! He rules the idea out at once. He's not going to crawl to that bitch like that.

Two can play at this game. If she wants to play silly buggers then he will do it too – where he can hurt her most. With money.

But then he knows that that's not the answer either. If he keeps money from her, then he is the one who will suffer. There won't be food on the table. He could always eat in the City, he tells himself, but what about the girls? He can make Clara feel some pain, not being able to buy clothes or things like that. But he has to admit she is quite frugal in that area. No, this won't do.

And now, for the first time, the thought that he might leave Clara makes its way into Henry's mind. Up until now, that has never occurred to him. Up until now, he has always pictured himself married to Clara with Mary or other bits on the side. But now he sees that marriage to Clara could become a sort of extended nightmare. She is quite capable of carrying on the way she is now for years. He could see her becoming more and more bitter as the years went by, becoming more and more hostile to him. Henry had an uncle and aunt who lived like that – two people who ended up completely detesting each other. He is not going to spend his life like that. Maybe now is the time to make a leap – to tell Mary he will forgive her and take her back and that he will now indeed leave Clara.

Maybe – and at this, Henry is somewhat alarmed – the thing now is for complete honesty with Mary.

Clara is having great difficulty sleeping. She finds herself waking in the middle of the night and thinking about James. It is like there are two parallel words – the one she exists in now and another with James. She spends most of her waking hours in that one with him. Often she pictures herself in France with him. She tries not to think of how she will cross from this world to that other one. Better by far just to imagine herself already there.

Tonight she is thinking about how the time is going so slowly. Was it really only three days ago that they were together? It seems so much longer. And how the hours of the weekend are dragging, and then four whole weekdays until she sees him again.

And wasn't it wonderful when James said that he really liked her?

Chapter 39
Sunday 27 July 1914

The notice in the *Times* seems innocent enough. It runs:

British Naval Measures
Orders to First and Second Fleets
No Manoeuvre Leave

We received the following statement from the Secretary of the Admiralty at an early hour this morning:

Orders have been given to the First Fleet, which is concentrated at Portland, not to disperse for manoeuvre leave for the present. All vessels of the Second Fleet are remaining at their home ports in proximity to their balance crews.

Early on Monday, Henry asks Mary to come to lunch with him today. Her demeanour is glacial and she refuses. However, later in the morning she comes by his office and says brusquely that she has changed her mind. She will come after all, but only to hear what he has to say. He says he will meet her at the ABC at one o'clock.

He arrives on time and takes a table. While he waits he rehearses the speech he intends to make to her. She is going to listen while he speaks. He's going to admonish her for writing the letter. He's going to tell her that the ball is in her court. There are plenty more fish in the sea, he keeps telling himself.

He gets plenty of time for his rehearsals because it is nearly half past one and Henry is on the point of leaving when she arrives. She apologises for being late but gives no reason why.

'Well,' she says. 'What is it you want to say to me?'

Henry's intention had been to be firm and businesslike with her, exactly as though he were dealing with a supplier who had made a mess of things. Instead he finds himself apologising for the way he behaved towards her on Friday. Mary's eyes are cold and this throws Henry off his stride. But he manages to get back on track and hears himself saying, 'You need to make your mind up. Do you want to be with me or not?'

'I want to be your wife and not your whore,' she says, her eyes drilling into him. 'If that's not what you want, then you can go and fuck yourself.'

Henry looks around in alarm to see if anybody at any of the neighbouring tables heard what Mary said. And now she pushes her chair back and begins to get up. Henry is afraid she will say something else even more loudly.

'Do you have anything else to say to me?' she demands, her voice rising a fraction.

She is standing now. Henry is terrified she will make a scene.

'Please. Sit down,' he says.

She stands over him, her eyes flaming.

'I'm going.'

'Please,' he says again, almost in a whisper.

Out of the corner of his eye, Henry is conscious that somebody is indeed looking at them. Mary hesitates.

'Please sit down,' he says, and this time it *is* a whisper. Henry indicates the chair. Slowly, Mary resumes her seat.

Henry says, 'I will go and speak with a solicitor to find out about a divorce. Will that satisfy you?'

'When?' she demands.

'As quickly as I can make an appointment.'

'And once you're divorced, we'll be married?'

'Yes.'

And now it is as though Mary has been transformed. Her eyes fill with warmth and she reaches a hand across to place it on top of Henry's.

'Say it,' she says.

'Say what? That once we're divorced we'll be married?'

'Ask me to marry you,' says Mary softly, correcting him.

Her lips, with their very red lipstick, are parted fractionally. He thinks she looks quite beautiful. She takes her hand away from his but leaves it on the table. Henry assumes he is meant to take it but he is too annoyed to give her the satisfaction of doing that.

'Please Mary, will you … when … once I'm divorced … will you marry me?'

'Do you really want me to?'

Henry is about to snap at her that of course he bloody well wants to, but instead he just says, 'Yes, I'd like that very much.'

Now Mary places both her hands on his and says, 'Yes, I will, Henry. I will.'

In London, Herbert Samuel, one of the younger members of the government, finds Grey alone in the Cabinet Room that looks out over the garden in Downing Street.

'There's some devilry going on in Berlin,' Grey says passionately.

Later the Cabinet is split over whether or not to become involved should a European-wide war break out. The only decision that's made is for Winston Churchill to put the British fleet on alert. His order reads: 'Secret. European political situation makes war … by no means impossible. This is *not* the Warning Telegram, but be prepared to shadow possible hostile men of war … Measure is purely precautionary.'

Der Kaiser arrives at the Wildpark Station at Potsdam looking fit, sunburnt and confident after his three-week cruise.

Isn't it funny, dear reader, how sometimes a person's name reflects some aspect of their character? So it is with Sir Edward Grey. We've all heard the expression, 'It's not black and white,' and some things in life aren't – they don't have one definitive answer. But many things do. And then there is the related expression, 'It's a grey area.' Maybe Sir Edward has spent too long dealing in diplomacy, because, right now, when plain talking – black and white language – is required, Grey lapses into the grey language of diplomacy.

Sir Edward summons the ambassadors of three countries – Russia, Austria and Germany – to the Foreign Office. The Russian Ambassador says that the time has come for Britain to declare itself. Grey's reply is grey. He says that 'Churchill's orders to the First Fleet will surely be plain enough to Germany.' To the Austrian he offers an almost contradictory view. 'There is no menace in what we are doing,' he says. 'But owing to the possibility of a conflagration, we cannot disperse our forces.' And finally he asks the German Ambassador to use his country's influence with Austria to take the Serbian reply as a basis for discussion. The Ambassador passes this on, even beefing up Sir Edward's words. 'The British government,' he says, 'is convinced that it lies entirely with us whether Austria shall jeopardise European peace by stubbornly pursuing a policy of prestige.'

Diplomacy. Fluffy words and phrases. It would have been perhaps asking too much, for Grey to have stood up, banged the table and said that if Austria continued with its present course, Britain would absolutely go to war.

The French Ministry of Foreign Affairs begins to call back its troops from its overseas colonies. One man who receives this summons is General Louis Lyautey, the man who runs Morocco. At the moment when the cable arrives, he is presiding over a meeting in Casablanca which is to do with promoting agriculture in Morocco.

The cable reads, 'In the event of a continental war all your efforts should be directed to keeping in Morocco only the minimum of indispensable forces. The fate of Morocco will be decided in Lorraine.' Lyautey is instructed to reduce the French occupation of Morocco to merely holding the principal sea ports.

'They are completely mad!' is Lyautey's response. 'A war among Europeans is a civil war. It is the most monumental folly the world has ever committed.'

There is a phenomenon known as 'groupthink.' It was first coined by a man called Irving Janis in 1972. Groupthink occurs when a group makes faulty decisions because pressures within the group lead to a reduction in 'mental efficiency, reality testing and moral judgement.'

Janis found that groups affected by groupthink tended to take irrational actions that dehumanise other groups. A group is especially vulnerable to groupthink when its members are similar in background, when the group is insulated from outside opinion and when there are no clear rules for decision making.

What a pity Janis wasn't around in 1914. On the other hand, maybe it wouldn't have made any difference – look at the invasion of Iraq.

In Paris, the French Foreign Minister tells the German Ambassador that France is anxious to find a peaceful solution. It will do its utmost to influence the Russians if the Germans will urge moderation on the Austrians.

Austria continues its preparations for war against Serbia. In Vienna, the British Ambassador reports that the 'country has gone wild with joy at prospect of war with Serbia.' He concludes that Austria wanted war all along.

In Berlin, the German Foreign Minister explains to the Austrian Ambassador that he is only pretending to consider the British offer of mediation, and that in reality he has no intention of stopping the war against Serbia. The Germans are anxious to keep the British from getting involved and so are treating them with the utmost deference. If Germany were to explicitly tell Sir Edward Grey that it wasn't pushing his mediation proposal with the Austrians, then world opinion would see Germany as being responsible for the war. In addition, German public opinion needs to see the war as having been forced on their country. The Germans wire Grey that they 'have immediately initiated mediation in Vienna in the sense desired by Sir Edward Grey.' And they do indeed pass on Grey's offer of mediation to their Ambassador in Vienna. However, they order him not to show it to anyone in the Austrian government for fear that it might be accepted.

The French President, Poincaré, is still at sea. (Just how much at sea he will find out when he eventually arrives in France.) On board the *France*, Captain Grandclement keeps her at a steady eighteen to nineteen knots, south westerly through the Skagerrak towards

Dunkirk. The seas are heavy, the ship rolls and President Poincaré's saloon ships a lot of salt water. During the day, a German torpedo boat operating out of Cuxhaven or Emden passes the *France* and fires a salute.

So at this stage, dear and maybe slightly perplexed reader, we can probably summarise the Group of Death like this. Austria wants to play a quick match against the Serbs and give them a jolly good hiding. The Austrians are only in the game because the Germans are backing them.

The Germans believe the Austria-Serbia war can be localised and will be over and done with before any of the rest of the big guns gets involved. Anyway, Russia isn't ready for a war – or so the Germans believe – the British aren't prepared to fight and the French – well, Poincaré is still at sea.

And Sir Edward Grey believes the Germans really don't want war and are clear that Britain would fight if it came to it. He could hardly be more wrong on both counts.

Far away from all this, Clara is missing James. She has become tired of goading Henry and now just wants it to be Thursday. Up to the morning she received the letter, Clara had envisioned the rest of her life as being a weary journey down to death, accompanied by Henry. Now all that has changed. She sees the chance of something new and bright and beautiful – like a rainbow glimpsed in the distance. Where she stands there are still purple, angry clouds and it is raining. But she now sees a little bit of brightness, a glimpse of sunlight, a ray of hope.

In her Atkinson Grimshaw fantasy, James has now become the man in the room. Those nights that Clara used to lie awake worrying, she now spends imagining what it would be like to be with him. And not just in that fantasy, but in real life. But she stays focussed on life *with* him, trying not to think about the terrible journey she will have to make before that can ever come about.

Clara has another night of broken sleep. She goes to bed about 11:30, sleeps soundly until three and then is wide awake after that until she hears the girls. (Today she lets Henry get up first and get his own breakfast.) 'It's such a long time until Thursday,' she writes later in her diary.

Chapter 40
Tuesday 28 July 1914

Der Kaiser rises early in the New Palace at Potsdam. He goes out riding in the park. He has at last read the Serbian reply to Austria and he is in a good mood. The note is a complete capitulation. Vienna has brought off a great victory. 'All reason for war is gone,' says Der Kaiser. He has written as much in the margin of the document containing the news. 'Every reason for war drops away. Giesl might have remained quietly in Belgrade.'

Der Kaiser notes that the Serbs have made 'a capitulation of the most humiliating kind. The few reservations which Serbia made with respect to certain points can in my opinion surely be cleared up by negotiation.' Der Kaiser says that 'the Serbs are Orientals, therefore liars, tricksters and masters of evasion,' and that therefore a temporary Austrian occupation of Belgrade is required until Serbia keeps its word.

Proving that he might not be barking mad at all, Der Kaiser sits down at his desk and drafts a proposal for a temporary Austrian occupation of Belgrade. Der Kaiser sees that it is the Austrian Army that feels most sensitive about the murder of the Archduke. After all, he was their commander-in-chief and their honour had been sullied by his murder. Der Kaiser feels that his 'Halt in Belgrade' idea will go a long way towards soothing their feelings.

The German Chancellor, military and diplomatic services are all appalled and angered at Der Kaiser's sudden change of mind. Accordingly, they do what all good civil servants would do under the circumstances. They sabotage his proposal.

The Chancellor sends the German Ambassador in Vienna a message that reads, 'You must most carefully avoid giving any impression that we want *to hold Austria back*. We are concerned only to find a *modus* to enable the realisation of Austria-Hungary's aim *without at the same time unleashing a world war*, and *should this after all prove unavoidable, to improve as far as possible the conditions under which it is to be waged.*'

In passing on Der Kaiser's message, the Chancellor excludes the parts wherein the Emperor told the Austrians not to go to war. The German Foreign Minister tells his diplomats to disregard Der Kaiser's peace offer and to continue to press for war. General Falkenhayn, the German Minister for War tells Der Kaiser that he no longer has control of the affair in his own hands. Falkenhayn implies that the military might even stage a coup if Der Kaiser continued to work for peace.

Also that morning, the German Ambassador in London forwards yet another British offer of mediation, this time from both King George V and Sir Edward Grey. Later that day the Ambassador tells his people in Berlin that nobody in Britain believes in the possibility of localising the war and he warns *them* against their believing it.

This time, when the British Ambassador in Berlin presents the mediation proposal to the Germans, it is totally rejected.

Austrian troops begin to concentrate in Bosnia as a preparatory step towards invading Serbia. Meanwhile in Vienna, the Austrians have run into a problem. They no longer have an ambassador in Belgrade. How then are they to declare war? Trust the postal service? Probably never a good idea. Send a messenger? Yes, but wouldn't he have to go under a flag of truce for his own protection? And how could you have a flag of truce when you don't yet have a war? These diplomatic difficulties!

Finally, they find a solution. A telegram is sent via Bucharest in Romania to Belgrade. It reads:

The Royal Serbian Government not having answered in a satisfactory manner the note of July 10–23, 1914, presented by the

> *Austro-Hungarian Minister at Belgrade, the Imperial and Royal Government are thus pledged to see to the safeguarding of their rights and interests and, with this object, to have recourse to force of arms. Austro-Hungary consequently considers herself henceforward in a state of war with Serbia.*

And so, at 11 a.m., Austria is at war with Serbia. An hour later – deliberately so – the German Ambassador presents Der Kaiser's 'Halt in Belgrade' proposal to the Austrians. Later that day, Austrian heavy warships begin to bombard Belgrade.

Der Kaiser sends a telegram to his cousin the Tsar asking for Russian support for the Austrian war against Serbia.

The Tsar replies to Der Kaiser's message: 'Am glad you are back ... I appeal to you to help me. An ignoble war has been declared on a weak country ... Soon I shall be overwhelmed by pressure brought upon me ... to take extreme measures which will lead to war. To try and avoid such a calamity as a European war, I beg you in the name of our old friendship to do what you can to stop your allies from going too far.'

Der Kaiser's brother, Henry, arrives at Kiel after his sojourn in England. He writes a letter to his brother.
'I had a short talk with Georgie, who said, "We shall try to keep out of this and shall remain neutral".'

In Berlin, the Social Democratic Party (SDP) denounces Austria for declaring war on Serbia. It orders street demonstrations in protest against Germany's actions in supporting Austria. However, privately the SDP leaders tell the Chancellor that they would support the government if Germany was faced with a Russian attack.

In St Petersburg, the Tsar signs two orders of mobilisation. One is for general mobilisation. The other is for mobilisation confined to the four military districts opposite the Austrian frontier – Moscow, Kiev,

Odessa and Kazan. Both documents are given to General Janushkevitch, the pornographer, anti–Semite and Chief of Staff.

Later that evening, Grey goes to a musical party at Pamela Glenconnor's. There, Mr Campbell McInnes sings pieces by Handel and notes the 'ashen misery' in Grey's face. Funny how that 'grey' thing keeps recurring, isn't it?

All leave is stopped in the British destroyer flotillas.

It is learned that since Saturday, no Orient Express has travelled beyond Budapest.

In Vienna, there are jubilant demonstrations in support of war with Serbia in front of the War Ministry. The streets are full of flags, ribbons, bands, processions and proud young soldiers in their new blue-grey uniforms. Food prices rise sharply but the only people who notice are the housewives out doing the day's shopping.

General von Falkenhayn orders German troops on manoeuvres to return to barracks.

Clara goes to bed with a headache. She has had quite a few headaches the last few days. She knows what it is. Yes, she feels huge anticipation about meeting James again. And now she so much wants things to go a certain way with him. She also has a terrible fear that things *will* go that way – because then she will be lost to her old life and committed to her new. And that prospect *terrifies* her.

She wakes at one and doesn't go back to sleep. It is during this time that she decides she cannot wait until Thursday. She will go to the park tomorrow and surprise James.

Chapter 41
Wednesday 29 July 1914

In case you'd been wondering where he was – because we hadn't heard from him in a while – President Poincaré has arrived back in France from Russia. The *France* docks at Dunkirk and his train speeds towards the Gare du Nord in Paris. The weather is warmer than it was when he left and seems to promise a summer that will be late but wonderful. On the train he has his first real chance to study the official reports. The situation is more serious than he thought.

His train pulls into the station at twenty past one. It seems that all Paris has turned out to greet him. Gorgeous tricolours are everywhere. The station is crammed with people and as Poincaré steps from the train, looking pale and tense, cries of '*Vive la France*' and '*Vive Poincaré*' go up. There is no mistaking the message – his people are ready for a war.

Once he gets to the Elysée, Poincaré doesn't waste any time. He convenes a meeting of the Council of Ministers. He has a simple question for them. Should Russia be promised French military support if she mobilises and war then ensues?

By six o'clock, assuming they will get the support of England, the ministers have answered yes.

In St Petersburg, events are moving swiftly like a train that has lost its driver. The German Ambassador has told the Russian Foreign Minister that if Russia goes on with its military preparations, Germany will have to mobilise in response. Not long afterwards the Prime Minister is talking to the Austrian Ambassador. The Prime Minister explains that Russia is engaging in a *partial* mobilisation but that it is only a precautionary measure.

Then the telephone rings on the Prime Minister's desk. The news is not good. Austrian ships on the Danube have fired shells into Belgrade.

In London, the Cabinet is still no closer to deciding whether to remain neutral or to become involved if France is attacked. It approves what is essentially another twenty-four hours' stalling to wait and see what happens. Meanwhile, the rest of Europe is hurtling down the helter skelter to war.

Der Kaiser receives his brother's letter from Kiel, with its news that 'Georgie' had told him Britain would stay neutral in the event of a European war. Here is something that goes way beyond the shabby dealings of politicians.

'I have the word of a king,' says Der Kaiser. 'That is sufficient for me.'

After lunch, Sir Edward Grey calls the German Ambassador to the Foreign Office. Grey repeats his suggestion that Britain, France and Germany should mediate in the conflict. He reiterates Der Kaiser's suggestion – proposed a day earlier – that the Austrians be content to stop in Belgrade. Diplomacy could then take over.

As long as the conflict is confined to Austria and Russia, Britain can remain neutral. But, Grey explains gravely, if Germany – as Austria's ally – and France – as Russia's ally – are drawn in, then the situation would be very different.

'If war breaks out,' Grey says. 'It will be the greatest catastrophe that the world has ever seen. It is far from my thoughts to express any kind of threat. I only want to save you from disappointment and myself from the reproach of insincerity.' To support Grey's warnings, the British government orders a general alert for its armed forces.

The Ambassador returns to the embassy and cables Berlin. When Der Kaiser sees the telegram he hits the roof. At the bottom he scribbles, 'England reveals herself in her true colours at a moment when she thinks we are caught in the toils and, so to speak, disposed of. That common crew of shopkeepers has tried to trick us with dinners and speeches … Grey proves the King a liar … common cur.

England alone bears the responsibility for peace and war ...' It is initialed 'W.'

Mad?

At a meeting with the German Chancellor late that night, both the Minister for War, Falkenhayn and the Chief of the General Staff, Moltke demand that Germany use Russian partial mobilisation as an excuse to go to war. The Chancellor insists that Germany must wait for Russian *general* mobilisation as it is the only way of ensuring German public support and that Britain remain neutral in the 'imminent war' against France and Russia.

At another meeting in Berlin that night, the Chancellor tells the British Ambassador that Germany will soon be going to war against France and Russia. To try to ensure British neutrality the Chancellor says that Germany will not annex any parts of France. He's not prepared to give the same guarantee about French colonies. During the same meeting, the Chancellor all but announces that Germany will soon violate Belgium's neutrality. (He adds that if Belgium doesn't resist, then Germany will not annex that country. It is at last clear to London that Germany has no interest in peace.)

After the British Ambassador leaves the meeting, the Chancellor receives a message from the German Ambassador in London. It says that Grey is most anxious for a four power conference, but that if Germany attacks France, Britain will have no other choice but to intervene in the war.

In response to the British warning, the Chancellor does a swift about-turn.

He writes to the German Ambassador in Vienna, 'If, therefore, Austria should reject all mediation, we are faced with a conflagration in which Britain would be against us, Italy and Romania in all probability not with us. We should be two powers against four. With Britain an enemy, the weight of the operations would fall on Germany ... Under these circumstances we must urgently and emphatically suggest to the Vienna Cabinet acceptance of mediation under the present honourable conditions. The responsibility falling on us and Austria for the consequences which would ensue in case of refusal would be uncommonly heavy.'

Five minutes later, the Chancellor sends a second message asking his man in Vienna to stop 'refusing any exchange of views with Russia,' and warning that we 'must refuse to allow Vienna to draw us into a world conflagration frivolously and without regard to our advice.'

In a third message, the Chancellor writes that, 'To avert a general catastrophe or *in any case* to put Russia in the wrong, we must urgently wish Vienna to begin and continue conversations with Russia.'

Horrified at what he sees as his ally's sudden about-face, Berchtold tells the German Ambassador that this is all coming far too late. He says he'll need a few days to think about what Germany is now saying. Until then, events will proceed.

Later in the evening, in St Petersburg, the Tsar receives a telegram from his cousin, Der Kaiser. Der Kaiser says that he believes his proposal for a halt in Belgrade is within sight of being accepted. He says that Russian mobilisations – even partial mobilisation against Austria alone – are going to compromise this.

The Tsar is badly shaken. In his nightshirt, he hurries downstairs to the hall where the telephone stands. Unused as he is to the instrument, he telephones the Minister of War and the Chief of Staff, Januskevitch, and orders that mobilisation should be stopped. The Minister explains that such a thing is technically impossible. He passes the phone to the Chief of Staff, General Janushkevitch. He too explains that this cannot be done.

'Stop it,' the Tsar snaps. Transmission of military telegrams ordering mobilisation is halted for the night.

The Tsar wires back to Der Kaiser that the military measures now coming into force – that is, the partial mobilisation that the Tsar thinks is continuing – are only for reasons of defence because of what Austria is doing.

And finally, after all this, dear reader, on this momentous day when the great leaders of Europe have been making their great decisions, let's not forget about a person for whom, hopefully, you have come to care about. For today was also a momentous day for Clara. It was the day when she couldn't wait any longer and went to meet James. Let's rewind the clock a few hours to the late morning.

Clara is on her way to St James's Park. She goes to this meeting with impunity now. If Henry is aware that she is doing this, he says nothing. Had he asked, Clara was ready to make some impertinent answer along the lines of 'I can do what I like' or 'What's it to you?' but in the end, he never said anything. She's not even sure he noticed, so caught up is he in his own sordid life.

She hopes she will just bump into James, but now that she has begun her journey, it occurs to her that maybe he won't be there. Austria has declared war on Serbia according to the newspaper sellers' posters. Maybe this means that, with things this serious, James won't be able to take a lunch break. She finds she is hurrying and is terribly anxious that he won't be there. She couldn't bear that. She *loves* his company.

Clara is also excited because he should have arranged the meeting with the solicitor. Now that she knows she is not alone, Clara is looking forward to that meeting. It will be a step further down the road she has chosen to take.

And here, dear reader, you'll forgive me if I interject. There is a moment in each of our lives that could be described as our most perfect moment. I use 'moment' in the poetic rather than the scientific sense. I don't mean an instant but rather a short space of time – probably not longer than a day. For Clara, that moment is about to come.

Because, as it turns out, James *is* there that day. He has snatched some time away from the madness of what is going on at the Foreign Office – the comings and goings of various ambassadors, the endless meetings to try to interpret what is being said and to phrase replies – to try to clear his head. He knows he will be there until late tonight so he told his secretary he might take a few hours.

The next time you are in London, dear reader, go to St James's Park. If you could locate it, it would be possible to find the very spot where James sat that day. And if it were possible to find a way to push open the door to the past, there he would be. The summer's day – the perfect backdrop to what is about to take place. The hot sun, the warm breeze just enough to caress the leaves and the skin, the sound of people and birds calling, the smell of warm earth and grass. A day when, instead of squashing insects which happen to land on us, we gently move them on their way.

There is James. He is five-foot-ten, trim and with tiny flecks of grey hair. He has left his hat at the office and has just removed his jacket, folded it and laid it on the seat. He is unwrapping his packet of sandwiches.

And now here comes Clara, in the distance, hurrying towards him. She wears the same hat, white blouse and cornflower blue skirt she wore last week. She is conscious of wearing the same outfit a second time but it's not like she has a vast wardrobe of good clothes and, anyway, she likes how she feels and how she looks in it. This morning, as she was dressing, she noticed that her face was becoming a little tanned. It suits her – makes her look like she is bursting with health.

She approaches James and from his face it is clear that he is both surprised and delighted to see her. He stands up. The expression on Clara's face is almost angelic – something not quite of this world. Unlike their previous encounters, James takes both her hands in his. We can hear the words he speaks next.

'There's something I must tell you, Clara.'

She looks anxiously up into his face. All sorts of thoughts go through her head. He is not divorced after all. He can't go through with his promise to be her ally. What is it?

'I love you,' he says. 'Ever since I met you I've loved you. I can't sleep properly at night for thinking about you. I want to help you get this wretched divorce out of the way as quickly as possible so that, then, I could ask you … you might do me the greatest possible honour of becoming my wife.'

Clara goes to say something, but James continues.

'If you say yes, I will be the best father I can be to your girls. I haven't met them but I want you to know that I love them already. And I will love and cherish you—'

Suddenly he seems to run out of things to say.

All Clara can say is, 'Oh James' before they kiss – oblivious to the people around them or any of the conventions of the day.

They sit down.

'I wondered about you from the moment I met you,' James says. 'I imagined you with this perfect life, perfect husband, perfect children. I found myself cursing fate that I had not met you earlier in my life. And then, when we agreed to meet again, you will never know how much I was looking forward to that second meeting.'

He is speaking quickly. There is so much he seems to wants to say. Clara is in a state of wonderment. She cannot believe the day is unfolding like this.

'And then when you asked me about becoming divorced … I knew then I might have a chance. But I thought that, even if I could only be your friend, I would help you through it – and that would have been enough for me. I wanted so much to be the one who helped you. If I could just be your friend and get to spend time in your company.'

By this time, they are turned towards each other on the bench and holding hands.

'And then when I said that I really liked you – and you responded with the same words, I knew then – or at least, I hoped I knew … That I hadn't misinterpreted.'

'You haven't misinterpreted,' she says, smiling.

She shakes her head. 'You haven't misinterpreted at all.'

And then, like all lovers everywhere, there are those first few hours. Hours that are like reading the first page of a big fat novel that you have not read before, hearing the opening bars of a symphony that you have never heard, seeing the first moments of a long film that you have not seen: there is so much to be discovered.

And that afternoon Clara and James each discover just a little. Their ages and their birthdays. Books they have read. Books they like. Their favourites. Amusing things that have happened in their lives. They find that they can make each other laugh. (Clara had always thought she had a good sense of humour. Now she has found somebody who thinks the same.) Places that they have visited that are important to them. 'You must see France,' he says. 'Learn a little French. It is such a thing to speak the language.' (Clara feels so unsophisticated and unworldly and inadequate in this regard.

James has seen so much and she so little. But he poo poo's that. 'You shall see all these places,' he says. 'And more.')

'Tell me about your girls,' he says to her, and here she feels on firmer ground. 'I don't have any children,' he adds. 'So I want to know all about them. (It is only afterwards, when she is replaying their afternoon together, that she realises he deliberately steered her away from the subject of travel because he knew how she was feeling. She is so grateful for that. How wonderful that he should have known – that he was so sensitive.)

She doesn't know how long they have been talking when he suddenly asks her if she is hungry. She is absolutely starving but hadn't noticed it until now. She laughs and they go to find a place where they can eat.

If this is the beginning of a book or a symphony or a film, then Clara is starting to feel that this book is going to have far more pages than she will ever have a chance to read; this symphony will just run on and on and on; this film will never end.

After they have eaten they walk in the park, seeking shade amongst the trees. They find a deserted bower and kiss and touch each other's faces. If anyone saw them they would be scandalised. It hardly costs Clara a thought.

She has never known such complete harmony. She has no fears about James, that he will fail her or do anything other than what he has promised. Neither is she concerned about the future. What will come will come and, good or bad, she will deal with it as it does. She feels as though a magic circle encloses them and that the world is in a state of blissful perfection. The ordinary world – worry about her girls, money, Henry, divorce, the crisis in Europe – none of these things matter this afternoon. It is possible that terrible things may lie waiting for her up ahead, but this afternoon, she finds that possibility as remote as the stars.

Instead she imagines things they will do together. Ideas tumble into her head. Bird watching in France. Buying James little surprises or cooking him beautiful food. Travelling with him. Eating in restaurants and staying in hotels. Exploring wherever they go, whether it's just a walk in the park as they are doing now or on a trip to some far off place. Reading. He is holding her hand and the warmth of him makes her wonder what making love with him would be like.

And so the afternoon shadows begin to lengthen as they walk in St James's Park in that far away time. Far away, yes, but close also, so very close – if only we could find the door to the past and push it open.

Eventually, the world calls Clara back as it always does. A distant bell strikes four.

'I'm going to have to go,' she says.

'I know,' he says, his voice scarcely more than a whisper. 'I'll see you to the Tube.' They take the long way out of the park so they can delay the moment of separation for as long as possible. They walk hand-in-hand, silent, sad at their impending parting. Occasionally, they look at one another and when their eyes meet, they smile.

'Oh, by the way,' he says. 'I nearly forgot. I've made the appointment with the solicitor for two weeks Thursday, the thirteenth. At noon. I couldn't get it any sooner because the man I would like you to see is on holiday until the tenth. And I assumed Thursday would suit you best.'

'Thank you,' she responds softly. 'I appreciate it. I don't know what I would have done otherwise. Without you. You're so very thoughtful.'

'It's nothing,' he replies. 'I can come with you, if you like. I mean, I'll take you there, but I'll come in with you, if you want me to.'

'Oh please, of course,' she says. 'That's exactly what I'd want – that's if you really don't mind becoming involved in my suddenly very complicated life.'

'I've wanted to become involved in your life from the moment I laid eyes on you.'

Clara sits on the train, unsure whether she wants to laugh or cry. Their beautiful afternoon is over. They've arranged that they'll meet again next Thursday and then James will take the rest of the day off. He tells her that he can't guarantee he can get any other time off before that – especially if the crisis in Europe intensifies. Clara is not sure how she'll get through the next week without seeing him. And she knows there will never be another day quite like today. There may be other days when they do similar things.

But this day, this day is just about the most perfect she has ever lived through. It is gone now but – in some ways – it can never go. She knows she will cherish it all the days of her life. She imagines it will be her last conscious thought in this world.

Interlude

One of the things you'll notice from now on, dear reader, is that the Austrians – the people who started the whole bloody thing – will figure less and less in our story as the (really) big boys in the Group of Death start to take over.

PART 2

Chapter 42
Thursday 30 July 1914

Upon hearing of Russia's partial mobilisation, Der Kaiser says that he too must mobilise. The German Ambassador in St Petersburg tells the Tsar that Germany will mobilise if Russia doesn't demobilise at once.

That afternoon, in the Tsar's study at Peterhof, its windows looking out onto the Gulf of Finland, Sazonov, the Russian Foreign Minister, accompanied by Russia's top generals all urge the Tsar to go for full mobilisation. Sazonov has finally understood that there is really no such thing as partial mobilisation and explains this to the Tsar. The Tsar agonises but eventually he tells his Foreign Minister to pass on the order for general mobilisation.

The German Chancellor, Bethmann Hollweg tells a meeting of the Prussian State Council that his only interest now, for domestic political reasons, is to '*represent* Russia as the guilty party' behind the war. If it appears to public opinion that Russian mobilisation has forced Germany into a war, then there is 'nothing to fear' from the Social Democrats and 'there will be no question of a general or partial strike or of sabotage.'

Later that day, the Chancellor sends a message to the German Ambassador to Vienna, increasing pressure to accept the 'Halt in Belgrade' proposal, saying that: 'If Vienna … refuses … to give way at all, it will hardly be possible to place the blame on Russia for the outbreak of the European conflagration.'

At 9:00 p.m. the German Chancellor gives in to Moltke and Falkenhayn's repeated demands and promises them that Germany will mobilise at noon the next day regardless of whether Russia begins general mobilisation or not.

But shortly afterwards the Chancellor is overjoyed to learn that Russia has indeed ordered general mobilisation, which allows him to present the war as something forced on Germany by Russia. He instructs the Ambassador in Vienna 'that all mediation attempts be stopped.'

The British Prime Minister, Asquith, writes: 'The European situation is at least one degree worse than it was yesterday, and has not been improved by a rather shameless attempt on the part of Germany to buy our neutrality during the war with promises that she will not annex French territory (except colonies) or Holland or Belgium. There is something very crude and childlike about German diplomacy. Meanwhile the French are beginning to press in the opposite sense, as the Russians have been doing for some time. The City, in a terrible state of depression and paralysis, is for the time being all against English intervention.'

In London, the price of wheat rises by four shillings a quarter.

In Acton, the girls are in bed, Henry is downstairs and Clara is having a long, hot bath. She can't remember the last time she took a bath for pleasure – for years it has just been about making herself clean. She knows that since yesterday there must be a glow around her but nobody seems to have noticed it or, if they have, have not remarked on it. There are times when she wonders whether yesterday was all just an illusion, but then she smiles and remembers how real and perfect it actually was.

She and James have arranged to write to each other. Since she doesn't want any letters arriving here in Horn Lane, they have arranged that she will write and James will reply. But he will keep his replies so she can read them when they meet. Clara thinks it's a beautiful idea and eventually, when they are together, they will have this wonderful sequence of love letters.

Clara is not the only one bathing before she goes to bed. The Tsar, after perhaps the most monumental day of his life, has a bath and then writes in his diary just before going to sleep, 'I went for a walk by myself. The weather was hot. Had a delightful bath.'

Chapter 43
Friday 31 July 1914

The weather is fine in Berlin, pale blue sky at early morning with the promise of a hot, uncomfortable day. Moltke, Chief of the General Staff, telephones General Hell, his man on the eastern frontier with Russia.

'Do you think Russia is mobilising?' Moltke asks.

'I have thought so for several days,' is the reply. 'The frontier is sealed. Nobody crosses either way. They are burning the frontier guardhouses. Red mobilisation notices are said to be posted up in Mlava.'

Moltke orders Hell to get his hands on one of the red mobilisation notices, and two hours later Hell has done exactly that.

On this basis Moltke telegraphs Conrad in Austria saying, 'Mobilise at once against Russia.'

And by half past noon, the Austrians have done so.

Taking an early lunch, Henry calls into a solicitor's not far from the office. He finds himself blushing as he explains he'd like to speak to a solicitor on a 'matter of family law.' The only other time Henry has been in a solicitor's was when they were dealing with Clara's father's estate. Then, about to become a man of property, he had felt confident, sure of himself. For some reason, he finds being here now, for *this* reason, somewhat humiliating.

He had thought he would get to speak to somebody right away and he is relieved when he is told that the partner who deals with such matters is not available today. Furthermore, he's about to depart on two weeks' holiday and so won't be back until the 17th. An appointment is made for the 17th.

As Henry returns to the office, not only is he relieved at this two-and-a-half week reprieve, he is delighted that this delay will probably annoy Mary. But he's already rehearsed his reply. 'He's their best fellow. A specialist in this kind of thing. You wouldn't want me to use anything less, would you?'

Henry's also going to push her for another night in a hotel next week. And she'd damn well better say yes, if she wants this whole business to continue.

Elsewhere in London, the Stock Exchange is closed – 'until further notice' says a notice on its door – and the bank rate goes up from four to eight per cent.

The Prime Minister, Asquith, writes that, 'the general opinion at present – particularly strong in the City – is to keep out at all costs.' The British Cabinet is badly divided with Lloyd George, the Chancellor of the Exchequer, strongly opposed to Britain becoming involved in a war. The Conservatives, on the other hand, say they will support a war against Germany if France is attacked.

Grey tells the German Ambassador that if France becomes involved in a war, then Britain will inevitably be drawn in. However, he tells the French Ambassador that, as far as Britain is concerned with regard to its relations with France, no treaties or obligations are involved. Grey describes the meeting as 'rather painful.'

That night, the Prime Minister asks the King to ask his cousin the Tsar to stop mobilisation.

The Tsar writes to Der Kaiser explaining that Russian general mobilisation is not intended to be a prelude to war. He thanks his cousin for his mediation efforts and says that he hopes all will still end peacefully. He explains what he has discovered about mobilisation – and what Der Kaiser will soon find out – that it is impossible to stop mobilisation once it is set in train. The mobilisation was necessary, the Tsar explains, because of Austria's mobilisation. 'We are far from wishing war,' the Tsar continues. 'As long as the negotiations with Austria on Serbia's account are taking place my troops shall not make any *provocative* action. I give you my solemn word for this.'

Later that night, the Tsar will write in his diary, 'A grey day, in keeping with my mood.'

In Paris, there is a run on the banks. Long queues form outside the Bank of France which announces that it will pay no more than fifty gold francs per depositor once a fortnight.

When word reaches Berlin of Russian general mobilisation, Der Kaiser agrees to sign the orders for German mobilisation, and German troops began preparations to enter Luxembourg and Belgium as a preliminary to invading France. The German Social Democrats support the government on the basis that it is Russia that has forced Germany to mobilise.

The Bavarian military attaché at the War Ministry writes, 'Beaming faces everywhere. Everyone is shaking hands in the corridors. People congratulate one another for being over the hurdle.'

Both Moltke and Falkenhayn tell the government that Germany should declare war even if Russia offers to negotiate.

And in Berlin, Der Kaiser writes, 'I no longer have any doubt that England, Russia and France have agreed among themselves – knowing that our treaty obligations compel us to support Austria – to use the Austro-Serb conflict as a pretext for waging a war of annihilation against us.'

At seven o'clock in the evening, the German government declares a state of *Kriegsgefahrdzustand* – 'preparation for war.' It is the preliminary step to mobilisation.

Clara writes in her diary. 'There is one form of love where people have things in common. There is another one – I don't know yet whether it's more or less intense – where you just love the other person for being themselves, for what they are and do.'

Chapter 44
Saturday 1 August 1914

At 3:45 in the afternoon, the telegrams of mobilisation are handed in at the Central Telegraph Office in Paris. The first notices of mobilisation start to appear, still wet from the billposter's brush.

Armée de Terre et Armée de Mer.
ORDRE DE MOBILISATION GÉNÉRALE.

It's a Saturday yet Paris is strangely deserted. There are no taxis and the Metro isn't running. Buses have been requisitioned to carry men to their mobilisation points.

The French General Staff had previously estimated that thirteen per cent of reservists would fail to turn up. They are delighted when they discover that the figure is closer to one and a half per cent.

At 4:23 p.m. a telegram from the German Ambassador in London arrives in Berlin. The British are proposing that they will guarantee the neutrality of France and thus limit the war to one fought in the east. Der Kaiser is delighted. 'That calls for champagne,' he says and immediately accepts. He then orders German forces to strike against Russia alone and demands that his generals shift the mobilisation to the east.

This leads to fierce protests from Moltke who says that it is not technically possible for Germany to do this. It's that old mobilisation problem again. The bulk of the German forces are already advancing into Luxembourg and Belgium. After a great deal of argument, it is decided to mobilise as planned but then to cancel the planned invasion of Luxembourg. The army will then redeploy to the east.

Like all military men who want to try out the thing they have created, Moltke is depressed beyond belief. 'Now it only remains for Russia to back out, too,' he says gloomily. However, he does manage to persuade Der Kaiser that the advance into Luxembourg needs to continue 'for technical reasons.' By 7:00 p.m. that evening, the first German troops are in Luxembourg.

Meanwhile, the German Chancellor announces that Germany has mobilised and delivers an ultimatum to France, telling her to renounce its alliance with Russia or face a German attack. In response to reports of German troops invading Luxembourg and Belgium, plus the German ultimatum, French mobilisation is authorised.

The Germans also declare war on Russia. When presenting his declaration of war, the German Ambassador accidentally gives the Russians two copies. One claims that Russia refuses to reply to Germany and the other says that said Russia's replies were unacceptable.

In Germany, there are exhilarated crowds on the Unter den Linden in Berlin. The same is true in Munich on the Odeonsplatz where a young Austrian called Adolf Hitler celebrates along with everybody else. Der Kaiser summons the Chief of General Staff to his palace and says, 'Now you can do as you wish. March into Luxembourg.'

In London, Grey still has no comfort for Cambon, the French Ambassador. Grey points out that Germany has said it will not attack France if the French stay out of the fight between Germany and Russia. He knows the French won't do this because of the alliance they have with the Russians. But, Sir Edward says, Britain doesn't even know the terms of this alliance. It's not going to send its troops to fight in France on that basis.

Cambon tries to argue that Britain has an obligation to help France but Grey is having none of it. Cambon talks about the 'obligation of British interests' but Grey replies that the Cabinet will make its own evaluation of British interests. The only thing

Grey offers is that he will remind his Cabinet colleagues about France's undefended Atlantic and Channel coastlines.

Clara is feeling terribly down. She's tormented by what she's about to put everybody through. She remembers that one time she loved Henry and now she is going to hurt him terribly. She wonders if he ever felt bad about the ways he used to hurt her.

And it isn't so much Henry as the girls. Their whole future is going to be radically altered now and it is all because of what Clara is about to do – actually, because of Clara's happiness. Does she have the right to do this? And to children. Her own children. Who she loves more than life itself. She would die rather than hurt them. But she realises now that this is not actually true. Because if it were, she would just get on with it and stay with Henry. But if she stayed with Henry, she believes – and of this she is quite convinced – that *she* would die. And it is this thought which keeps her facing resolutely down the road she has chosen to take.

She wishes there was some way she could make it easier for all of them, but she knows that they will each have to deal with it themselves. It may not be so difficult for Virginia, but it's going to be awful for Ursula. Clara feels terrible that she is the cause of visiting this unhappiness on people she loves – or, in Henry's case, used to love.

Even the thought of knowing that James is in her life brings her no comfort.

That evening in London, when Winston Churchill learns that Germany has declared war on Russia, he issues the order to mobilise the British fleet.

Chapter 45
Sunday 2 August 1914

The German Army occupies Luxembourg as a preliminary step to the invasion of Belgium and then France.

On the platform at the top of the Eiffel Tower, French soldiers have mounted a lookout for German aircraft.

At three o'clock in the Winter Palace in St Petersburg, a solemn ceremony takes place. In front of six thousand people dressed in gala costumes, the Tsar takes the gospel in his right hand. He takes the same oath that his ancestor took in 1812 just before going out to face Napoleon's *Grande Armée*: 'Officers of my guard here present, I salute and bless in you all my army. Solemnly I swear that I will not conclude peace as long as there is one enemy on the soil of our country.' A wave of cheering that lasts ten minutes shakes the hall.

Now, even though it was probably the last thing he wanted, it is game on for the Tsar in the Group of Death.

The British Cabinet, sitting around the long table with its covering of green baize, is being pushed for a decision by Sir Edward Grey. He argues that Britain has 'both moral obligations of honour and substantial obligations of policy in taking sides with France.' He tells his colleagues that if Britain remains neutral, he will resign. The meeting, which began at eleven, is still sitting at a quarter to two. Eventually Grey is authorised to tell the French Ambassador that if the German fleet comes into the Channel, the British fleet will give France all the protection it can muster.

The Cabinet meeting resumes at 6:30 p.m. Grey, pushing again, gets agreement that if the Germans violate Belgian neutrality, Britain will take action.

After the meeting, Grey promises the French Ambassador that the Royal Navy will protect France's coast from German attack. The Ambassador is delighted, reporting to his people that he now feels Britain will enter the war. 'In truth,' he writes, 'a great country does not wage war by halves. Once it decided to fight the war at sea it would necessarily be led into fighting it on land as well.'

That evening, Grey is dining when a red dispatch box comes in from the Foreign Office. It contains the news that, since six o'clock this morning, German troop trains have been leaving Cologne station at the rate of one every three or four minutes. They are headed not south-west towards France but towards Aix-la-Chapelle, the direction of Belgium.

In addition, the Germans have given the Belgians an ultimatum that German troops should be allowed to pass through Belgium to counter 'the threat of a French invasion.' The Belgians are given twelve hours to reply. King Albert of Belgium refuses the German request to violate his country's neutrality.

Clara writes in her diary, 'If I were to say no to this now, I would be saying no to the only opportunity for love I will get in this lifetime. There won't be another.'

Then she adds, 'I wonder whether Henry will try nasty things involving the children.'

Finally, she writes, 'I have set my face to doing this and the decision is now made, the door is closed, the Rubicon has been crossed.'

Clara finds that when she is feeling very, very small, writing in her diary helps. When she does it she feels like the Clara of the time before she met Henry, the Clara of when she is with James.

Chapter 46
Monday 3 August 1914

A Cabinet meeting is held at 11 a.m. in London. The Cabinet approves the mobilisation of the Army and the Navy. It is Bank Holiday Monday.

In the afternoon, sometime after half past three, Sir Edward Grey, wearing a light grey summer suit, rises from the front bench in the House of Commons. His face is pale. He begins by telling a packed house that, even though he has consistently worked to preserve peace, the peace of Europe cannot be saved. Now that this is the case, he wants to make it clear that the House is free to decide what its response should be. He wants to make it clear that there is no 'secret engagement' into which Britain has entered with other countries which it is now bound to honour.

Grey explains that, up until yesterday, no promise of anything more than diplomatic support had been given to anybody.

Uh oh, is our reaction to the beginning of this speech. While we may not have heard this *particular* speech before, the style of speech is very well known to us, if we've ever listened to a politician speak. It begins with a categorical denial. So then, you'd have to ask, why say anything else? But of course politicians, being politicians, *always* have to say something else. Obviously, one of the great drivers of politicians is the need for power. But surely another one has to be that they love to hear what they have to say and assume that other people have that same crying need.

So after the categorical denial comes the beginning of the watering down of the categorical denial. And here it comes: After the 1906 Morocco Crisis, Grey explains, he was asked whether, if France and Germany had gone to war over Morocco,

Britain would have given her support to France. His reply at the time was that it would have if public opinion supported that course of action. So then when the crisis had blown over, the French pointed out that, even if Britain had wanted to give that support, it wouldn't have been able to unless some 'conversations had already taken place between naval and military experts.'

So such conversations had taken place but purely on the understanding that they didn't bind or restrict the government in any way.

Grey goes on to read a letter he sent to the French Ambassador, confirming this situation in writing. The silence in the House is complete as it learns for the first time of this document that doesn't commit the government to anything. No – of course, not!

Grey is interrupted at this point. 'What is the date of that?' a member asks. 'The 22nd November, 1912,' Grey replies. Sir Edward goes on about the previous Morocco and Agadir crises, and then how the current crisis is different. But he ends by saying that he now feels that he has 'faithfully and completely cleared the ground with regard to the question of obligation.'

Having explained then that Britain has no obligations arising from any of the preceding history, Grey's next sentence is rather extraordinary: 'I now come to what we think the situation requires of us.' And there is a sense of 'here it comes,' when he goes on to say, 'For many years we have had a long-standing friendship with France—'

'And with Germany!' a member interrupts.

Grey sails on. He recalls how, when the agreement with Britain and France was put in place, 'the warm and cordial feeling resulting from the fact that these two nations, who had had perpetual differences in the past, had cleared these differences away … But how far that friendship entails obligation … let every man look into his own heart, and his own feelings, and construe the extent of the obligation for himself.'

So now – very deftly – we've gone from no obligation at all to – hey – an obligation. Sound of turning one hundred and eighty degrees. Grey then goes on to read out the letter he sent to the French Ambassador yesterday, what he referred to earlier as 'up until yesterday.'

'*I am authorised to give an assurance that, if the German fleet comes into the Channel or through the North Sea to undertake hostile operations against the French coasts or shipping, the British fleet will give all the protection in its power. This assurance is, of course, subject to the policy of his Majesty's Government receiving the support of Parliament, and must not be taken as binding his Majesty's Government to take any action until the above contingency of action by the German fleet takes place.*'

And so, as Grey's non-obligation is rapidly transformed into an obligation, the British Parliament and nation and Empire slide down the slipway to war.

Soon after seven, the House reassembles and Grey tells it that Belgium has rejected the German ultimatum.

In Austria, as in all the other countries in the Group of Death, the army begins commandeering horses, taking them from carriages, ploughs, carts and – basically – wherever they can find them.

In Berlin, Germany declares war on France.

In Paris, the streets are black with people singing *La Marseillaise* and carrying tricolours. German food shops are ransacked. There is a coolness bordering on hostility to British visitors as it is still not really clear if Britain will enter the war on the side of France.

Clara writes, 'My life is filled with total happiness and I am joyous and free. Things are always difficult after difficult decisions. You make the right decision – to those affected by it, it may not seem so at the time but only in the fullness of time.'

Chapter 47
Tuesday 4 August 1914

The first of the thousands of trains that will carry the French Army to meet their enemy have begun running. The carriages are decorated with flowers and tricolours. Slogans have been chalked on the outside. 'Excursion to Berlin,' one of them reads. The soldiers are in high spirits. *La Marseillaise* is sung endlessly.

The French General Staff believe they will be facing sixty-eight German divisions. In fact, they will be opposed by at least eighty-eight divisions. It will be the first of many, many surprises that not just the French Army but all the contestants in the Group of Death are going to experience over the next four and a bit years.

Clara is out early to do her grocery shopping for the day. Mr Evans, the grocer, tells her that the price of butter and eggs has gone up by nearly fifty per cent. She's astonished.

'It's all this talk of war, you see, Mrs Kenton. I'll charge you the old price today but I'm afraid from tomorrow on, it will have to be the new one.'

Clara buys extra.

'And if I were you, Mrs Kenton, I'd lay in stocks of any non-perishables as well.'

Clara does so. Late in the afternoon, she will take the girls out for a walk and they will happen to go by the grocers. To their surprise, it will be closed. A note on the door will read, 'Sold out of everything – please come back tomorrow.'

In Berlin, Germany declares war on Belgium. Later that evening the German Chancellor tells the Reichstag that the German invasions of Belgium and Luxembourg are in violation of international law, but he argues that Germany is 'in a state of necessity, and necessity knows no law.'

The declaration of war on Belgium violates Belgian neutrality, the status of which Germany, France and Britain are all committed to by treaty. So now Britain delivers an ultimatum to Germany, asking for an assurance that Belgian neutrality be respected. This is done via the British Ambassador in Berlin.

In Berlin, at 7 p.m. that evening he delivers the ultimatum to Bethmann at the Ministry for Foreign Affairs. The ultimatum demands a commitment to go no further with Germany's violation of Belgian neutrality. Britain will wait until midnight for a reply. The British Ambassador goes back to the Embassy to pack.

Der Kaiser says, 'To think that George and Nicky should have played me false! If my grandmother had been alive, she would never have allowed it.'

In the Cabinet room at 10 Downing Street, Prime Minister Asquith and his wife, Sir Edward Grey and Lord Crewe sit in the gathering darkness. The portrait of Sir Robert Walpole by Van Loo looks down on them as they smoke and wait. Finally, the clock on the white marble mantelpiece strikes eleven – midnight, Central European Time. No reply has come. The ultimatum has run out.

As the British ultimatum runs out, so too does Henry's semen, having just a little while earlier climaxed inside Mary.

Chapter 48
Thursday 6 August 1914

Clara meets James as they had arranged. He is very apologetic – he can only spend a couple of hours with her.

'Things are quite mad,' he says. 'So many English people on the Continent who we're trying to get home. Never mind dealing with our new best friends, the French and the Russians. Anyway, how have you been, my beautiful girl?' he asks her, as they find a seat.

'I've missed you' she replies. 'I thought today would never come.'

'It's probably good that I've been spending every waking moment over there,' he says, indicating the long tiers of windows of the Foreign Office. 'If I'd had time on my hands, I don't think I should have been able to stop myself from slipping round to Horn Lane in the hope of catching sight of you.'

All Clara can think to say is, 'I love you so much, James – even though I hardly know you.'

'You know all the important things,' he says.

"Yes, I do, don't I?'

After a pause, she asks, 'And do you know all the important things about me?'

'I'll never know everything about you,' he says. 'That's why I want to spend the rest of my life finding out.'

'And have you been in good spirits?' he asks. 'What with that husband of yours and everything?'

'Oh, Henry – it's almost like he's not there. I'm fearful about next week … the solicitor … you know, the divorce and all that.'

'And you must be grieving,' he says.

'Grieving?'

'For your marriage. At least that's what I remember. Not so much for the reality of it, but for the idea. We all go in expecting it's going to be perfect and forever. And when it's not, it's like a death. Something we loved is gone. And so we grieve.'

'Maybe that's what I've been feeling,' says Clara. 'I've been up one day and down the next.'

James nods.

'That sounds like it,' he says. 'I hope the thought that I'm here whenever you need me … I hope … maybe that helps a little. I hope so.'

'Oh James, you know it does. I don't think I'd have had the courage to do it without you.'

'And how is your boss's boss doing?' asks Clara, changing the subject.

'He's not happy. He's like a bear with a sore head. And gone quite in on himself. Brooding on everything that's happened. What he needs now are a few chums to take him out, get him inconsolably drunk and tell him he did the best he could.

But he's a solitary cove and so he won't do that. Instead he'll continue to brood. He blames himself. Reckons he failed. Of course he doesn't say that. No, he keeps saying that the only people who could have prevented war were the Germans. I suppose if he says it often enough, he might end up believing it himself. In actual fact, in those dark hours of the night when we lie awake, I'm certain he keeps wondering if he could have done something different and, if so, that it might have turned out differently.'

'And could it?'

'Fact is, my dearest Clara, I think it could. Right at the beginning if he'd made clear where Britain stood, then I don't think it would have come to this at all. Of course, he'll argue that he couldn't because the Cabinet was divided or that Parliament hadn't approved this or that or something or other, but damn it all, look what was at stake. Even if he'd acted without Cabinet backing or the approval of the House, even if it had destroyed his career. I fear we're all going to pay a very high price for the man's prevarication. And you know what the worst thing is?'

'What's that?' asks Clara as she sees that James is smiling.

'It looks like it's going to be some considerable time before you and I get to go to France.'

Chapter 49
Wednesday 12 August 1914

Henry and Mary spend the night of Tuesday the 11th in a hotel. Earlier that morning, when Henry told Clara he would be staying up in town, she replied, 'Of course, dear.' Her face told a different story – quite the most withering, disdainful, disgusted look that Henry had ever been on the receiving end of.

'Bitch!' he muttered to himself as he headed out the door carrying his overnight bag. He soon puts all thought of Clara out of his head as he anticipates the night ahead with Mary.

And indeed it turns out to be quite perfect.

He is starting to get used to her now and, in some ways, it feels like they are already married. But it is not the tired marriage he has with Clara. Rather it is alive and vibrant and everything he imagines a marriage should be but hardly ever is. This may actually be the best thing that has ever happened to him, Henry finds himself thinking, while they are eating a quite magnificent dinner.

Mary seems to be completely happy and is full of fun, as he finds out later, when they get back to the hotel room. They get hardly any sleep that night. Henry wakes in the morning with a vague memory of Mary having asked him, 'So how do you like your first night of continuous sex?' The fact is Henry liked it very much and hopes there will be a lot more of them.

When Mary wakes, all Henry wants to do is to talk about the night they have just passed. But for some unfortunate reason, Mary becomes colossally angry with Henry. Who knows why this should happen? Perhaps the closest we can come to an answer is that, hard as steel as Mary may appear to be, she is just like the rest of us. She just wants to be happy and with Henry seems to have found that happiness.

However, she now fears that it will be snatched away from her. She is terrified that he *does* only want to bed her and that all this talk of solicitors and divorce is only stringing her along. After all, he could *pretend* to go to a solicitor and *pretend* that the legal things have been put in train. The legal profession is a byword for doing things as slowly as possible. It could be months. It could run well into 1915 before she suddenly woke up to the fact that he had been stringing her along all this time. And then he could drop her like a hot potato. And then where would she be, having invested all this time? A year older. Her body a year older. And nothing to show for it.

Whatever the reason, Mary starts shouting and Henry shouts back. The end result is that he storms out of the room, goes downstairs, is too angry to take breakfast, pays the bill and goes off in the direction of the office.

Fucking women, he thinks. That bitch at home waiting for him and that other bitch never seems to be happy no matter what he does for her or what kind of lengths he is prepared to go to. And here he is working like a dog so that they can enjoy the high life. Well, fuck them. Fuck them both. Fuck all women.

Henry is in this frame of mind when he walks past a post office and his eye is caught by a large buff-coloured poster in the window. He stops to read it. The Royal Crest is at the top and then it says in huge type, 'YOUR KING & COUNTRY NEED YOU.'

'A CALL TO ARMS,' it goes on in slightly smaller type. And then it continues, 'An addition of 100,000 MEN to His Majesty's Regular Army is immediately needed in the present grave National Emergency. LORD KITCHENER IS CONFIDENT THAT THIS APPEAL WILL BE AT ONCE RESPONDED TO BY ALL THOSE WHO HAVE THE SAFETY OF OUR EMPIRE AT HEART.

TERMS OF SERVICE. General Service for a period of 3 years or until the war is concluded. Age of Enlistment, between 19 and 30.

HOW TO JOIN. Full information can be obtained at any POST OFFICE in the kingdom or at ANY MILITARY DEPOT. GOD SAVE THE KING.'

Henry is twenty nine. It's a sign!

He wonders where the nearest military depot is. Looking around, he sees a policeman and asks him.

'I don't know where the closest one is, sir, but there's certainly one off Whitehall in Great Scotland Yard.'

Henry strides off in the direction the policeman indicated. He begins to imagine the scene when he walks in tonight and tells Clara what he has done. He pictures telling Mary. That will serve the bitches right. Perhaps now that it's going to be taken from them they'll realise what they had and what they should have been so damn grateful for.

When Henry turns into Great Scotland Yard, he is stopped in his tracks. He had been imagining that, on a weekday morning like this, he would encounter a handful of likeminded souls at the recruiting office. Instead, from where Henry stands to an overhead sign that reads 'London Recruiting Offices,' the street is thronged with men. Police, including several on horseback, try to keep the crowd of men on the pavement but it is so great that it keeps spilling onto the cobblestones. A car turns into the street and the police try again to move men out of the way. There is a cheer from the crowd as the car pulls up outside the recruiting office. Somebody gets out and hurries inside. Another cheer. It all seems terribly good humoured – even the police are smiling and are exchanging banter with the crowd.

It takes several hours for Henry to reach the door of the recruiting office and slowly snake his way up the steps and inside. But by lunchtime, he is a soldier. They explain to him that he will earn army rates of pay and his wife will get a Separation Allowance. He's told that they have no uniforms or weapons or barracks or anything else at the moment, so for the present he is to continue living at home. But he will be getting a letter from them in the next few days and then he will begin his training.

Henry can't wait to begin telling people. But first he goes to a pub for lunch and a few pints with a couple of men he met in the queue. After that, remembering that nobody at the office knows where he is, he decides he'd better go there. He buys some peppermints to cover the smell of alcohol on his breath. He is not drunk by any means but feels a great sense of bravado. He will ask to see Mr Faber, but when he arrives, he is told that Mr Faber is already asking to see him.

Of course he is. Well, Henry's got a surprise for him.

When he is ushered into Faber's presence, Henry is left standing while Faber sits, head down and pen scratching on a piece of paper. He is well aware that Henry is there but pretends not to notice. It's common knowledge that Faber has no other interest except work – no wife, no children, no friends – only business acquaintances, no hobbies. He takes no holidays and works all of the public holidays.

After several minutes, without looking up and continuing to write, he says, 'I believe you were missing this morning, Kenton. And no message sent or reason given.'

It really is an outrageous way to treat a manager, Henry thinks. It's the kind of thing you would say to a junior clerk. Now Faber puts the pen down and looks up, sitting back in his chair and joining his hands. Henry reckons he is in his fifties but looks much older, with grey, papery skin. Does he ever get any sunlight? Henry wonders.

'I presume you do *have* a reason, Kenton.'

There's an expression Mary is fond of using – 'a face like a smacked arse' – and it pops into Henry's head now. He smiles at the thought and says, 'I do, sir.'

He lets the suspense last a few moments longer.

'Well, come on, out with it, man. I'm intrigued to know what could have kept you from us for most of the day and without a word by way of apology or excuse.'

'Well, I hope you'll approve, sir. I've enlisted.'

The change that comes over Faber is remarkable.

'My dear fellow,' he says, standing up. 'Let me be the first to shake your hand.'

And with that Henry is asked to sit down.

He is probably in Faber's office for half an hour. When he emerges it is all very satisfactory. His job will be kept for him for when he returns. They will pay his salary until the end of the month whether he is available for work or not, and then give him an extra month on top of that. Add to that his holiday pay and any other entitlements.

Henry wants so much to tell Mary, so he calls down to New Policies to arrange to see her after work. When she sees him coming through the door, she indicates with her eyes that he should go back out. He does so, stepping back into the corridor. She follows him out.

'I'm so sorry about this morning,' she says. 'I don't know what came over me. You're so precious to me and I think I'm just afraid of losing you. Please – can you forgive me?'

Henry realises that it is the first time she has ever apologised to him. What a good feeling that is.

'Of course,' he says. 'Think nothing of it.'

Henry had intended to ask her to meet him after work and to tell her then but he knows now that the news of his having enlisted will go through the office like wildfire. He has to tell her straight away, right here and now.

'There's something I need to tell you,' he says. 'I've joined the army.'

Henry does arrange to meet Mary after work. As he waits for her he reflects on how she reacted as he broke the news to her. It was like he had kicked her in the stomach. It was such a satisfying moment.

When she arrives, it is clear that she has been crying. She doesn't want to go to a café or any place where there are people so they just walk. She goes on about how devastated she is and bursts into tears several times. She keeps asking him why and Henry responds with wonderfully patriotic sentiments which in no way calm Mary, nor are they intended to. It is nearly eight before they part, and by then Henry has given her plenty of 'who knows what the future holds' and 'as long as we have each other' and 'making the most of each day – and night!' He reckons there won't be a peep out of *her* for the next few months. Indeed, they should be quite splendid indeed.

The war will be short. This was the firm view of everybody he spoke to today, even the recruiting sergeant. Henry will spend a few months as a soldier. He may not even see any action. Then the war will end, he will come home a hero whether he is involved in any fighting or not. And then he will decide what he wants to do about Mary.

His feeling is that there will be plenty of Marys interested in returned heroes. But that will certainly not be a worry for this year. Now, for the rest of 1914, he sees a fretful Mary anxious to satisfy him in every way. And his fun is only half over. He still gets to tell Clara.

Clara lies in bed unable to sleep. Henry is snoring beside her. It is several hours since he told her he joined the army. She still can't quite believe it. He will be here for several more weeks, was what he said, and then he'll be going away. She will have the house to herself. She'll be able to do as she pleases. She'll be able to see James as often as she likes.

And even though she tries not to let it, another thought loiters on the edge of her consciousness trying to force its way in. Supposing he weren't to come back at all. Maybe she doesn't need to have that meeting with the solicitor tomorrow. Maybe she can just spend the time with James. They'll probably only have a couple of hours. Why spend it in some dusty solicitor's when they could just be together?

And there's no fear of James having to enlist. He is thirty-four so he's over the age. Everything has turned out so perfectly. Clara can hardly believe how her life has so utterly changed in a few short weeks. She is *so* happy. So very, very happy.

Outside she hears the first birds of dawn twittering. She's so excited she doesn't think she'll get back to sleep now, but she doesn't care. Life is so wonderful.

Chapter 50
Thursday 13 August 1914

'All set?' asks James, as he greets Clara. It is quarter to twelve and their appointment with the solicitor is at twelve.

'I was thinking,' says Clara. 'Perhaps we don't need to go today.'

'Are you getting cold feet?' asks James, and she notices the anxious tone in his voice.

'No, it isn't that. It's just that … well, I have some news. Something's happened.'

'Oh?'

'Yes. Look – could we cancel the appointment, send a note or something. And maybe get some lunch and I'll tell you.'

She notices for the first time that he doesn't seem anywhere near as cheery as he normally is. His face is clouded.

'Don't worry,' she says, touching his arm. 'It's a good thing. The most wonderful thing.'

James takes one of his calling cards and scribbles a note on the back. Then he calls one of a group of boys who are passing carrying a football and asks if he'll deliver the card to a particular address. The boy says, 'Righteo, guv,' touches his cap and disappears with the note and the coin James gives him.

'Sandwiches?' James asks. 'Or a café?'

'Café,' she says. 'I feel like celebrating.'

As they turn in the direction of the nearest café, Clara can't keep the news to herself any longer.

'Henry has enlisted. He's joined the army. In a few weeks he'll be gone and then I can see you as often as we want. Maybe we could spend a night together,' she says daringly.

She wonders if James will be outraged by what she has just said. He certainly appears very disturbed by it. It is not at all the reaction she was expecting.

And now she is alarmed. Has he just been going along with her and now that there's the possibility that they could be together, he's getting cold feet?

'There's something I have to tell you too, Clara,' he says sombrely.

Oh God, she thinks. He's married after all. It has all been a game for him. Oh no. Oh my God. Just when she thought she had been given everything she could have possibly wanted.

She hears James say, 'Darling Clara, I have to enlist too.'

She feels herself flooded with relief. Silly old James. He's obviously so caught up in his job that he doesn't know about it being nineteen to thirty.

'But you can't,' she says happily. 'Don't you know the age limit is thirty?'

He suddenly looks terribly weary.

'It's thirty now but that will change very quickly. This is going to be a terribly long war, Clara dearest.'

'But you can't go,' she says. 'What about your job? The work you do. It's important—'

James smiles but it is a tired smile.

'It's not *that* important. And even if it was – we didn't do a very good job, now did we? Look where we've ended up.'

'But—'

'I *have* to go. Don't you see? Everything I hold dear is threatened. England. My beloved France. You, Clara, my darling. What if the Germans were to invade here? What would happen to you?'

'The Germans won't invade,' Clara scoffs. 'I may not know much about war but I know we have the biggest navy in the world. They'd never get across the Channel.'

'Maybe you're right,' he says. 'But I still have to fight for the things I care about. And anyway, in six months' time, every proper man in this country will be in uniform. You'll see. I'm not going to wait and then join because I feel guilty. No, Clara, I have to go. Don't you see? Please tell me you do.'

'But what about us?' she asks.

'When I come back,' he replies. 'Then we'll have us.'

'But suppose something happens to you?'

'Nothing will happen,' he says. 'You and I will grow old together. You know this, don't you?'

Clara shakes her head as she feels a tear slide down her cheek.

'I had hoped so,' she murmurs. 'But now I don't know.'

They stop walking and he turns to hold her. She is crying now.

'I will,' he says. 'I wouldn't miss the rest of *our* lives for anything.'

Eventually Clara stops crying and takes James's proffered handkerchief. She dries her eyes and blows her nose in it.

'Sorry,' she says, holding it in her hand and trying to smile.

'Come on,' he says softly. 'Let's get you a cup of tea.'

'I know what it is. I know why you're enlisting.'

Puzzled, he says, 'I've told you why.'

'No, I know the real reason.'

'Oh,' he says, still puzzled. 'And what's that?'

'You just wanted to get back to France, didn't you?' she says with the biggest smile she can manage.

It is after midnight in Horn Lane. Henry and the children are asleep and Clara stands in the back garden, barefoot and in her nightdress. A half moon hangs in the sky.

Clara has always loved the moon. She feels it is so like herself. Alone, unremarked on, taken for granted, ignored. She feels a closeness to it. It is her friend. She imagines it shining on the statue of the naked woman, bathing it in a blue-grey light.

Really – to be honest – Clara is not sure she believes in God. Oh yes, she goes through the motions – with the children especially. She talks to them about God and goes to church at Christmas and on some Sundays, but all of that really has no meaning for her. But the moon – the moon she can believe in.

And so now she speaks to it, softly but aloud, and says, 'Please, sacred moon, bring him home safely to me.'

And she knows – the moon knows – of whom she speaks.

To be continued in Part 4 of
The Four Lights Quartet, Candlelight.

Lightning Source UK Ltd.
Milton Keynes UK
UKOW05f0731220813

215761UK00001B/2/P